NIGHT WAKING

He hesitated, the piece of rope coarse in his hands. He saw his own face reflected in her eye. Her face was split white with the gag. He could feel the blood pulsing out into his spread fingertips and he saw the cry on her face, unable to reach her lips as the rope tightened. She thrashed beneath him and he could feel the heaving wetness of her terror as the rope bit through and he could feel her neck give. There was a sound but it wasn't a live thing at all, it felt soft and hollow as a rubber doll.

NIGHT WAKING

KATHLEEN SNOW

ARROW BOOKS

Arrow Books Ltd
3 Fitzroy Square, London W1P 6JD

An imprint of the Hutchinson Publishing Group

London Melbourne Sydney Auckland
Wellington Johannesburg and agencies
throughout the world

First published in Great Britain 1980
© Kathleen Snow 1978

ISBN 0 09 922320 1

The Random House Group Limited supports The Forest Stewardship
Council (FSC®), the leading international forest certification organisation.
Our books carrying the FSC label are printed on FSC® certified paper.
FSC is the only forest certification scheme endorsed by the leading
environmental organisations, including Greenpeace. Our
paper procurement policy can be found at
www.randomhouse.co.uk/environment

Printed and bound in Great Britain by Clays Ltd, St Ives PLC

Thanks to the many who helped this book
on its path,
with special gratitude to my writing group:
Mary Epes, Carole Spearin McCauley,
Lillian Perinciolo

Watchman, what of the night?
The watchman said, The morning
cometh, and also the night.

Isaiah 21:11–12

Night Waking

Prologue

Wednesday, June 16, 1976
11:59 p.m.

The car eased off Long Island's Highway 27, homing in on the sound of surf. The tires drilled upon asphalt, turned right, crackled onto a hard-sand roadbed. Hollies, then the mittens and gloves of sassafras flogged the car's sides. It burrowed deeper. The roadbed became path, engulfed by masses of catbrier and twisted lianas of grape and poison ivy.

Dalroi snapped off the ignition. The car shivered into silence. Beyond the cicadas he heard the ocean, pounding under the starless dark. Through the open window came

11

the iodine breeze, and with it the realization: they were alone, no one would bother them here.

He turned to the girl, his body flushing with the expected sweetness.

She was beautiful. Long hair lay loose down her back, a sheaf of frizzled wheat. Jeans, bleached thin and soft as chamois, rounded her thighs and dove between. He could see the sand, dark and damp, white and dry, between her toes.

He wanted to tell her how long he had waited. The times he had seen her, loving her even from afar. He wanted to tell her how his love had grown.

Up in his head the soft words sounded. But it was his body that spoke.

He reached for her, fingers searching for the nub of her breast. She was unyielding, as if to resist him. But that was an old game: *No I will.*

His fingers played *Yes you will* on buttons, zippers, hooks. Calluses rasped on denim. Then he gathered a handful of pink nylon waistband elastic, feeling the urgency tighten, sweaty damp as his palm. He yanked down.

The cicadas roared.

Her legs tangled for a moment inside the pink hobbles— a netted fish, he thought as he stripped her panties over ankles, toes, and off. *Angelfish.*

But it was too dark in the car. Reaching behind him, he opened the door. The light blinked yellow across the tangled vegetation.

He stretched out on his belly, feet in the breeze.

Her eyes were dark and wide, liquid as he stared into them. Her body spilled up to him like a ripe fruit.

Did she know, he thought, the power she held? The control over him—past, present, future? That he would crawl over broken glass this last six inches, just to please her?

His mouth found her other mouth. With slow reverence he worked headfirst into the blackness.

Pain filled his mouth. An ache, he traced it, at his tongue's root. He could taste the dark scent of her, rolling on his tongue. He felt her thighs, smooth and unresisting beneath his palms.

Awareness returned, and with it gratitude, tenderness. And then the urgency, the need to feel her fully accept him.

He unzipped his trousers, held himself up against her. His thrust sent her head against the car door. But she did not complain.

He reached over her, yanked the door handle. Her flag of hair spilled off the seat as his rockings moved her head back, back, and over the edge into the cool salt night.

When he had finished, the girl's hair was moving, silver as quaking aspen in the wind. His hand smoothed down along the cool strands. Then he raised his body, balancing above her on whitened knuckles.

The light pooled yellow from inside the car. Looking out at the sweep of dunes, he saw an answering yellow. Across the bushy shapes of beach heather and bearberry came the far stab of a flashlight. Its beam blinked and wavered toward the car.

The fear rose, choking as vomit.

The ignition key chattered on metal, serrated edge grating impotently. Then it slid home.

He gunned the engine, wheeling the car's front end through a curtain of sand. The tires pulsed back along the hard-packed path, the flashlight fading in the mirror to firefly insignificance.

Air sighed deep and long into his lungs. He looked down at the girl beside him on the vinyl seat. He was sorry he hadn't pleased her. He wanted to tell her so.

But she was already dead.

Chapter One

Monday, August 8, 1977
10:14 a.m.

The phone rang in their apartment, the phone that no one picked up.

Where was Alex?

Gone back to sleep? Francie wondered. Sprawled on her back in a pool of sunlight? Limp-legged as what-was-his-name, Dad's old blue heeler, and just as dead to the world?

(That hound could sleep through ants on his balls. She had watched him once behind the barn twitching on through his dream.)

Or was Alex padding around their apartment, brown silk hair in her eyes, wearing her red silk kimono with the raised black-and-white dragon belching blue flames on the back (if she was wearing anything at all), thinking, "To hell with the phone, fuck Francie"?

Because she would know it was Francie.

Counting the eleventh ring, Francie Perry imagined the metal-on-metal sound scraping down through layers of sleep.

She has to answer it. She can sleep through work, sleep with as many men in a month as I meet in a year, sleep like the dead. But when the telephone rings, your father could be dying and you have to answer it.

Two seconds of ringing, four seconds of silence, two seconds of ringing—it was rhythmic as life. No human being despite having been out all night Sunday night doing God knows what and with whom could sleep through such Pavlovian, predictable ringing.

Except someone once said the ringing you hear in the earpiece isn't the ringing at the other end at all. No, to pacify you, Ma Bell feeds you this phony ringing from down in central switching somewhere, because the truth is, there's no connection between you and the number you call until they pick up the receiver, so how could you hear the ringing?

The truth is there's no connection between appearance and reality.

Even right now on the twentieth ring there was no guarantee that the telephone in their apartment was ringing. Or even working at all.

"You haven't got anything to do out there but make calls, Francine," Cyrus Vetter shouted, "I've filing in here."

She punched the lighted cube still on Hold. "Kandis?" (The woman had even spelled it for her: "Hi, I sit behind Alex, Alex Baskin, your roommate? I'm Kandis. K-a-n-

16

d-i-s?") "I don't know what to tell you," Francie said into the receiver. "She's not at home. Maybe a doctor's appointment . . ."

There was a condemnatory silence.

As if *I* were the one, Francie thought, sleeping late, skipping work, arrogant enough not even to call in an excuse.

"Well, she better haul her ass in here," said the voice, whose accent now sounded like an angry Bryn Mawr, "or Tibor's going to fire her. And, sweetie, I *don't* mean fire her with enthusiasm."

"She'll be in, don't worry. Maybe some family emergen—"

"Fran*cine*. Come in, please."

Francie dropped the receiver onto the black plastic cradle, whose hairline fracture widened to a crevasse. She stood up —a short girl with a thin trunk and muscular calves, wearing a blue-and-white shirtwaist dress with makeup on the collar. Her thick shoulder-length hair—the pale brown that suggested a glorious blond childhood—was parted in the middle and pinned back on each side by a gold barrette. She walked out of her cubicle, last in a line of cubicles over whose breast-high walls every word circulated along with the air-conditioning, and paused at the open office door.

"Yes, Mr. Vetter?"

The editor of *Nebula* magazine was bending over an army-green filing cabinet whose bottom drawer was crazily askew. His too-short trousers strained up over sagging white socks.

"Coffee cups," he said, not pausing in his search through the drawer. "Be a good girl, huh? Thanks."

She looked down at his desk. Four yellow cups and saucers were in the Out box. Brown stains scalloped the sides, one held a Vesuvius of ash, and in another Vetter's cigar butt floated belly up in oily liquid.

For *this* she had apprenticed four years at Iowa Wesleyan College, Mount *un*-Pleasant, Iowa? She felt like walking out.

But she had already walked from two other secretarial-cum-trainee jobs in the past year.

She stacked the cups and carried them out to the door in the hall whose sign someone had amended to "*ma*Ladies Room."

Can't job-skip, she thought, squirting the yellow-green soap from the dispenser into the cups, rubbing the stains with her fingers. It was her father's phrase, reducing her to a child playing a game. *Looks unstable. What did we send you to college for, anyway, and you the first in the family?*

She saw Harold Perry's shoulders pinch together as he turned away—always turning away—his hand coming up to rub the back of his neck—always irritated there, bad as chiggers the way the skin burned and itched. She saw the stump of the index finger he had caught in the baler, out in the field two miles from anyone and only the crows to hear his scream. He had pulled out his pocketknife, lopped off the finger, and walked home.

If thy right hand offend thee, cut it off: Reverend Athol Eskerson, circa 1971, eyeballs like peeled grapes seeking her out in the third pew. Elmer Gantry? she had always wondered. *For it is profitable for thee that one of thy members should perish, and not that thy whole body should be cast into hell.*

But didn't it take just as much courage to come out here hanging off the eastern seaboard over the sharks, trying to live in New York City?

She returned the cups and typed two letters, the cheap scent of the soap rising from the keys. Then finally she spread out the long, ink-stained galleys still to be proofread. She loved the neat, exacting, absorbing quest for the typo, the misspelled, misused word. She positioned the gray metal ruler beneath the line with the pencil tick beside it.

"The two green-scaled Arrusthenes, antennae tracking, pursued Jarl down the"

She moved the ruler to the line below.

"pedway. He reached for his blaster."

But where was Alex? What if she had killed herself?

Ridiculous.

Suicide because you told her at the kitchen table just this morning that it hadn't worked out, trying not to hurt, to wound, but that she might be happier finding another apartment, moving out?

"So who's going to tell her?" Paige had said Sunday night from the opposite twin bed, when it was obvious Alex was staying out all night. With another man. Again.

The only reply appeared to be "I will, I guess." She had always been the one with sympathy for Alex, when Paige had grown impatient. But the thought of the confrontation had kept her sleepless.

Under the bright gloss there was something sad reaching out from Alexandra Baskin. And she had her good, generous side. Coming out into the living room all those nights after Dad died, making cocoa and talking until dawn. She was a person you could like, get on with, other than *that*. But the that was the problem.

She and Paige had agreed: it *was* intolerable, wasn't it? For ten months Alex's sexuality had blanketed the apartment like a raincloud. Precipitation of pubic hairs on the soap. . . . Men on the phone, voices soft when they think you're Alex, wheedling and yet barbed with threat. . . . G-strings flying on the shower rod. . . . Men in the living room, hallway, bathroom, Alex's bedroom. . . . The toilet seat left upright. . . . Jockey shorts, size thirty-four, furred with dust under the couch.

And then there was that raw, underground sensation that prickled up your back when Alex came home in the mornings, face jaunty, lips swollen. Her voice, hoarsened and throaty: "I'm in love, Francie. This time it's love."

And then sometimes, jauntier than ever, it was just

"Well, kid, I got laid."

All right. Envy, maybe. Fascination, it was true. But also revulsion. Indignation.

But how do you tell someone her presence is so disturbing two women can't live with her? How do you tell her she gives you the creeps, with her flabby, maybe gonococcal douche bag and the look of something hunted about her shoulder blades? That her promiscuity sometimes excites you, enthralls you with the taste of destruction, like copper in the mouth? That you hate yourself for wondering, wondering, wondering what they do to her and how, and who makes the first overture to part? That her life plays like porno, which draws yet sickens?

How do you tell anyone, even yourself, that the worst thing is she's vivacious when you're not, beautiful when you're not, even with those odd eyes so dark the pupils don't show, and not quite in alignment, either—one eye looking off while the other is on you, giving that disconcerting irony to her face. As if she holds back from you, doesn't give a damn, and laughs.

That she was Beverly all over again, Beverly the cheerleader, prom queen, National Honor Society member, star of *You Can't Take It with You* on the auditorium stage. Beverly two years older, preceding everywhere, firstborn, Daddy's favorite, the tomboy he loved ("Look at that girl *corner*," he bragged when Beverly rode the tractor, "that little girl corners good as me"). And then Beverly sprung overnight into a beauty, her features kin-close, sister-shared, but one sister was beautiful. And the other—Suann O'Neill had said it—"What happened to Francie?"

But no matter how much the guilt, it was over. Alex had agreed to move out. The tears had glinted, fusing with her lashes, then double-streaking toward her mouth as their eyes had met.

But by the end of August the thing with Alex would be finished, scoured from the apartment. The way Alex threw herself at Spy would be buried in the past.

I might even, Francie thought, meet someone more scintillating than one Spyros Aristotle Xanthakis, who after all had bad breath.

She looked back down at the galleys, checking the spelling of "Arrusthenes" against her neatly scripted alphabetical list of proper nouns, even as the question surfaced again in her mind.

Where *was* Alex?

1:15 p.m.

Victor Amspoker stared at the shirt in his closet. He had never seen it before: red-and-green plaid—garish, ridiculous —sleeves stiffly at attention the way Maddie always starched them.

Who the hell did she think she was fooling?

Each disk of his spinal column seemed to grind down on the one below—bone powdering, spurs arrowing into his flesh. He opened his mouth, sucking air.

Not his. It was not his shirt she had ironed and laundered so lovingly, rubbing out the stiffened sweat marks, soured after-shave.

Amspoker withdrew his hand. He didn't want to touch it, this shirt of his careless wife's lover.

In his underwear he sank back onto the bed. The white gauze curtains bellied in the breeze, drawing in the voice of his elder daughter, Laurel, who shrieked from across the yard with a child's abandon.

He still had a family. Hold to that, he had to, get a grip

on, think things out. Couldn't blow a sixteen-year marriage in one afternoon.

Seeing the shirt, the surprise of it, wasn't the worst part anyway. For three months now his suspicions had cut muscle-deep as a knife.

Amspoker felt the first touch of an absolute aloneness. It began at his toes, welling slowly higher, squeezing his chest. No one cared about him, no one even knew him except for Maddie. Every man and wife had problems, have to find a way to work them out was all.

But how do you negotiate loss of desire?

He remembered how she looked on their first date, sitting in the chilly diner with a very small, sad smile. God, he'd wanted to make her laugh. Blundered, said something stupid about a pretty girl like her not being married yet.

"But getting married means the end," she had said. "I was always interested in beginnings."

"What do you mean?" he said as she stirred her coffee.

She drank, brown eyes focusing past him on an oil painting of the Acropolis. "In high school I used to feel . . . oh, like I was standing in the center of a huge circle—all possibilities rayed out. You start down one path and it ends up with the others closed off. So I didn't want to start. Just wanted to go on standing there."

"Yeah, I felt that way, you know?" He spoke too quickly, cutting her off. But her words made him lonely. He wanted to share, whatever it was she meant, feeling her going out there somewhere beyond him.

"I used to go riding in Van Cortlandt Park," she continued, eyes everywhere but on him. "Even there, it was the same thing. The most fun was just as you left the stable, the day all new and bright, nothing tarnished. No end in sight."

Well, it was finished now, Amspoker thought, looking

22

across at the closet. But where had it gone, the beginnings she had talked about, the juice to life? Forty-two years slipped past you like signs on the highway before you can read them. And love—he had never had that, whatever it was you were supposed to feel. Like, respect, lust—those he had known. Maddie was pregnant when he married her. Then she lost the baby—a boy, too.

The question was, what now? Confront her? Sicilian rage? Threaten mayhem, pledge violent love? He felt utterly without energy for such a task—he, Victor Amspoker, who knocked out Branislav Malowski's front teeth because he walked Carol Ann home from P.S. 194. Twelve months later Carol Ann was knocked up, she married the big Pole, last he heard she weighed two hundred pounds.

Amspoker pulled a blue shirt from the closet. Under the tails he buckled the belly holster of his off-duty Smith and Wesson, snuggling the gun beneath the roll of flab. He left the buttons open under his tie, as always, so he could get quickly at the hard wooden butt, against which he could feel the sweat starting. Still, it was better than the ankle holster, which felt funny when you were walking.

He raked the square hairbrush over his thick dark brown hair, then laid it down on the bureau top beside his comb and bullet.

It was *the* bullet, of course. From the same make of gun used to wound Joe Colombo—a 7.65 mm. Menta automatic bullet.

Amspoker picked it up, rolling it between his palms, enjoying the heavy feel of the metal. The nose was as flat as a mushroom.

The citation had been a cinch that year. He remembered that and the sound of the gun—short, sharp, flat—which registered only after the bullet caromed toward him, red-hot and malleable, twisting left down the barrel and out where he stood on stakeout at the finance company. He remembered the blow like a sledgehammer plunging into the Model P armor vest.

That was the answer, he thought, pulling on gray trousers, cinching the belt. He would throw himself into things at work, stop slacking off, trading stories in the coop. The work always nourished him, even with the cold winter concrete through your shoes, the paperwork, and now this damned reform-minded hairbag of a chief of detectives.

Well, he would make the work yield up a whole meal this time, three courses of chicken soup, chicken soup for dessert. He would get back between the traces, maybe lose the pounds, leave it to Maddie to make the next move.

What he needed, he thought as he walked out to the red Plymouth two-door, was a meat-and-potatoes case. One of those A-priority headline makers that sent a detective everywhere but home.

2:07 p.m.

In her tiny fluorescent-lit office near Wall Street, Paige MacLeish felt a stab of annoyance. It had nothing to do with her.

She took a deep drag on her True, letting the smoke out in sharp puffs. The thought of her roommates and their squabble seemed to drag at her like wet skirts. Women were supposed to get along together. Wasn't that what feminism was for?

"This girl, Kandis, at Gilbert, Levensky, has called *twice*," came Francie's voice over the receiver. "No one answers at home. I think it's ominous."

"Ominous?" Paige laughed. "The only thing ominous is how you get so tied up in knots over Alex this, Alex that. She's always got a cold, cramps, some damned thing Fridays and Mondays. Just doesn't want to answer the phone."

"I can't—"

"Let her alone, okay?"

"Paige. I'm worried."

"Why are you worrying she skips work? For God's sake, Francie. It's almost two-thirty, Dornbush is waiting for a crapping report . . ."

"What should I tell this Kandis, then?"

"You don't know where Alex is and you don't care. I'm taking in a movie with Heidi tonight, so I'll see you later. And, Francie . . ."

"Huh?"

"Don't worry."

Paige could hear the exasperation leaking through her voice, harshening the "Don't worry." As she replaced the receiver she felt a stab of guilt.

But it was all so difficult. It seemed that with people, she never knew what to say or do. Just kept blundering on through.

Paige's hands were very large, with unpolished, bitten nails. She ran one hand through her short, crinkly auburn hair, fluffing it out from her ears. She felt the pulse of emotion mottle the whiteness of her throat, blotching up like a birthmark. So bad that, like wearing your heart on your sleeve, anybody could look at you and know your business.

Paige lit another cigarette, staring down at the sprawl of ink-corrected pages, the title sheet that read "Textured Vegetable Protein: Identifying New Market Opportunities."

It was making her hungry. She opened her drawer, unwrapped the foil-covered sandwich—tomatoes, salad, mushrooms, zucchini and Tahini-spread on whole-wheat *pita*. It was funny, she thought, biting down into the crisp layers. Since she had switched to health food in order to reduce her 140 pounds, she had gained ten.

She put the sandwich down and read the opening page again.

The time was now—she felt it rich and immediate: convince Dornbush, now that Hank Blaise had left, to promote her to senior research associate. Not to hire some off-the-street blunderer (a man, of course, the type in a three-piece chalk-stripe suit and paisley tie) who knew nothing about how things were done at Hornblower, Weeks, Noyes & Trask. Not like she had made it her business to.

Paige MacLeish, Senior Research Associate. Maybe even Hank's office with the window, acceptance at Harry's Bar, where she would breeze past the round table at the door where all the snobbish OTC securities traders sat and go right up to the bar where head bartender Daniel Bugarija would say "Hi, Paige," and write "MacLeish" on the back of her tab.

Yeah, and if horses were wishes, riders would beg.

"But I don't want to learn to type," Paige remembered telling her mother her freshman year at Sarah Lawrence. The thought made her smile.

"I don't care," Tessa MacLeish had said. "You get at least fifty words a minute under your belt. Then you can always leave your husband."

But it was all so difficult.

The job pressures, and this incessant third-roommate problem (remember Elinor, who never took a bath?). Thank God she and Francie got along, although they had nothing in common, but Francie was just *nice*.

Either they would have to move out of a great bargain of an apartment or put another ad in the New York *Times:* "Woman coll grad to shr w/2 othrs. Own bedr. $76.40."

But how had they been so wrong about Alexandra Baskin?

She had, of course, seemed a vision of normal female personhood after the last three applicants. Paige remembered the meek voice on the telephone clumping in in combat boots with her ponytailed boyfriend; they were planning on taking the room *together*. Then there was the greasy-haired asthmatic, and the girl whose obvious intention was to treat the apartment like a hotel. But they wanted a friend, not a paying guest.

Enter Alex. She was neat, clean, employed, although suspiciously gorgeous. The breasts should have told them something, Paige thought. Large ones that bobbled free in a ribbon-knit V-neck sweater—the shelf of breasts you never saw except on a Lana Turner pinup but you thought such bosoms were as dead as the word "bosoms" and the forties.

But even librarians might innocently inherit such breasts. Except on Alex they seemed to move with an animal abandon, like a force of nature that ought to be harnessed to produce electricity.

And you could scarcely expect someone with breasts like that not to use them.

After the prescribed tour of the apartment, Alex had flopped onto the sofa, one platform-soled sandal up on her knee.

"Like, I love it," she said, smoothing her long straight bangs sideways out of her eyes. "Feels homey, you know?" Her eyes were dark and jumpy and very bright.

"Want a gin and tonic?" Francie asked.

Paige felt a start of surprise. It was their agreed-upon

27

go-ahead sign. The other applicants had been offered Coke.

"You two are, like, really lucky," Alex said as they studied her. She appeared unconcerned under their gaze, dunking the lime slice with her little finger.

"Well, I'm glad someone thinks so," Paige said.

Alex sucked her finger. "No, you're really into your own thing, you know? You've got your own apartment, a place where you can, like, hang out, listen to music with your friends. I've been living with the parents in Manhasset. A drag, ov course. Like, you're still a baby when you live at home, no matter how ancient you get. I turned twenty-one last month, I want to be independent now, you know?"

There had followed the usual verbal résumés.

"I'm an exec secretary at Gilbert, Levensky—the Avon ad agency, ov course. No money. But lots of gorgeous Young Turks out to be the next Jerry Della Femina." She smiled. "You know?"

And then Alex had clinched it.

"J'ever think," she had said, "that women can click, I mean, like the way a woman clicks with a man? I mean, I'm independent. You're both independent. I can see that. I think it would work. I'd like to move in, if you guys agree."

Paige had thought about Rosalie, the asthmatic. In a way, she had liked her best of the applicants—down-to-earth, friendly, shy. But that was it. She wasn't independent. She was a sad-eyed frumpy-looking introvert who would probably tag after them every evening. The third woman out.

Alex was something else again. Although it was true she had a suspiciously sexy mouth—the kind you saw in close-ups on lipstick ads or performing fellatio in porn flicks—

still she obviously had an outside life and friends. Unattached male friends, parties to which they might be invited. A contributor, not just a taker.

Paige had looked at Francie, who nodded.

"Okay, sure. Fine," Paige had said.

Within forty-eight hours the error was evident: the time it took Alex to move in with eleven boxes, "Pandora's boxes," Paige had whispered to Francie.

It was true, Paige thought, that all her own clothes consisted of blazers and matching skirts and trousers (the covered-up executive look), that she herself was prejudiced in the direction of *tailored*. But Alex was the only girl she had ever known who owned three satin dressing gowns—power blue, silver gray, and Lana Turner (or was it Jean Harlow?) white.

And then there were the pills: birth control, Flagyl, Quaalude, Placidyl, Tuinal, Valium, Seconal, giant Welch-grape-blue unidentified capsules, and a bottle economically labeled "Speed." Packed beneath was a copy of *The Physician's Desk Reference*, with a lot of bent-down page corners.

Then the men began calling.

Paige remembered sitting trapped in the living room with one of Alex's admirers, while in the bedroom Alex was dressing. She had tried to think of something to say. She had told him about walking on West Ninth Street, the trees with new celery-green leaves, walking and then stopping before a brownstone with a painting on an easel in its window. The painting showed a brownstone with an easel in its window on a street with new celery-green leaves. Alex's admirer had been remarkably handsome, and his brown eyes had turned warm. Paige remembered the jump—of what? Hope? That he might like you, want you instead? "Don't let Alex spoil you," he had said.

In her office, Paige felt the knife prick of pain bore above her nape. She shook her head, and the pain shook with her. Then it settled down to a steady throb, throb—in time to her heart.

It was foreign as Latin, undecipherable as cuneiform: how some women knew how to attract men.

Paige remembered the voices in the kitchen, Francie telling Alex to move out. And then Alex disappearing into the bathroom. Paige had walked past the steam writhing from under the closed door, heard the sound of falling soap inside. The door to Alex's bedroom, just to the right, was open.

She had peered inside. The window was a pale square behind the curtain. Alex's unslept-in bed lay empty, ruffled spread pulled up to its chin. White trousers and tunic were thrown on the floor, and there was a blue stain on one limp leg. What was it? Blueberry Joy Jell (An Orgy's Delite) or the leaky pen with which he'd written down her number? Silver kid heels had been kicked off, and the soles inside were soiled.

I'll have to put on my makeup in the goddamned office, Paige had thought. Then she heard the cracked, off-key soprano from the shower.

Paige stared down at her desktop, uncapped her pen over the waiting pages of the report. Alex had agreed to move out by the end of August. She wouldn't have to feel this . . . this *what?* Confusion about Alex, this sense of something unfinished, something she should have said or done but didn't.

If only, she thought, she could remember the name of that blasted song Alex had sung.

Maybe then she could get it out of her mind.

The clean scent of orange peel drifted across the city room of the New York *Post*, past soiled gray metal desks, smudged plastic typewriters, speckled floor tiles, the sooty AP ticker that shook grime like dark dandruff with every whir and click.

What the fuck was it with these vitamin-C freaks? Orange peels were everywhere—in the ashtrays, damp piles in the dented wastebaskets.

Miles Kendrick Overby III looked up from his typewriter to see who was at it this time. Harry Beinsdorf, the rewrite slob at the round wooden copy desk, saluted him with a dripping section, then gave him the finger.

Miles returned it with feeling. Then he swiveled his chair around, a smile tangling the corners of his overgrown rusty-brown mustache. He tapped out "Overby - Assigned" and slugged the story "MUG." When he flipped the final take of copy from the machine and read it over, he felt the familiar rush at seeing his own order corraling an event, making it permanently his.

"NAB TWO IN ELDERLY MUGGING" the headline read. But below was the nice touch (exclusive, he hoped)—an interview with the hospitalized old lady's sister out in Flatbush. He'd had to really hoof it to bring that one home.

"But don't you feel like a jackal," the girl last night at Maxwell's Plum had asked, "hounding people in the midst of tragedy?" Such serious big green eyes.

Of course he did. He felt terrible for five minutes. But his job was to scoop, and if he took the other guys, the euphoria lasted two days.

The girl hadn't seemed to go for that answer. Adonis Overby scores again. Okay, next time he would reverse the proportions, say he bled for the old dame for two days; Christ, he was a sensitive, feeling bastard.

She was too tall for him anyway. And where the fuck was all this sexual revolution, sport-fucking, girls asking you for a change? He could write an extended ode on a Grecian yearn.

The closest he'd come to sexual contact in the last month was watching the Burger King counter girl give idle head to her microphone while he fumbled for change.

Miles stubbed out his unfiltered Camel in the overflowing ashtray. Just make the 3:45-P.M. last-copy deadline. He walked over and dropped the pink carbon in the overnight editor's box, the original and yellow carbon at the copy desk.

Then he stretched, flexing stiff fingers—a slight, sandy-haired man in a wrinkled blue workshirt and tan chinos—and pulled the plaid sport jacket from his chair.

Good timing, he thought. Lacing into a couple of Heinekens was just what he needed.

Four floors below he stepped out on South Street, relishing the fish-laden breeze off the waterfront. Then he turned south toward Moriarty's, a bar a few blocks from One Police Plaza, where he was meeting Gerald A. Dunning, deputy commissioner for whatever info he could pry from the cops this week.

A barrage of playground noise and radios swelled from the tract housing on his right. Nothing like New York City to cut men down to size, Overby thought as he turned from the Puerto Rican block down the Chinese street. It was wonderful. Not a man in sight over five-foot-eight, nothing like Memphis, where it had seemed every other high-school junior was pushing six-three and had a fantastic jump shot. What made them sprout like that out there—Frisch's Big Boy burgers, fluoridated water? Heredity, of course, but it didn't work in his case, since Judge Miles K. Overby Jr., six-one, made the grievous error of marrying tiny.

He didn't have his father's looks, either, he thought. Or success.

Okay, the brain. What would you rather be, tall and dumb? Rather tall and bald, tall with pimples and bad breath—but tall and dumb, no. So settle: short, homely, but smart.

And he would settle, if he could make it to the New York *Times*, which, as Gay Talese had pointed out, was indeed the kingdom and the power.

The words, in his boy's falsetto at the 8:15-A.M. school assembly, came back to him: "For dying is the kingdom and the power and the glory forever. Amen."

For years he had thought "thine" in the Lord's Prayer was "dying"—probably had had some dark, deleterious impact on his id. But as the song went: "... who wants Freud's advice? I'm sure it works with mice."

He began to sing as he walked, enjoying the eyes that swiveled toward him.

The only trouble was he was thirty-two and on the verge of no longer being the promising young man.

He stopped singing.

Well, Joe Alsop had started as a police reporter, doing character sketches of witnesses at the trial of Bruno Richard Hauptmann for the murder of the Lindbergh baby. After that, for Joe Alsop, it was Washington all the way.

What he, Miles III, needed—God forbid—was a Lindbergh baby.

5:22 p.m.

Relax, Francie told herself.

It wasn't Thursday. She was only groped on Thursdays.

And she was only groped *going* to work, not coming

33

home, like now, and only between the Fifty-seventh Street and Fifth Avenue stops, where the BMT subway swung shrieking around the bend, hurling hips into hips, knees into knees, mashers into mashees.

To mash: to reduce to a soft, pulpy state by beating or pressure.

Her left hand strained to hold on to the strap. With her right, she opened the paperback cover of *Lady Ingram's Retreat.* "Chapter One. Mr. Briggs shrugged up the collar of his shabby greatcoat and turned his tanned face to the west. The wind, he thought, with a pang of nostalgia, was blowing from Ireland. . . ."

She pressed the book closed against her side. Impossible to concentrate. The tension had begun when she had told Alex this morning, and had built, crescendoed through the day. Where was Alex? So hurt by their rejection she was unable to go to work? Now she would have to face Alex— alone—once again. What could she say? Apologize? Beg her to stay?

Forty-second Street stop. Forty-ninth Street next, and not a masher in sight.

But "masher" wasn't the right word anyway; what had the dictionary said? *Frotteur,* that was it. Oh, she was getting to be a real expert, could get a Ph.D. in *frotteurism* (*frottage?*). He who rubs against clothing or anatomical parts (usually buttocks), from the French *frotter,* to rub; also, to create a design by rubbing (as with a pencil) over an object placed under paper. But why was sex always *à la française?* French kiss . . . French postcard . . . French tickler. On the fourth day of Christmas my true love sent to me four Frenched hens.

And why did the masher have a route, a schedule, like a paperboy? It would be unions next.

Forty-ninth Street now. Fifty-seventh Street next.

Maybe he wasn't a masher/*frotteur* at all, but only a *toucheur*, one who indecently touches (feels, palpates, handles, paws). And anyway, why her? Because she was short? Because she still looked too Midwestern, too Main Street-corny, naive? Because her hair was the color of hay dust, not New York-dark over knowing New York coal-scuttle eyes?

Fifty-seventh Street. Fifth Avenue next, then Lexington Avenue, and she'd be out—unmolested, unfrotted, untouchered. She would go home, talk to Alex—yes, that's what she would do. Maybe they could still work things out.

Lexington Avenue was a wall of noise.

Francie climbed toward it up the subway stairs. Her dress slid over her wet body. A buzzing fullness crowded behind her eyes.

She crossed the street and pushed open the door of Dumas Patisserie. It was cool inside. She took a deep breath of the yeast and butter smells, country-fresh and clean. She stared into the mirrored cases at revolving cakes on paper doilies, waiting for the salesgirl with her metal tray. She wanted something exquisite, she decided—candied violets on ivory frosting—something too cosmetic to be food.

"Yes?" the salesgirl said.

She pointed out two petits fours, watched them wrapped in a white box. A peace offering for Alex, she thought. I'll make us some coffee and we'll talk.

Then the memory bore in: *"Little kaffeeklatsch?" Alex had said, emerging from the dusk of the hall out where old Mrs. Hanshaw from 5-H sat under lamplight, holding a steaming china cup sprigged with flowers. The coffee had splashed painfully over Mrs. Hanshaw's thumb. Alex was without kimono. Or anything else.*

In the heat outside, the bakery box was a plumb bob, dragging toward the center of the earth. The knotted string reddened her fingers. It was only August 8, Francie thought. Alex would be in the apartment like bad air until the end of the month. Like a pimple or a scab you can't stop picking, back and back to the same hurt.

Her legs moved slower toward the East River—a gray ribbon washing in metallic swells at the foot of Sixtieth Street. She had reached Second Avenue before the other memory came: *"Oh, hi!" Alex silhouetted in the bathroom doorway, wearing nothing but a T-shirt and that drunk-with-something devil on her face. Behind her by the wash-basin a man tugging up his jeans. Alex running down the hall toward her room, giving Spy a long look at her long, slim legs, her hard little cheeks peeping from the hem like melons from a sack. Spy's face following her, eyes hard and rutty as the Duroc Red boar's, the sow shrieking under his jackknifing back. Herself staring at Spy, staring and staring until finally he looked back, eyes brilliant with defiance.*

And then nothing had been the same between her and Spy.

At the corner of First Avenue Francie turned north. The street was crowded with singles bars—Adam's Apple, Thank God It's Friday, Koatails—and was known as The Strip, or so the media had dubbed it, sending crews to film the pop message. It was just, Francie thought, that she could never decide exactly what the message *was.*

People alone? The Friday-night girls climbing out of cars from Queens or Jersey? The Friday-night men appraising their crotches, leaning against parked cars that required no cover charge? Except that by Saturday all you saw was couples clambering up the evening like salmon, spawned out by Sunday—you saw them staring, surprised by crow's-feet in the coffee-shop morning.

And then on Mondays all the stunning young women emerging onto streetcorners with ugly older men not their husbands. The stunning young men emerged with other stunning young men. And every night of the week the bum balanced on his crate under the bistro vent, sniffing escargots, the garlic made him cry.

Francie climbed the sagging stone steps of their red-brick apartment building. Inside the entryway she stopped. Through the slit of the mailbox labeled "MacLeish—Perry—Baskin," a fold of white showed.

Alex hadn't picked up the mail.

Where was Alex?

Things you imagined, of course, were always worse than reality. Like that movie *The Thing,* the shape hinted through the ice, melting drop by drop, rising clearer as the music swelled. And then the shape finally shambling into view—James Arness in tinfoil.

If only she were still going with Spy, she could call him, he would know what to do. Or not call him, not have to because they might have been married by now, even in front of a justice of the peace, and she could have been out of this whole roommate mess, three girls barely able to pay the rent.

But then that thing had set in, that point where you can see him moving away, interest waning (waxing on Alex?). And you try harder and harder to please him, catch his eye, amuse him. But you're not Alex. And it's all gone out of your control.

Francie's footsteps rang sharply down the tiled hall, whose walls were painted a flaking pea color. As always, she conjured up a green octagonal door waiting at the end, cyanide eggs ready to drop. ("Dear Mom, my building's really a gas.") She glanced through the windows at the courtyard—a concrete patch bare as a prison exercise yard, crumbling walls penning it in. A dresser skeleton sprawled in the center—drawers smashed beside it, white knobs scattered in the wreck. Easier to drop than to carry, the maintenance men figured when faced with the detritus of moved-out tenants. And once it had cupped the broken body of a woman who flung herself from a sixth-story window. Human detritus. Francie remembered arriving home that Wednesday to see a sheet-covered hump, pale in the window-lit darkness.

The hallway turned right toward the back stairs. She climbed to the fifth floor through the warm, stuffy layers of pot roast, finnan haddie, kielbasa. She moved faster, eager now. Before her nerve failed, she would tell Alex she was sorry. It was not too late.

At the top of the stairs she stopped. By the light of the one remaining bulb in the hall fixture she saw that their front door—which Paige had double-locked behind them that morning—stood a hairsbreadth ajar.

The edges of the keys bit into her palm. She pushed the door wider. It was heavy, metal-covered, swung slowly inward on the narrow entrance hall.

After a moment she stepped inside. The walls seemed padded, stanched from sound. She strained to hear. Stale, chilled air moved on her face, and now she could make out the misrhythm of the air-conditioner—*whir, lump, whir*—drifting down from the living room. But that was usual, they always left it on, electric bill included, thank God, in the rent.

She thought: Apartment always was too dark.

She felt for the switch on the table lamp, smelling something fruity as she leaned over, that reminded her of apples.

The light clicked on over twelve yellow roses, beads of moisture glinting up from the tight, unopened petals. She picked up the card propped against the vase. In thick black capitals, as with a marking pen, someone had printed "LOVE, DALROI."

For Alex, of course.

Maybe they were here now, had just walked in, intent on what they would soon be doing, had carelessly left the door ajar.

"Alex?" she called. "*Alex?*"

The apartment was silent.

To her left was the living room, the bedroom she and Paige shared, and the kitchen. To her right was the door to the bathroom. And beyond it, at the end of the hall, Alex's bedroom.

Burglary, she thought, sick with the sudden certainty. She headed for the living room and the spots with no dust where the stereo, her sewing machine, and the new television had stood.

She snapped on the overhead light. Nothing was disturbed.

She felt suddenly exposed in front of the two tall windows. She remembered the unprotected doorway, open out into the hall.

Through the door to the kitchen: everything the same here. On the dinette table a half-eaten doughnut. Fuchsia-colored jelly had oozed out of the center, congealing on the chipped china plate.

What had the burglar taken? They had nothing, really, no jewelry to speak of. Of furs there was only Alex's raccoon with the rip under the left sleeve.

Francie peered into the bedroom she shared with Paige. It looked exactly as they had left it: a large room in tailored brown and white, with twin beds, two night tables and dressers. A narrow band of light fell between the unevenly hung curtains onto an aging blue-tweed carpet.

Francie crossed to her dresser. She opened the tall mahogany jewelry box, its layers of purple velvet platforms swinging out under the light. "It's beautiful," she had told Alex, when it stood on Alex's dresser. "It's yours," Alex had said.

The few pairs of pierced earrings, the Drake Relays shot-put medal Ron had given her back in college, gleamed obvious as Woolworth's in a Tiffany case.

She thought: Alex ate in a rush, left half a doughnut, slammed the door that had not caught, forgot to double-lock it, although we *told* her ninety-nine times. An accident, a simple accident. And Paige would be home soon, after the movie, they could laugh together over coffee and petits fours at her stupid, asinine fears, blown like always out of all proportion.

Everything was okay.

She stared down at the plain brown corduroy bed-spreads. She really hated this room. Something made her buy these practical unadorned things (Paige made her buy?), when what she had always wanted, longed for, was a real *boudoir*, with crisp white ruffles and those little neckroll pillows edged with lace.

This room, she thought, was more a stranger's room to her—a stranger she didn't particularly care to know—than Alex's room, whose every smallest detail was so perfect and pretty. She remembered the mirrored top of Alex's dressing table glinting up the stairs under the movers' tattooed, hairy forearms—*Paige, where's she getting this stuff? Looks real, almost like antiques.* The mirrored top set in place, reflecting the ivory cup holding sable makeup brushes, the heavy silver mirror-and-brush set, backs inlaid with opal milky-cool to your fingertip. The drawers and drawers of lingerie thin and pale as moth wings, so pungent with potpourri in satin covers that when you sniffed them they made you sneeze. On the tiny, carved oriental table the bronze fish arched on its tail, spouting four silk roses from its mouth.

Yellow silk roses.

Francie retreated to the living room. She could feel the wrongness; it had been there all along, but now it clotted the air.

Advice, heard and read, filled her mind: "Never enter an apartment when you have reason to suspect a burglary. You may surprise the intruder in the act, bringing harm to yourself."

Her eye caught a splash of red. Blood?

No, Alex's kimono on the gray-and-white carpet, beside the sagging black high-riser couch.

Francie walked over, stared down, unable to touch the silken folds.

Run!

She felt her heart hesitate, saw herself running.

But be sensible. Run where? Tell them what? That the apartment had been unlocked? Clothing was out of place? How could she live in New York City without being rational about a mere odd turn of events?

Francie walked out to the hallway. Its narrow length seemed to have unfolded, rolled onward. Alex's bedroom beyond lay deep in shadow. The door was closed.

Where was Alex?

Just check it out, she thought. Then go on, do what you should have done in the first place and call the police.

She walked down the hall and grasped the knob, the metal sliding wet in her palm. She pushed the door a few inches.

From the darkness within, music played softly. She could make out the radium dials of the clock-radio.

Anger filled her. Alex was sleeping, that was all. The fear, the worry, the calls from work had been for *nothing*.

41

"Alex."

Her hand swabbed down the bumpy plaster for the switch. The overhead light stabbed on.

Alex was not on the bed. Beyond the bed two bare feet, spread apart, extended on the floor. They appeared as waxen as a department-store mannequin.

The air seemed to dance. Francie stepped forward on feet that compressed a distance below her, without feeling. In the space beyond the bed sprawled naked shins, knees, thighs, pubic hair, breasts. Above lay a face, contorted, unfamiliar, the toe of a stocking lolling from the mouth onto the chin. The eyes were open.

They were the color of bitter coffee, wide and staring, eyes that were not quite in alignment, the right looking up at the ceiling while the left focused outward. It stared back at Francie with a curious glaring shine.

She felt the scream rip up from her chest.

Chapter Two

"If you're interested in seeing dead, naked bodies, become a detective," former Chief Albert Seedman had once said. The memory, cigar-scented, broke fresh as Detective Third Grade Victor Amspoker stared down at the bedroom floor.

The girl had been beautiful.

She was a brunette, with long, slim legs and large, lovely breasts. She reminded him, in just a small glancing way, of Maddie when she had been young.

The girl was lying on her back between the bed and the wall, hands above her head, fingers curled. Her face was blotchy and gorged dark. A gag of nylon stockings bulged her lips. She wore a tangled rope of stockings, beige and navy, wrapped tightly around her neck.

She was deeply tanned, with a bikini triangle of white skin at the hips, a white triangle over each breast. Beneath the surface of her skin, where it contacted the rug, there were the purple-pink streaks of settled blood.

Surrounding her left nipple, which stood dark in the triangle of white, was the clear imprint of teeth.

Near her feet lay a used Tampax.

Like an ailing queen bee, he thought, she was attended at both ends. By her legs squatted two detectives from the local precinct house, one beaming his flashlight down on her thick, dark bush, the other squinting for a gleam of foreign pubic hair. By her bitten breast the police photographer's assistant held a fifty-millimeter ruler. The camera whirred.

She was an element out of place, a pretty young girl now dead, lying in a tangle of evidence he would have to sort into order. She was a job to be performed, analyzed, written up, a problem to be solved.

Hardening of the feeling arteries, Maddie had accused him. Yet they had all seen so many stiffs a callousness had to set in. It was that or occupational depression. After twenty years on the force, only the bodies of children still affected him. He remembered his first body: the ten-year-old Negro—correction, *black*—kid lying on his side in the middle of Third Avenue, smashed to hell among the pieces of a bicycle. O'Shaugnessy's had seen plenty of him that night, drinking under the TV, staring up until the screen softened and dimmed.

By the twenty-fourth body he had watched without comment as two fellow patrolmen, older and wiser than he, tossed the wino stiff over the park wall into the neighboring precinct.

As for the pretty young girls, anyone on the force had seen plenty of young girls dead. Then you discovered they were prostitutes or had been sleeping around all over town.

Amspoker held up his Polaroid camera, backed it against his eye and squinted through. On the worn brown carpet the forensics man was kneeling, joints popping—a bulky man with a receding black Brillo hairline. He opened a leather case on rows of neat leather-bound instruments, cotton swabs, stoppered glass tubes. Selecting a swab, he wiped the red bitten area of the girl's breast in a circular motion toward the nipple, then sealed the swab in a tube. His fingers, plump and hair-covered, moved with prissy precision. He began again with another swab, sweat ring darkening under his arm.

Horror seized Amspoker. Even as he felt it he examined the emotion, surprised by its sudden and complete invasion. Routine horror, after all, was his job: bodies rotted into their beds, bodies fished from the bottom of the harbor, blood pouring from their noses and mouths at the change in pressure. Even birth, he thought, was a horror: a memory of purples, blues, and reds. His rookie hands trembling between the woman's knees, his jaw struggling to keep from her watering eyes the fear, inadequacy, ill-remembered academy instruction: "Place the baby on the mother's abdomen..." But her belly was a mountain of waves, the baby locked within. It wouldn't come, couldn't come, probably cross-breech or some breech, cord around its neck, probably dying like my own son dying... Jesus Christ, it was coming... Jesus Jesus Christ, *help me place the baby on the mother's abdomen.*

And then he had. And the mother smiled.

Amspoker pressed the shutter. He moved for another view, pressed the shutter again. He exhaled, then felt an edge of anger suck in, basic as air.

Get him. Whatever it took, however long it took, he would get him. The shit-gutted animal who had done this to this girl.

Already he could feel the satisfaction in his hands, raw and real as the baby.

"I don't make it as burglary, even burglary gone wrong," Detective First Grade Frank Quinn said at his elbow.

The voice irritated Amspoker, the voice that was one turn higher than a man's voice ought to be. He turned to look at him, keeping his face impassive. Frank Quinn had a weight problem supported by short legs. This was despite his constant consumption of diet gum, diet soda, diet hard candies, coffee yogurt and pineapple cottage cheese. His mouth, beneath the thick brush of wiry red on his upper lip, was constantly in motion.

But his real hunger was for promotion.

Why in hell had Jimmy tapped Quinn to head up the case? Too damn young, for starters, all of thirty-one, even if he had made first grade already, earning near a lieutenant's pay after only nine years on the force. Of course, he was a college kid—St. John's, business administration—and working and letting everyone know it on a master's in crim at John Jay. Such things counted for more today.

He had two habits: the wearing of a tietack in the shape of a pistol, and the constant two-fingered combing of his past-regulation-length mustache—a practice he was engaged in now.

Your own damn fault, Amspoker thought. No one had forced him into partnering with Quinn. He had volunteered. He had seen the understanding looks being passed. So the entire fucking squad knew it—he was no longer

46

eager to go home nights. It was a problem most of them had from time to time.

"Billy done the job on the door yet?" Amspoker said, squinting down through the Polaroid again.

"His guess is it wasn't forced," Quinn said. "No signs, but they're taking the cylinders in."

"So she let him in. What—deliveryman, boyfriend?"

"Or he grabbed her in the hall, lobby, somewhere, forced his way in."

Amspoker lowered the Polaroid. The voice detonating from the front hall was unmistakably that of John J. Donoghue, chief of detectives.

A-priority, Amspoker thought. But then, it had been obvious. The girl was young, white, attractive. And sex was involved.

Donoghue's choleric face, topped by a thick crest of white hair, took in the A-priority on the floor. Every man in the room stared down with him, Donoghue's new young aide struggling not to gawk.

"You're Reid, Jimmy Reid, am I right?" Donoghue's eyes, colorless as quartz, fastened on the Fourth Zone Homicide Squad's lieutenant. "How many guys you got on this?"

"Six, sir."

"Load the bases. Those damn reporters out there right now are screaming for blood. The girl's father is Samuel Baskin, yeah, that's right. City Hall, the *Times*, they all go sucking to real estate these days, I have to spell it out?"

There was silence.

Donoghue departed as abruptly as he came.

Lieutenant James C. Reid, a tall robust man in navy slacks, blue-and-white-plaid jacket and red tie, turned to Quinn. "Frank, you and Vic see how the roommate's coming along. Maybe that trank's worn off a bit, she'll be able to talk about it now."

47

Amspoker nodded.

Quinn's face remained set, a glistening mask. He was looking back at the space between the bed and the wall, at the feet lying high-arched and vulnerable, toenails painted lacquer red.

"A girl with class that keeps her feet like that, Vic," he said. "Somehow it disturbs me more."

"What disturbs you more?"

"When a girl that classy gets it."

Among his other shortcomings, Frank was a still-unmarried romantic.

7:16 p.m.

Francie could hear Nyree Attenbury and the doctor talking, voices lowered, in the kitchen. The needle's prick had threaded velvet ribbons through her veins. The hot panic had receded to a red-tinged core, around which her body swam.

The door to the bedroom in which she was lying opened, and two curly little heads peered in. They eyed Francie with unabashed awe.

The door crack disappeared as someone walked by to answer the buzz from the front door.

She swam for a time.

"Miss Perry?"

She opened her eyes. Two men were standing by her side, Nyree just beyond.

"Miss Perry?"

She focused on the light that gleamed like an oil slick at the top of the room. She pushed for it, feeling her thighs bunch with the thrust.

"Here now. Don't sit up. Take it easy."

The speaker had a broad open face, Irish-potato nose, and vivid blue eyes. His balding brown hair was compensated for by a red jungle of sideburns and mustache.

"I'm Frank Quinn, with the Fourth Homicide Squad, heading the investigation. We'll get you out of here soon's we can, okay?"

She stared at the white card with the blue-and-yellow seal as if it were an artifact from Atlantis.

"Miss Perry, we need to ask you some things—about the apartment, Miss Baskin, if anything's missing. Think you can help us out with that now?"

Alex. On the matted brown rug, in the bedroom. Tears rushed up. She felt her face contract, tight and hard, into a baby's grimace.

A hand cut off the light. Large and warm and dry, it covered her forehead. She felt her face relax. She opened her eyes.

The man was tall, in his forties, with thick dark hair, black eyebrows that met over a wedge-shaped nose, cinnamon eyes. He looked like a football player gone to flab. His upper lip was pointed, like the beak of a tricornered hat, was moving but she didn't hear.

She closed her eyes. She was back on the second story of the old white frame house, the Iowa fields beyond, sweating into the night with flu, hearing her mother walk down the hall toward her room. Everything was going to be all right.

"Can you get up now?" the first man said.

She nodded.

The two detectives walked with her down the hall.

Five-M was like a strange apartment, no place she had ever lived. The dusky half-light, the silence, all familiarity were gone.

Men and activity crowded the walls—men in shirt-sleeves, suits, uniforms, bending over cameras on tripods, dusting the doorknobs, the tables, the can of Tab with a chalky powder, dismantling the bathroom-sink trap, sorting through the trash baskets, dictating into whirring tape recorders.

As she hesitated inside the front door, their eyes measured her with frank curiosity, slid to their tasks, darted back once more.

"Would you mind identifying her in our presence?" The detective with the mustache gestured toward Alex's bedroom. "We have to keep the chain of evidence intact. And I'd rather ask you than her parents. Help us out and we can spare them."

"Yes," Francie said. Her pulse struck within her throat like a fist.

The bedroom was crowded with yet more men, and this seemed somehow more shocking than seeing Alex again. Among the clothed men she looked pitifully exposed, inner thighs thin, pubic hair dark, obscene.

Somebody cover her.

But Alex lay unabashed, inviting with her splay of legs even in death. On her toe hung a piece of thick, linen-like paper about four by seven inches. There seemed to be writing on it, as if she were a piece of luggage waiting for its owner.

"It's her. Alexandra Baskin. My roommate."

The fabric of the couch scratched the backs of her bare calves. Her feet—suddenly wet—slid in her sandals. "Dalroi?" *That name. Again.* "I never heard Alex mention it."

"First name? Last name?" Detective Quinn prompted. "A nickname, maybe?"

"It was with the flowers."

"Yes. We want to talk to him."

"I never heard her mention him. It's an odd name. Sure I would have remembered it."

Detective Amspoker was handing her a small book.

Francie stared down at the worn blue-leather cover in her hands. It was stamped with flaking gold fleurs-de-lis. They didn't need to tell her whose it was, where they had found it. Alex had often stood with it open in her hands at the telephone in the hall—voice whispery, breathy with promise.

Francie remembered the gold-on-blue of it sliding out with Alex's night-table drawer, remembered looking up, listening to hear if Paige had heard the creak of wood against wood. She had, in fact, pored over this book many times. For what? For the same reason that sent her to broken-spined dictionaries to find the meaning of *auto-da-fe?*

"It's Miss Baskin's address book," Amspoker said. A mannerism—nerves, stiff neck?—followed his words: mouth squaring down and back, shoulders hitching up as if seeking a more comfortable fit. "Tell us about anyone you know, heard her mention."

Tell them what? she thought. That Alex slept with dozens, legions, hundreds? Tell them she undoubtedly slept with every name in here?

She opened the book at the plastic A tab. The pages were a mosaic of different-colored inks and pencils, numbers scratched out and written above, lacy doodlings, secrets blacked out in impenetrable squares.

"I'm sorry," she said when she had passed the R's. "She never talked about her dates much." *Let them find out from someone else.*

"How did you three get along?" Quinn asked.

Francie waited until the impulse to spill it all out

51

subsided. "I . . . she moved in just last October—the fourth, I think. Paige and I ran an ad in the *Times*. Like I told you, Paige and I've lived together two years. Alex was nice, but really, she was out so much. We hardly saw her."

"Well, just look on through the rest," Quinn said.

It was a new-looking notation on the blank page, written in red pencil with a lead as smeary as lipstick: S.X. Below was the familiar address and phone number.

"Miss Perry. What is it?" Amspoker said.

She looked at them, their strange faces walling in her emotions. She wondered for a moment where she was.

"You know him?" Quinn said.

"I know him. He was my boyfriend."

"Was?"

"We broke up at the end of July."

"He started seeing your roommate then?"

The colors of Quinn's face seemed to wash outward, like oil on water.

"Hey," Amspoker said. "Hey." His palms rasped her hand, rough and dry, comforting as her father's.

Quinn was standing beside her with a glass of water. She gripped the cool, pebbled plastic. The water tasted like iron.

"I hate to suggest this," Quinn said. "But is it possible? I mean, do you think he could be the perpetrator?"

"*No*." She felt herself pulling back, back behind the wall. "That's absurd. No."

But now she was considering the thought, its implications, mental prongs teasing it as it invaded her mind.

But she *knew* Spy. Knew the way he sounded at the moment of orgasm, his rhythms, his sweats, the way he smelled. The way he slept, belly down, face sideways on the pillow, waves of crinkled red-brown hair released from the rubber band down his neck, feet moving through

52

some dream. She had heard him cry out in some dream, and his hand, sleeping, had sought and cupped her breast. And she had lain beside him, not moving, tears tracking from her eyes down into her ears.

Spy a murderer?

She had trusted him, opened herself up to him, unpacked an attic full of old fears and odd-shaped vanities, spread them out, happy as a child, with no thought that he wouldn't like them.

But now she was remembering certain cruel things he had said. Could a cruel person be driven to murder? How he had forced her to see herself in the worst light through his eyes, how he had battered on the door one night for two hours, demanding she let him in.

But all that was the usual stuff of failed affairs, wasn't it? Spy was a usual man, raging sometimes, but not capable of murder.

Because if she could believe Spy had done that to Alex in there, then she had never known anything about anyone.

11:34 p.m.

The two hospital orderlies lifted the body onto the stretcher, forced the stiffened legs together, folded the four canvas corners, cinched the belts tight, and hauled it away.

Paige MacLeish, climbing the stairs beside the young patrolman, saw the covered bundle emerge from their open apartment door. She flattened herself against the wall as it passed.

Beneath the white canvas, lumps and peaks reared, like a plaster replica of a mountain range. But she could not tell which end had been Alex's head, and which her feet.

So this is what it is like, she thought.

The thing she had most feared had happened. Not to her, but to one close enough to stir a sense of fate narrowly missing, rushing by. She was the survivor, but why? What had saved her from taking Alex's place on the stretcher? What had she done, what had she *ever* done to deserve it—to be the one left alive?

While she had been at work, oblivious to Francie's worry, there was *this*. While she had been at the departmental meeting—cheeks aflame, with papers and theories of investment strewn about, too much coffee oversweet, sharp criticisms and the brief courage and then joy as half the group supported her view—there had been *this*.

Inside their apartment hall a short, bull-bodied man was talking to a group of men, dark eyes moving rapidly from one to another. He stood erect, in a dove-gray Brooks Brothers suit whose trousers, though cut full, did not conceal badly bowed legs. His eyes caught her face as she passed.

"You are Paige?"

"Yes."

"I am Alexandra's father. I'm sorry to meet you in such a way. Anything I can do for you, and Francine, you give me a call."

He handed her a gray business card with the heavy texture of linen. In embossed dark blue script it read "Samuel R. Baskin and Son—Real Estate."

"Thank you, Mr. Baskin." She thought: *Cold-blooded as hell.*

She walked into the living room and saw Francie's face.

It was the first time they had ever touched, she thought, hugging Francie to her. Francie felt short, her body stiff. Beyond her hair Paige saw two men in suits watching them.

54

It was past one A.M. when the detectives finished their questions. "I'm afraid we'll have to ask you two girls to come over to the Twentieth Precinct house," Quinn said. "We'll make it short as possible. Promise. But we have to fingerprint you—"

"Us?" Paige said. "Why on earth *us*?"

The other detective, the older one, gave her a sympathetic look. "Eliminate your prints from the others."

"And a piece of advice before we go downstairs," Quinn said. "Don't talk with the media. We're after the perpetrator. But they're after a story."

It seemed that every neighbor for five floors was peering out at them—old men with silver stubble and pouched eyes, old women in stained bathrobes, young men and women in jeans. As the two detectives and two women approached, footsteps loud on the worn marble stairs, the doors were snatched toward the jambs. As they passed, Paige could hear the outflow of breath, the whisper of speculation. Their audience was afraid to ask them for details. They would wait for Mrs. Ushenko, the busybody with the Welsh corgi on the third floor, who always knew what man had a live-in girlfriend and who was illegally subletting. Or they would read all about it in tomorrow's *Daily News*.

Outside, it was worse. Night was day under banks of television floodlights. Over a hundred people waited, spilling over the front steps, hanging on to the spikes of the iron fence, trailing down the sidewalk, massing across the street. Paige could see McDonald's hamburger sacks in children's hands, mouths sucking at straws, a couple in white shorts holding tennis rackets, a jogger in sweatsuit gray over from the East River pathway. At the back of the crowd a man yelled, waving across to discovered friends.

So this is what it is like, Paige thought again.

As they descended the front steps, blinding lights flashed and bulbous, fabric-covered microphones pressed into their faces. A torrent of questions broke over their heads.

"Who found the body, Captain?"

"I'm not a captain."

"Was the girl raped?"

"Knifed or strangled?"

"Hold the questions. One of our men will be down shortly with a statement."

"We got deadlines, Lieutenant."

"What's the situation at this minute?"

"Any leads?"

"Any connection with that rape-murder over on Eighty-third Street?"

"You heard him, no questions!" a patrolman said, elbowing two reporters, one hunchbacked under a minicam.

At the curb a sky-blue-and-white patrol car was waiting, motor running.

As she stepped forward, Francie close behind, Paige felt fingers touch lightly, then more insistently on her arm. She looked up.

The fingers belonged to a short man with an intense young face that seemed a calico of colors: blond hair sprouting in whorls, a reddish-brown mustache and sideburns, black hornrims pinching a long nose.

"What kind of girl was she?" Miles Kendrick Overby III said, his voice soft, penetrating the noise.

Paige looked at Francie, whose eyes were staring at the reporter, dark holes under the glare of lights. Paige jerked her hand upward, shaking off the touch. "Damn you, just leave us alone. *Please.*"

"Wait," Francie said, "I want to tell him. She was a . . . a wonderful person."

It was a Muriel cigar box, the pasted decal worn to suede by his fingertips.

Dalroi smiled down at the Muriel face, whose colors had faded like old, familiar shirts on a line. He raised the lid.

But they were stirring up above.

He listened to the footsteps that clicked sharply down through the linoleum tiles, the rafters, concrete, asbestos, nails. The sound hammered into his head.

Those who lived above him were still up, still walking around, producing yet more noise. They might even come tapping down here at his door.

He wondered what would happen if some morning, just one morning, he left his door open . . .

No.

He would be solitary, a root pointing down, fleshy pale with fibers that knotted around rocks, secure in his own basement room.

He remembered his Aunt Helen's pickles and preserves cellar, where huge roots thrust through the damp stone walls, rotting the air with the smell of earth and carrots gone bad.

They had locked him into the cellar once.

Not they.

The she person.

He had stared up from the bottom of the stairs as the she stood silhouetted in the warm kitchen light. He had looked for, had seen the dark triangle under the thin white slip.

The door boomed shut.

And there was dark.

Stop that. You little monster. Mommee loves you. I'll whup you good. Stop that, you hear? Mommee loves her precious. Takeyourthumboutofyourmouth. Now! Or I'll cut it off. With my scissors. Nice sharp sewing scissors, see how sharp? Mommee loves you.

Dalroi opened the lid of the cigar box.

Once it had held the older treasures. He had slept with the box under his pillow, the hard cardboard corner pressing through to his skull. He had reached beneath his pillow every time he turned over, just to touch it and know it was there.

But he had dumped those treasures, forgotten and mummified, in a wastebasket.

The new treasures were so much better.

Dalroi picked up the gold bobby clip, turning it beneath the beam from the small gooseneck lamp. It was tarnished now, gilt peeling back from the dark pronged edges. He remembered sliding it out from her hair.

Sally Teising's gold hair, Rapunzel, so long he could climb up into, lose himself in it.

He laid the clip back down in the box, studying the metallic shine against the red silk of the kimono sash.

He thought about she-flesh, the parts they kept jealously hidden, known only to the shes. He felt the urgency dawn on him again.

If only they understood he wanted to please them.

If only Alexandra Baskin had understood, had let him please her.

He could have. He knew he could have.

He remembered the shiny glass wall of the coffee shop, just off Lexington Avenue near Bloomingdale's. The three girls sitting at a table right by the glass, he could see everything, their crossed legs (then uncrossed), the three pretty young girls. One was short, one was plump, one was beautiful. They were bright, exotic, weaving color and movement like fish behind an aquarium. Talking talking talking talking. Crossing uncrossing crossing uncrossing.

The picture burned into his brain.

They didn't know he was standing out there, across the street, watching them from the dark.

The three pretty young girls, they didn't care.

He had followed them home. And then the morning only two had emerged. It had been so easy. He had pressed the buzzer, her voice rattling hollow from the metal plate: "Yes? Who it is?"

"Florist. Delivery."

And the door had buzzed free.

Dalroi dropped the lid of the cigar box. The sound had a clacking emptiness like his grandmother's dentures.

Now there were two pretty young girls. As he thought about them, the conviction grew.

He knew he could please Paige MacLeish.

Chapter Three

Robert Lee, M.D., a small man in a crisp tan suit, straight black hair polished as his wingtip cordovans, crossed the street toward the Institute of Forensic Medicine. Already the asphalt gave spongily beneath his feet.

Mother it was hot, Lee thought, opening the door of the blue-tiled six-story building at 520 First Avenue. The refrigerated air enveloped him, lifting off the sweat that curled behind his neat small ears and down his hairless forearms.

Lee walked quickly past the brown marble wall in the entranceway, into which were hammered the words he knew by heart: *Taceant colloquia effugiat risus hic locus est ubi mors gaudet succurrere vitae.* (Let conversation cease. Let laughter flee. This is the place where death delights to help the living.)

He unlocked the glass-paned door to his office, sat down on the needlepoint cushion his wife had made, and opened the folder on his desk.

Homicide, he read. Young, white, female. Probable strangulation and rape. Bite mark on left breast. Serological grouping from saliva by T. H. Marnell (*a good man, but a buffoon*). Assailant blood type O.

Lee took the elevator down to Autopsy, one level below the main floor, and changed from his still-warm suit jacket into a starched white coat.

While he did so, an attendant walked to one of 128 compartments in the refrigerated wall and slid a drawer out, revealing fingers, glossy brown hair, shaven armpits, finally scarlet-polished toenails.

Lee entered the long, narrow autopsy room with its pale-yellow-tiled walls. The sinus-piercing scent of formaldehyde assailed him. Glaring white lights hung suspended above eight steel-mesh tables, three of which were already occupied. Lee could hear the faint sound of water irrigating the runoff troughs under each table, the soft murmur of the doctors as they dictated their findings into tape recorders or directed an assistant to take a sample to the lab.

While he waited, Lee idly studied the young white male corpse on the end table, noting the tattoo of doves above the nipples. A homosexual, of course. Tattoos interested him, such a pictorial grab bag of information: sexual bent, social class, even antisocial tendencies like "Born to Lose" and that one on Richard Speck, killer of eight student nurses, yes—"Born to Raise Hell." Just this past Wednesday he had

61

seen another cross with three dots, the possessor of which had committed murder, arson, and rape—or wanted to boast he had.

At the squealing of ungreased wheels, Lee looked up. His first case of the day—the "cut-'em-up," as some insisted on referring to it—entered the room and took its place on a table, the white-and-black tag drooping from its ankle.

Rigor mortis, Lee noted, had left the body, which was now limp, meaning that death had occurred at least fifteen to twenty hours before. Probably, then, prior to six o'clock Monday evening.

Lee opened the file folder, then checked the writing on the tag. Yes. Alexandra Elizabeth Baskin.

He nodded to Joshua Gant, an interning M.D. and his new assistant. (*Smart boy, but perhaps not sufficiently devoted to the trade.*)

"Body is that of a well-developed and well-nourished young white female," Lee began, dictating into the tape recorder, "approximately twenty-one years of age, measuring sixty-five inches in length and weighing one hundred and nineteen pounds. Head hair is somewhat matted and brown in color. The irises are brown.

"In the right forehead is a horizontal recent linear laceration, one-fourth inch in length and located vertically one and one-half inches above the lateral aspect of the right eyelid and one inch horizontally and to the right of the lateral aspect of the eyelid. This laceration appears somewhat deep.

"The cheeks and tip of the nose appear somewhat mottled and purplish in color.

"The mouth is stuffed with portions of a woman's nylon pantyhose—beige in color—which I now remove."

With two rubber-gloved fingers, Lee fished out the still-damp gag. Then he paused, looking down at the mouth that gaped beneath the lights. His eyes met those of Gant. He saw the sweat bead upon Gant's forehead, glinting among the curly light-brown hairs.

"Examination of the mouth discloses upper and lower natural teeth. A quantity of blood is present on the upper and lower incisors."

Lee picked up a scalpel, examining its edge.

"There is a tight ligature encircling the neck. The ligature consists of two nylon pantyhose, beige and navy in color, doubly tied anteriorly. I now remove this ligature by cutting, and with preservation of the knots."

Lee's scalpel gnawed the fibers below the chin.

"The neck is of average proportion. Examination of the neck discloses a distinct dark-purplish impression beginning at a point just below the prominence of the thyroid cartilage extending laterally to the left and in this area having a width of approximately one inch. In the left antelateral aspect of this impression are multiple petechiae. As the impression circumvents the neck, it narrows in width in the left-lateral aspect and makes a deeper impression in the neck averaging up to one-eighth of an inch in depth. The width in this area is approximately one-fourth of an inch. The impression continues around the neck and in the left-posterior aspect begins to flatten out. There is no distinguishable impression in the right-posterior aspect of the neck. As the impression encircles the neck, it becomes slightly wider in the right-lateral aspect, very faint, and again becomes apparent in the right-anterior-lateral aspect of the neck."

Lee paused, reminding himself to pronounce clearly. Nothing more annoying than missing words on the transcript, which the secretaries, of course, blamed on garbled tape.

"The chest is symmetrical and discloses two very firm mammae with areas of light-pink areolar pigmentation.

On the left mamma and completely surrounding the nipple is a recent bite mark, round in shape and one and five-sixteenths of an inch in diameter. The mark exhibits a central ecchymotic area, or suck mark, and a diverging linear abrasion pattern typical of sexually inflicted bites."

Lee moved down along the side of the steel table.

"Examination of the external genitalia discloses a non-virginal introitus." Methodically he collected the semen deposited within, describing its color, consistency, and quantity.

Then his scalpel flashed beneath the lights, drawing the thoracoabdominal—the Y-shaped incision from shoulder to shoulder and down the midline of the flat abdomen past the navel.

Working faster now, but with an economy of motion, he removed and described the contents of the last meal.

He weighed the liver: 1620 grams.

He noted the condition of the heart, lungs, gall bladder, spleen, pancreas, adrenals, and ovaries. He sliced open the uterus: no fetus was within.

He made a mold of the bitten left breast. Then his blade sliced deep, severing the breast, lifting it from the sagging chest wall. He slid it into the wide-mouthed bottle of formaldehyde.

It was almost twice the size of his wife's breast, Lee thought. He watched it swim toward the bottom of the jar.

9:24 a.m.

In his office on East Twenty-third Street, Emmanuel Gold, DDS, P.C., consultant in forensic dentistry, was looking at a photographic blowup of the same breast.

"This was taken with a fingerprint camera at the scene, Miles," he said, pushing it across the desk. "But your word on this—not for print, not for nothing."

"Trust me, Manny. I'm just trying to get the outlines of this. Put it in focus, right?" Miles tapped a cigarette on his watch face, struck a match, and stared down through smoke at the glossy black-and-white image.

The wound was circular, with lines radiating out from its center, and triangular and square puncture marks rimming its edge. Like a bull's-eye from the center rose the nipple.

"Looks like a sunburst," Miles said.

"Yeh. Classic example, really. You get those diverging abrasion lines when the guy sucks in a mouthful, past the incisal angles of the teeth. When he lets go, the compressed tissue and the marks spread back out."

"This kind of thing rare?" Miles said, feeling his stomach tighten.

"Hardly. Hell, you see them in fifty percent of the sexual-assault homicides in the city. In the gay cases, you see bites on the back, also the arms, shoulders, axillae, face, even the scrotum. With the straights, it's usually on the breast"—he covered his right breast with his hand—"or on the thighs. Albert De Salvo, the Boston Strangler, was a biter. Bite marks were found on his victims' breasts, abdomens, thighs, genitals. What us goddamn civilized types forget, Miles, is that teeth are weapons. The most primitive weapons of all."

"Just in sex cases?"

"You see them in two types of homicides. The sex cases, like I said. And the battered children. Take this bite, now. It's like most sex bites—we term that an 'excellent' impression. The biting is done in a·slow, sadistic manner, you get this nice sharp mark. With the kids, though, there's a rapid, random, enraged attack, you get tissue laceration, diffuse marks. Hell, Miles, don't go green on me now. Anyway, for your purpose, here's the clincher. The wound pattern left by a bite is unique to that set of teeth."

"Like fingerprints, you mean?"

"Yeh. Exactly. The guy did this has his own shape, size, malalignment, wear, diastemata. Might be a good subject for a *Post* article, but make sure as hell you leave out the Baskin case." Gold looked across the desk at Miles. His face was aureoled by black hair crimped in rows, as if between a waffle press. Behind the black-rimmed glasses his eyes were eager.

"You got something there. Sunday-supplement story they can read over fucking bagels: 'Man Bites Woman.' "

"I helped solve a homicide last year," Gold said quickly. "The Richards case, remember it? My findings let the cops rule out two of three suspects. I had them bite down into wax. Of course, I can only say a suspect's teeth either *are* or *are not* consistent with the wound mark. But with Richards, the blood grouping from the dried saliva, the tooth impressions and the motive were enough to get an indictment. And then the sucker confessed."

"Where's he now?" Miles said, writing rapidly on his notepad.

"Brushing his pearlies in Attica." Gold leaned back in his chair, the cracked leather padding creaking. "Then I gotta tell you about this old woman the cops brought in from one of those West Side single-residency hotels. They're all hot it's a homicide, want to pick up this delivery boy. Why? There was this damn bite mark on her upper left arm. Wait a minute, perfectly even marks. Turned out she died of an infarct and fell over on her own goddamn dentures."

"What about this bite?" Miles said, looking back down at the photograph. "What does it tell you about the killer?"

"Guy's got two hypoplastic lower front teeth—lean in toward the tongue. I told the cops to look for someone with crowded lower front teeth. You got crowded lower front teeth, Miles?"

"Very funny. What else?"

"He was facing her head, not her feet. And he used his top teeth more for holding—there's a more diffused mark there—and the bottom teeth for the real biting. Ever seen a male cat ream a female? Bites her damn neck to hold her in position. So we're not so damn far from beasthood after all." Gold unwrapped a Reese's Peanut Butter Cup, held it out to Miles, who shook his head, then dropped the entire candy in his mouth. He chewed rapidly. "Ironic, really, all this breast stuff. I was always an ass man myself."

"So how's Gloria these days?" Miles said. Gold had remarried just two months before.

"Tolerable. Last night she turns her little tushy toward me, says, 'Feel that, hard as a rock, right?' "

"Women," Miles said. "They're all alike. Just after one thing."

"Makes you wonder if this Baskin number's ass was as nice as her breast."

Miles stared again into the photograph. He was looking at a real breast, he reminded himself. Part of a human being. Only yesterday it had belonged to a young woman with corpuscles, adrenaline, someone full of life, he liked to imagine. Someone's daughter, sister, lover. From the picture in the *News* this morning she had been beautiful, too. It was incomprehensible that someone had murdered her, all her life, twenty-one years' worth, ending up here, a severed part passed around from hand to hand.

He wondered suddenly what she had been like. In her wholeness, and deep in her mind.

"This the right or left?" Miles said.

"Left." Gold swung his long legs down from the scratched wooden desktop. "Always the left breast, for some reason. We see a bitten *right* breast around here, we get scared the guy's a damn pervert."

Hand a baby to a woman—Miles remembered reading it somewhere—and instinctively she'll rest it in the crook of her left arm, up against the beat of her heart. *Up against her left breast.* Then the baby would nurse more from the left, too, it stood to reason. From the left breast love and warmth and food, spat back here in some infantile rage? The littlest assassin, still after his mother?

"Gold's theorem," Gold said, "is they bite the left breast because they're lying on top of her. And most people are right-handed, so probably right-bited, too."

"The thought of it," Miles said, laying down the photograph as Gold dug in the back of his desk drawer. "That a man could bite a woman like that. It—"

"Makes you glad you're not a broad, right? And here's another little tidbit you can tuck away. Statistics prove it." Gold withdrew another peanut-butter cup, unwrapped it and wadded the paper. He bit down into the circle of chocolate.

"Cancer prefers the left breast, too."

9:42 a.m.

"*Wipe your fingers with this cotton ball, Miss Perry.*"
Yes. Cool with something damp, already evaporating.
"*Sign your name, please. Right here.*"
Yes. On an eight-inch white card held by metal strips in wood.
"*Now, then, just relax your fingers, look away from the card, let me do the work.*"

Like getting a shot, look away from it, yes.

Two fingers gripped her finger (wrinkled tube all hairs and pores like an elephant's trunk), pressed her finger down, rolling, rolling onto the inked glass plate, up, rolling onto the card, up.

Francie looked back and down. The topology of her finger showed black on white, valleys between ridges, furrowed swirls like a plowed field in a snowfall seen from the air.

But now they would know.

Her fingers, ten rubber stamps, had branded her name all over Alex's room, in her drawers, through the closet, down among the lingerie. Now they would think . . .

"Tell us why you killed her, Miss Perry."

"No."

"We know you did it, fingerprints don't lie."

"No. You don't understand. I'm—"

"Guilty?"

Francie came awake in a rush, the dream still vivid, noisy in her head. Her body was wet, heart loud in the dark room. But what room? Where was she?

The ceiling was a gray ocean of movement. Across the window, blinds clicked, swayed in the updraft from a vent.

The room was freezing. Under her back, cold pressed up through the mattress, spreading wide and hard as February earth. Her fingers and toes tingled. She moved her arms and legs out from her body, then in, out, and then in. She had made angels in the snow like this, being careful to get up from the imprint without marring the edges, looking back at the angel with her wings and skirt.

But that had been Red Oak, Iowa.

And this was the Summit Hotel at Fifty-first Street and Lexington Avenue, where the lobby drugstore sold dwarf toothpaste tubes and the bar sold dwarf bottles of Coke.

It was sometime Tuesday. Sometime toward dawn she

had drunk down the Dalmane, feeling its tubed slickness wedge through her throat, tumble out into her gut. She had lain in bed, heart beating faster, waiting to feel the first effects. She had never thought she would take it, or any drug. But "You'll sleep like a baby," Dr. Reiss had promised.

Now she had waked, helpless as a baby.

"Paige?"

"Yeah."

"You awake?"

"No."

"Paige, what time is it?"

"Almost ten. In the ungodly A.M."

Francie looked across at the second bed. Paige was sitting up, rubbing her arms, a tall figure with pendulous breasts, the pink of her nightgown phosphorescent in the dim light. Her face was a pale, unreadable disk.

"Francie . . . I'm going home."

The fear was immediate. "What do you mean?"

"I'm going to tell Max today—screw Hornblower." Paige sawed the sheet hem back and forth across her palm. "And I want you to come home with me. We'll get jobs there—something, I don't know what."

The old white colonial house in Hopewell, New Jersey, came into Francie's mind as she had first seen it—fragmented between elms up the long driveway in Paige's red Volkswagen. It stood on a hill fifteen minutes from Princeton University, where Willis MacLeish taught, wrote, and sculptured arcane anthropological theories. Mrs. MacLeish was an artist, wore jeans with watercolor spatters, and was the sort of mother who was always pushing lemonade on you. Homemade lemonade.

It was inconceivable, but there it was: "Will" and "Tessa," Paige called them. She wondered what it must feel

70

like to be an only child of such parents—cherished, lavished with presents and ideas.

But Hopewell, New Jersey? No matter how beautiful, it was like Red Oak—a place you left, not came back to.

And then there were the bills, Francie thought. Two weeks in London, the new pantsuit from Bonwit's, three cavities, solid-gold filled—all arriving "Payment Overdue" in the mailbox on the first. Already the hotel room had entered the Visa computers.

"You can't leave New York," Francie said. "You have a real career, for God's sake, not like me. You know you'll make senior associate now Hank's gone."

Paige's head dropped back into the white pillow. "Hornblower—it just doesn't seem to matter anymore. And without that, there's nothing else—just the city. Even the karate hasn't made me feel better about it. Hell, all the muggers probably know karate, too. And then, I haven't been able to go out with anyone for a year. The whole sick sexual scene. Every time now I see a guy with a girl, I get this vision. Like a man with a dog. All over the city—girls on leashes, bought and paid for. All those men are into it— the dominance trip. All those men with rape in their eyes. You know yourself. We talked about that—no one we know hasn't been raped on a date."

"I wish you wouldn't talk like that," Francie said.

"Now it's rape *and* murder."

There. It had been said, Francie thought. *It was real.*

"It could have been you," Paige said. "It could have been me. But I'll be damned if it's *going* to be me." She threw aside the covers and paced back and forth at the foot of her bed. She crossed to the window blinds, held a plastic slat open, peered out, let it snap back. "So help me God, Francie, I'll kill first. I'm going to get a gun in Hopewell."

"But you remember what that Detective Amspoker said.

It was an isolated thing—a thing like that, it won't happen again."

"And you believed that crap?" Paige's eyes stared out of mascara smudges. "What do you expect him to say: we'll be dead tomorrow too? That's his job—feed platitudes to the frightened roomies, pat their heads with that phony father routine. Bullshit."

"Wait a minute. He *is* concerned. He's doing everything he can—all of them are. Anyway, what happened had nothing to do with us. In a sense Alex brought this on herself."

"Don't say that! *Asking for it.* That's what they'll all say. 'Oh, that slut was just asking for it, sleeping around all over town.'"

Paige sat abruptly on the edge of the bed, her fingers tight on Francie's arm. "We can't tell anyone those things about her. Not the fuzz. Not anyone."

"But what can possibly matter now except to *catch*—"

"No." Paige's head leaned close. "Don't you see? That's the kind of thing that encourages murder. Can you imagine the headlines? PLAYGIRL SLAIN. EX-LOVERS SOUGHT. Her parents would suffer, and what the hell for? So people could say, 'Oh, well, that was one victim just asking for it.' So another pervert could kill another girl and go home and think, 'Oh, well, she was asking for it.' To encourage talk like *that* is asking for it. And the cops are no different. Four kids in Bensonhurst, Mass on Sunday. Hell, you think the cops'll bust a gut for a promiscuous broad? No, but they'll work all night if she reminds them of their daughter."

Francie could see the tears in Paige's eyes.

"Okay, you're right. We'll say she went out, as far as we know, just on casual dates, never mentioned guys' names or brought them home. We didn't know her that well, but we liked her. I did that already, with that reporter. And we'll find a new apartment, Paige, in a really high-security building, just the two of us. Maybe get a dog, a German shepherd, you know you always wanted one. A sexy blond in lederhosen."

"And a gun," Paige said. But the anger had sagged from her face.

"Yeah, okay. Maybe a gun."

Paige pushed herself to her feet, walked over to the bathroom.

The fluorescent tube rustled on with the sound of mice. The light hesitated, then glared whitely out the door. There was the rush of the sink tap.

"And nobody knows we wanted her to move out," Francie said over the sound of the water. "Nobody knows what we really thought of her."

Paige stood silhouetted in the door of the bathroom, a plastic tumbler in her hand. She waited until Francie looked up.

"Hey. Forget about that."

The shower droned against porcelain.

Francie lay on her back, watching the steam drift cloud-like across the ceiling. Faces appeared, disappeared in the mist.

He was out there, she thought, walking around right now. Maybe eating breakfast somewhere, mopping up egg.

Or was he too staring up at a ceiling, thinking of that other ceiling that had frowned down on Alex, her fingers limp as fabric on the rug.

Had it been an isolated act? An explosion of rage, jealousy—never to be repeated, always to be regretted? Or did he plan to do it again?

But why, Mother? Why do we die? How can God love us and yet make us die? "*But of the tree of the knowledge*

73

of good and evil, thou shalt not eat of it: for in the day that thou eatest thereof thou shalt surely die." That's Genesis 2:17, Francie. Death was not planned by God, he didn't want it. Death came as a result of our disobedience, which is sin.

In one motion Francie was out of the bed.

"Paige," she said at the bathroom door. "Going out for a walk. I need some air."

"Well, don't be long."

Outside, the sky was pale and clear, the humid sun pressing down. Two women were idling along, looking in store windows and pushing strollers. Francie fell into step behind them. They were turning the corner when she saw Alex peering up at her, almost unrecognizable behind false eyelashes and shoulder-length hair.

BRUNETTE EX-MODEL FOUND SLAIN, said the *Daily News* in banner type across page one. CAREER GIRL IS SLAIN IN HER EAST SIDE APARTMENT, the *Times* version read, without photograph and relegated to the bottom-right corner.

"Help you, miss?" the newsman asked, wiping inky fingers on his soiled canvas apron.

Had she stared down too long? Had he guessed?

Francie dug twenty cents from her handbag, grabbing up a *Times*. She felt his eyes on her until she turned the corner. She walked south to Fifty-first Street, turned the corner again. Then she unfolded the paper.

CAREER GIRL IS SLAIN IN HER EAST SIDE APARTMENT

Daughter of Real-Estate Czar Samuel R. Baskin Found With Pantyhose Around Her Neck

A 21-year-old advertising-agency secretary, who moved to the city

> only ten months ago from her
> family's home in Manhasset, Long
> Island, was found apparently stran-
> gled yesterday evening in her fifth-
> floor apartment at 403 East 63rd
> Street.
>
> The victim, Alexandra Elizabeth
> Baskin, was found at 5:45 P.M. by
> one of her two roommates, Francine
> Perry. Miss Baskin was lying nude
> on the floor, pantyhose in her mouth
> and tightened about her neck.
>
> Lieutenant James C. Reid of the
> Fourth Homicide Squad, who is in
> charge of the investigation, said
> there was no immediate indication of
> forcible entry by door or window. . . .

Her own name, like an obscenity, leaped from the page.
She would be indexed now, microfilmed, permanently entwined and embalmed with Alex. But why this terrible
shame, as if she had been caught in some lurid act?

She had walked two blocks before she realized that the
other footsteps were with her, footsteps that turned just
where she did.

She walked faster, heading back toward the Summit
Hotel.

"People are really good at heart," Anne Frank had told
her diary, even as the Germans cried over Goethe while
pushing Jews in the oven. But Anne Frank had known
what she now knew. You had no choice. You had to believe
people were really good at heart, or else how could you dare
to leave your parents' home, come to the city, get a job,
walk down a street?

You had no choice but to trust, walk on, keep on trust-
ing.

The footsteps behind her continued.

You had to trust the way she trusted, lying in her bikini on Tar Beach—the asphalt-covered roof that softened in the summer, leaking tea-colored water into the apartments below. Trust the way she trusted looking out at the sun haze through her straw-hat fringe, telling herself no sniper on an opposite roof or leaning from a window was drawing a bead on her forehead, or when she turned over to brown her back, sighting down his barrel onto the nape of her neck.

The footsteps sounded louder, closing the gap.

It was trust or be a prisoner in your own apartment, staring out at the sun through the barred gates on your windows. It was trust or give up living, you had to trust that this time too nothing would happen. And just walk on.

Francie whirled.

A scant five yards behind her she saw the same short man from the night before, the reporter with hornrims who had pushed through the crowd with his question.

"*What are you doing?*" Her voice was shrill in her ears.

"Hey, don't be scared. You scared *me.* I saw you leave the hotel. Aren't there any police, plainclothes keeping a lookout?"

She stared at him.

"Sorry. Didn't mean to frighten you. I'm Miles Overby, of the *Post.* But I'm not after a story, don't get the wrong idea. Sure, I was in the lobby to ring and ask for an interview. Then I saw you walk out alone and got worried. I just don't think you should go strolling around like this by yourself. Want some coffee?"

"Why shouldn't I take a walk when I want in broad daylight?" she said as his fingers closed on her elbow, easing her toward a corner coffee shop.

"C'mon inside," he said, opening the door, "and I'll tell you."

From the uneven vantage point of the sprung booth seat, she looked across at Miles Kendrick Overby III.

"So how are you doing?" he said. "You and uh, Paige, isn't it?"

"We're all right, I guess. Actually I don't know. Don't know how we're doing. You must have talked to plenty of people after a murder. You'd know better than me."

"No. No, I don't know. Never had to go through what you're going through."

He was looking down at his interlaced fingers on the table. He had a thin chest under an open-necked sport shirt and blue madras jacket. Cowlicks sprouted from his scalp, his pale hair whorling east, west, and on top of his head, north. But his eyes, which were gray behind the glasses, were warm and intelligent.

"Yeah, whatya havin'." A large waitress stood beside them on one soiled white shoe, rubbing the other up the back of her calf like a misplaced flamingo.

"Just tea," Francie said. "With lemon."

"Seventy-five-cent minimum at booths."

"Just tea."

"And I'll have coffee," Miles said. "And two eggs—lookin' at me."

The waitress lowered her foot.

"He *means*," Francie said, looking at the waitress, "sunny-side-up."

Miles was smiling at her. "Oh, yeah. Midwestern hayseed, same's you. Well, not perxactly Midwest, but close enough. *T*ennessee, *Mem*phis, *T*ennessee, border state actually, but God's country just the same—you know, out there where crops grows thicker'n people. And I know all about your fair Red Oak, Iowa. 'Prettiest eyes,' according to your high-school yearbook. But that doesn't do them justice."

"How did you—"

He waved her to silence. "Now, Francie—can I call you

Francie?—you know you can't ask a reporter to reveal his sources. Supreme Court still says that's a no-no in this man's democracy."

She felt the tension flow from her body. He was not another Easterner, he spoke and understood the way she did. It was like finding a friend in the middle of a party where everyone knew everyone, except for her. "What's Memphis like?" she asked as the tea and coffee arrived, splashing over into the saucers.

"Dull place, really. Only downtown business making bucks is the Avant Garde Cinema"—his voice rose— "Pornucopia of the World's Finest Aaadult Entertainment, Twenty-Three Private Movie Rooms with Sound and Memphis' Largest Selection of Aaadult Films and Eeerotic Paraphernalia, Couples Welcome."

She felt laughter tunnel up, almost making it to her lips. But she knew what Paige would say. He was a reporter. Not interested in her, just the story. "You were going to tell me why taking walks in the morning isn't healthy," she said.

"Yeah. Well, look, one of the prime suspects skipped town. I'm not trying to scare you with this, just caution you. How do you know he doesn't worry you may know something to connect him?"

"What suspect?"

"Her boyfriend. This guy Xanthakis . . . What's the matter, you know him?"

She felt a burning sensation flush upward, scalding her eyes. "What do you mean, skipped town?"

"Cops went to his apartment early this A.M., Upper West Side. He'd packed up and cleaned out sometime last night, parts unknown. July rent still due."

"Coincidence, probably."

"So you don't think he had anything to do with it?"

Francie took a worn leather wallet from her purse. She opened it at the plastic sleeves. "I knew him pretty well."

"Rock climber, huh?" Miles said, staring at the snapshot. It showed a virile-looking young man leaning one hand against a near-vertical wall of gray stone, reaching down with his other hand for something out of the picture. He had a broad chest in a red plaid shirt, and his narrow hips were hung with metal—rectangular carabiners, triangular chocks—and twisted lengths of orange and lilac nylon. Through an orange harness that circled his waist and each thigh threaded a royal-blue climbing rope. He wore glasses, and a white terry sweatband that held back waves of reddish-brown shoulder-length hair.

"What do you mean, 'knew him,' Francie?"

"We broke up end of July."

She could hear his breathing—soft, a little ragged.

"Look, I'm sorry I brought this up. But someone's gotta look after you, right? Jesus, you worried me this morning, alone like that. I just want to help. I like to walk in the mornings, next time you get the ole urge, give me a call." He wrote something on his napkin and handed it to her as a thick white china platter arrived. The eggs were scrambled.

She looked down at the white square of napkin. "Clark Kent," he had printed, along with his work and home telephone numbers.

"Regale me with life on the farm," he said, upending the salt shaker. "I get homesick as hell for cowpats."

She remembered the alfalfa ready in the field, dew on the tractor seat soaking cool through her jeaned bottom. The sun beginning to burn on her neck, steering wheel vibrating, nails white, cutting alfalfa at ten miles an hour. Hen pheasant up, down, up again, tries to lead away from her brood. The fourteen-year-old down in the tall alfalfa,

79

fingers through, smell of dry black soil, green soft alfalfa scent, searching out the fluffs of speckled brown that beat in her palms like a heart, carrying them one by one to the fence row.

She drank her tea, then put the cup down. "My father died and we lost the place."

"*Lost* it, Francie? Why?"

"Estate taxes. Dad built it up too good, I guess. In the end it was twelve hundred acres, one hundred thirty thousand dollars' worth of heavy equipment—we even had a computer service with printouts to show what was profitable. We had everything but the cash for the taxes."

"That's the worst thing I ever heard."

"It's worse now. I really need him now and he's gone, Dad's gone. This probably all sounds self-pitying."

His hand came down on top of hers. "Hey, you have reason. I can't believe how well you're handling this thing. Where's your mother live now, Francie?"

"In California with Beverly. My oldest sister. She's married and has two kids. I don't believe this. Yesterday morning Alex was okay. And now she's gone. Just like that. Just like Dad. Just *gone*."

"Did you like Alex?"

"Yes. Of course I liked her."

"*De mortuis nil nisi bonum*. Of the dead, speak nothing but good, right?"

She looked down. He had very attractive hands, she thought. Large for his size, strong-looking, with neat broad clipped nails. She had liked many men other people thought unattractive. It was always possible to find something you liked—ripe olive eyes, long supple hands, charisma that overcame pimples, arrogant male pride that overcame bad breath. There was always something, some chemistry that hung veillike, shielding her eyes from whatever they weren't. You could spend your whole life waiting for Rhett Butler to sweep you up some dark staircase of desire. Or you could settle for the men who were really out there.

"How long do you think it'll take them to find the . . . the one responsible?" Francie said.

"Well, it's a funny thing about these front-page murders. See, there's two investigations—the public one and what's really going on. The public thing reassures the panicked populace the mad dog's almost caught. But behind the scenes—hell, the boys've got other cases, too, you know. They don't nab this guy in the first forty-eight hours, their chances plummet. By a month they got a snowball's chance in hell and the case is all but dropped. Your friend could end up in a file labeled 'back burner.' And that's really being buried."

"Why are you telling me this?"

"So you'll keep after them, prod them a little. They can use it. Rand Corp study last year said in half the cases solved there's no question who the guy is anyway. Either he's arrested at the scene, or somebody got his name or license number. So much for Kojak."

"One of the detectives—Amspoker—seems very concerned about it," she said, voice angry. "I don't think . . . Let's get the check, all right?"

He turned toward the waitress, who was deep in conversation with a man at the counter. She seemed impervious to his signalings and sheepish muttered sounds.

How could Miles ever have become a reporter? Francie thought. He couldn't even summon a waitress.

"On to something more pleasant," Miles said. "I might be able to interest my editor in a piece starring you. You know, the all-American girl in the big city, apple pie versus crime and grime, screened-in porch versus doorman—"

"We didn't have a screened-in porch."

81

"Take maybe two hours. We'll get a photog. And you'll be famous. Read all about it."

She felt vanity charging down the track, plucking her right off the ground.

"Seriously, it would be totally sympathetic to you, and all the 'yous'"—his voice rose in mock drama—"young pretty career girls who come to the city with dreams."

"What are you going to call it? 'I *Had* a Dream'?"

He laughed. "Titles always come to me down the pike. Usually in the bathtub down the pike."

"But Detective Amspoker said—"

"Nothing will be printed about the case beyond old news, what's been in the papers. This is about you, you're what's interesting, trying to live in the city after all this."

"I'll have to ask Detective Amspoker."

"We could get started tonight, over dinner if you'd like."

If it was just for the story, she wasn't interested. But he seemed nice somehow, sympathetic. She wanted to ask if he were just after her for a story. But that implied she wasn't desirable enough to attract a man just with herself.

The sun was blinding after the dimness of the coffee shop. They hesitated on the sidewalk.

"Tonight, your place or mine?" Miles said. He was smiling at her.

Like a small boy, she thought, utterly without weapon but trying to look wicked. It was repartee, requiring only a light, equally barbed response. The kind she could never think of.

"I'll get in touch with you," she said.

He took her hand, and to her surprise, kissed it. "Been a pleasure meeting a fellow Bible-belter," he said.

At the entrance to the hotel she watched him walk down Lexington Avenue, ankles showing just like Mr. Vetter's always did—weren't there any men in New York who bought pants long enough? But it made him look boyish, vulnerable —certainly no one to be feared.

She walked inside, where the man at the desk motioned her over. "Uh, you're Francine Perry, right? Wanted to ask you . . . Don't take no offense. But I been looking for a good two-bedroom I can afford for three months now. Been wondering, that is, when your apartment might be available? Up for rent?"

7:43 p.m.

John Doe #126, about 20, black, found dead of a gunshot wound at the corner of Fox and Kelly streets, Bronx. Unsolved.

Angel Ruiz, 19, Hispanic, stabbed to death during an altercation at a 14th Street bar, Manhattan. Investigators believe this was a narcotics-related crime. Unsolved.

Darryl Tunney, 39, black, shot to death after being robbed in a fifth-floor hallway at Gowanus Houses, Brooklyn. Ora Morrison, 17, black, was arrested at scene.

Alexandra Baskin, 21, white, found raped and strangled in her apartment at East 63rd Street, Manhattan. Unsolved.

Unsolved. Victor Amspoker pushed aside the copy of the chief's log for Monday, August 8. He felt depression settle onto his shoulders, pinching his chest. Why did he keep having this feeling the Baskin case would never *get* solved?

They were working in relays, somebody doing something right around the clock. Brune Corolla, the squad sergeant, had handed down the assignments: "Frank, you and Vic take the address book." Three hundred and twelve names, mostly men. Others got the canvassing, calling every Baskin in the book, distributing leaflets asking tenants to list all businesses that delivered to them, checking the hospitals—any new admissions, the BCI for someone with that kind of M.O., the psycho wards, any suicides, the transit cops, subway token booths, an ad in the cabdrivers' newspaper. The call had gone down to the chief's office: request each command to report rapes, sodomies, burglaries, robberies, homicides bearing any similar features.

Then there was the matter of the paperwork: the least-wanted, most thankless task of all. "Vic, you got neat writing," Frank had said.

He had been neatly at it until four A.M., when he grabbed a few horizontal hours in the dormitory, listening to Frank snore. But at least there hadn't been Maddie, oiled from another man, face washed innocent on the other pillow.

He wondered if she had missed him.

He knuckled his eyes until they stung, then dropped his forehead into his palms. He opened his eyes. He felt old, tired, out of shape as Frank. The bulge of his gut bisected the straight edge of the green table, which was second in a line of three pushed end to end down the center of the "coffee room," which doubled as the conference room. The Baskin conference was over, leaving filled ashtrays, half-filled mugs, and a new pile of waiting paperwork. He picked up his pen, glanced over the form.

MEDICAL EXAMINER'S REPORT
M.E. No.   Dr.
Cause:
If required:
Last time victim ate:
Consumed alcohol:
Used narcotics:
Prescription drugs/medication:
Under present doctor's care:
Consistent with facts:

No. of wounds:
Type:
Trajectory of wound:
Sex (oral-anus etc.):

"Rape is indicated," Detective Second Grade Ron Diamond had said at the conference, reporting back from the medical examiner's office. "Bite mark on left breast, saliva on and about the labia. Blood type from the semen and saliva is O. Uh-huh—the Nazis *said* type O meant a lack of character. Acid-phosphatase test shows the guy dropped his wax sometime between nine A.M. and three P.M."

"Somebody's lunch break?" Lieutenant Reid said.

"But semen for which the blood type could *not* be determined but dating from the previous evening was also present."

Pens scratched on paper.

"Xanthakis," Frank Quinn said, his thumb and forefinger flicking his mustache up, then smoothing it down. "She saw him Sunday night, again Monday, they had a fight . . ."

"We can be ninety-five percent certain," Diamond continued, "that two guys are involved. The semen samples were tested for fifteen discriminatory substances—five in the seminal plasma, seven in sperm, and three in both plasma and sperm."

"Yay for science," the assistant district attorney said.

"Also," Diamond said, "rape occurred *after* the homicide."

"What the fuck," Quinn said. "Boston Strangler all over again. But would somebody tell me why these rape guys always strangle? How come no knife work, no guns?"

"Point of legality," the ADA said. "Can't charge rape if it occurs after death."

"Well, we sure as hell ain't gonna put down necrophilia," Quinn said.

The ADA flipped open a small black vinyl notebook. "Uh, let me find it here. Yeah. Quote: One-thirty-point-twenty: Sexual misconduct. A person is guilty of sexual misconduct when: three, being a male, he engages in sexual conduct with an animal or a dead human being. Unquote. Sexual misconduct, for your edification, is a Class A misdemeanor."

"Oh, swell," Quinn had said.

Amspoker began filling out the form, his left hand searching blindly into the soup bowl of Cheese Nips. Christ they were bad. The cavity in his right molar protested. He scooped another handful, eyes on the poster of "Desiderata" taped against the yellow cinder-block wall.

> Go placidly amid the noise and haste, and remember
> what peace there may be in silence. As far as possible
> without surrender be on good terms with all per-
> sons . . .

On the bottom was printed "Compliments of Louis DeLuca & Sons Funeral Home."

Be on good terms with all persons, he thought, looking down at the rectangular blue case folder in front of him. It was not easy. Frank was dropping hairs these days like a blimp shooting howitzers. A long pale-brown S crossed the printed black line headed VICTIM, on which he had written "Alexandra Elizabeth Baskin," curved down over TIME, PLACE OF OCCURRENCE, METHOD, COMPLAINT NO., DET. ASSIGNED, and ended at DET. ASSISTING, the tail bisecting his own neatly entered name.

He brushed the hair onto the scuffed green tile floor.

DET. ASSISTING. Right there. That was what had been nagging at him. A kid like Frank horning in, knowing there was a promotion for whoever grandstanded a big case like this one. *If* it ever got solved. While he, Victor, would be bypassed yet again—swept into some backwater out of the corridor of power. Okay, he was no Eddie Egan, promoted to detective after only nineteen months in uniform. It had taken Amspoker fifteen *years* to wear the gold (four apprenticing in plainclothes on the Pussy Posse—two collars per man-night—a job he had despised). Having a good hook like McDarrah in headquarters hadn't seemed to hurry things up at all.

According to Maddie he had achieved his goal, the ambition of every patrolman—to carry a gold shield instead of the white, to be a member of the Bureau, one among 3,109 men in the largest municipal detective force in the country. According to Maddie he should be satisfied: career, family, house in the suburbs—he'd gotten them all. But 81 detectives (including Frank) had gone on to first grade, 400 to second. The rest were still with him: third grade, that sounded (and paid) like third rate.

He thought about the police commissioner's office, empty at the time, which McDarrah had shown him once: huge and ornate, dark paneled walls, brass chandelier, red velvet drapes. Facing Amspoker were two blackened and grease-encrusted broilers, a coffeemaker whose product was legend, chipped china dishes, and economy-sized jars of sugar, Nestlé's Quik, Sanka, and A&P Eight O'Clock coffee.

He looked up. Frank was standing in the doorway, face flushed from a douse under the bathroom faucet. "Girls are here," Frank said. "Any coffee left?"

"Robbery stole it." The squad on the floor below was notorious.

"Want to make some more?" Frank said.

MacLeish and Perry were sitting in front of Frank's desk when he carried the coffee out. He set the cups down on the desktop and drew up his own chair.

Frank was leaning back in his swivel chair, tapping his fingertips against the blue-leather address book. "So it's a good bet the killer's in here," he said. "Sixteen hundred homicides a year in New York City. Fortunately for us, maybe seventy-five percent of victims knew the perpetrator. So the odds with Miss Baskin are some kind of personal motive. Wrapped up with her life. What we have to do now is unwrap her life. Know it in and out—better than she did."

The two women exchanged glances.

Frank was going about this all ass-backwards. You eased into something like this, didn't he have eyes? The girls looked tired and drawn, frightened as all civilians in a station house.

"So we start like this," Frank continued. "Assume she knew the perpetrator. No sign of forced entry. Lock report's back and says it wasn't picked. Ergo, she let him in. Now, then." His thick hand, with its tufts of hair, smoothed the book's cover. "There are a lot of names in here. Men's names. Hardly any women. This would seem to be a little girl who liked men."

"She was twenty-one," Paige MacLeish said. "Hardly a little girl."

Amspoker's eyes moved to her face. She had a blotch of color on her neck, angry as a birthmark. Bossy, you could tell who dominated things. He wondered if she let Francine out without supervision. If he could talk to Francine alone, he felt he could convince her to trust him, open up a bit.

Francine's round face had gone bloodless under the tan, her stubby hands—nails clipped short, no rings, bracelets, or watch—darting in her lap. He remembered her face staring down at the body on the floor. She had seemed very young, a nice girl, scrubbed-looking, head above the city crud. Until last night, he corrected. It made you want to cry.

"Quite right," Quinn was saying to Paige. "My apologies. Now the question is, who was the man who didn't like her? Enough to kill her, that is?"

There was a silence.

"Girls," Quinn said, "I understand you're probably both scared to get involved. But anything you remember about these boyfriends may be crucial. You have to know something. She has to have had one of these guys up. You have to have talked to one of them over the phone, something, right?"

"What about you, Miss Perry?" Amspoker said.

"Well, she really didn't bring her dates home. Yeah, she went out a lot. But as far as we know, not with one single man."

"Was she promiscuous?" Quinn said.

Paige crossed her leg sharply at the knee. " 'Promiscuous' is a value judgment."

Amspoker looked across at Quinn, whose jaw was stiffening with anger. "More coffee?" Amspoker said into the silence. Both girls shook their heads.

Quinn's fingers massaged the thinning spot on the top of his head, then flipped to one of the tabs in the address book. He sat forward, voice crisp. "This Tibor Nagy, now. He was her boss. This number she's got down here is his Fifth Avenue apartment. She must have mentioned him, so how about it?"

Paige shook her head. "We weren't close, that's what you have to understand. We didn't usually talk about things with her—Francie or me."

Francine was studying the palms of her hands, then the backs.

"Is that all?" Paige said. "We're very tired."

"All right, I know you are," Quinn said. "If you do think of anything—either of you—give me a call, okay? Appreciate it. You have my card. *Ron,*" he called. "One of the boys is going over that way. He'll give you a lift."

"I'll take them," Amspoker said.

It was nearing midnight. For the past two hours Amspoker, Quinn, and Tim Arendt of the Sex Crimes Squad had been poring over descriptions of rapes, sodomies, molestations—even yellow sheets on a housebreaker who stole only women's undergarments, a kid who cut the crotches out out of his mother's briefs—looking for something, anything similar to the details surrounding the death of Alexandra Elizabeth Baskin.

The results had been nil.

At his desk, the last in a row of six, Amspoker closed his eyes on the sand beneath his lids. His mind struggled, as if through mist, to discern a shape, a face, an occupation, a motive.

But that was the problem. Sex meant motive, and the more sex, the more motives: jealousy, hostility, rejection, ridicule. He stared down at the color and black-and-white photographs of the girl spread-eagled on his desk. She had had everything—looks, youth, money. Maybe she had had too many men.

He thought of the two roommates. Girls like that, he thought, they would be better off, happier, if they were out of the city, married. So why weren't they? Perry, now, could have a bit more off at the ankle, but she was a looker. Obviously had been asked. The other one, MacLeish, looked a bit like a dressed-up Wac. Still, they were young, naive. They had no idea, he thought, of the absolute sewer of many men's minds. What went on in the heads of tens of thousands of punks, degenerates, pervos, methadone junkies who stood around on corners, sat on stoops, drank, pissed, called out as girls passed in those cut-out summer dresses, those thin T-shirts with their nipples like raisins poking through. MacLeish, Perry, all the young women of the city had no idea what it did to those men when they walked by.

He turned in his chair to look out the window.

He wondered if he could ever accept it: his own daughters and men, the chances they would take, moving out on their own.

"I hate it—you and Mommy fighting." The memory made his fingers go cold. Laurel had been standing in her green nightgown printed with pink elephants, nine-year-old eyes already older than they should be. "Me and Ninny, we hate that fighting, Daddy."

"Kitten." He had pulled her up, her face burrowing under the edge of his chin, her hair smelling clean, as sweet as bubble gum. "Grown-ups are just dumb sometimes," he had said. He turned her face up to him, but she had squirmed in his palm, and he felt the moisture scald against his throat.

"Grown-ups have dumb problems but they work them out, kitten. You got to give us grown-ups a chance. Things'll be better, you'll see."

"Bobby Aronowitz' parents are getting a deevorce."

"Well, Bobby's parents aren't your parents. Anyhow, we're all staying here together for years and years and years. You'll be the first one to leave—all grown up, a real heartbreaker, you'll see. Every boy in the neighborhood'll be after you. Peter what's-his-name that you like—him, too."

"No, Daddy. I'm staying right here with you. Forever."

"Yes, kitten."

He was still looking out the window when the telephone on his desk rang.

"Detective Amspoker? It's Francie Perry. I didn't know if either of you'd still be there. But Mr. Quinn said we should call if—"

"What is it, Miss Perry? Anything wrong?"

"This reporter from the *Post*. He wants to do a story on me. My roommate talked me out of it, but I—"

"What reporter?"

"He's from the *Post*. Miles Overby."

"I know him. He calls relatives of homicide victims and poses as a detective."

"Oh."

"Stay clear of him. And absolutely no story. Plenty of nuts around the city, and it could focus the wrong kind of attention on you. Okay? Aside from all that, how are you doing?"

"Fine, I guess. Going to be looking for a new apartment, of course. When do you think we can get our stuff out of the old one?"

"Just another few days. I know it's inconvenient. Give me a call when you move. We've got a couple of lazy bums around here and we'll put 'em to work for you."

"Thanks. That's really nice."

"Anything else you might have recalled, any of her boyfriends that came around?"

"I've tried to think, but I just don't remember anyone."

"Well, take care of yourself, Miss Perry. Try to get some rest."

He sat for several minutes staring at the room's closed door, to which was taped a blowup of an apartment floor plan. A small stick figure lay prone in one of the two bedrooms. As the door opened, the stick figure moved to face the wall.

"Think I've maybe got something," Quinn said from the doorway. "An officer in Suffolk County brought this in." He was holding up several white pages covered with typewriting.

"Montauk," he said, slapping the pages down on Amspoker's desk. "June seventeen. Seventy-six."

92

It was a small resort town on the farthermost tip of Long Island, Amspoker thought, picking up the top page. He had been there once for the Fourth of July, Maddie had burned lobster-red but still they had made love, then fallen asleep under the wet sheet. But that was a long time ago.

July 2, 1976

SUBJECT: Investigation of Death, Sally Ann Teising
Lab Case 421-F-378

TO: Captain R. F. Morgenthau
New York State Police, Troop "C"

EVIDENCE: Brought to laboratory on June 21, 1976
by Trooper Arnold Whittaker for
Investigator A. M. Hopkins

HISTORY
OF CASE: Submitted with evidence

Body of Sally Ann Teising, age 18, of 120 Dune Road, Montauk, New York, was found by two local bird-watchers on Thursday, June 17, 1976, just west of the Highway 27 access road, town of Montauk, Suffolk County. Body facedown in heavy underbrush and completely nude. Evidence of strangulation by rope. 1¼" bite mark on left breast. No physical evidence at scene, excepting for shrubbery and dirt samples secured. Articles of clothing and personal papers found on June 17 in an area about one-quarter mile south of location where body was found.

Amspoker handed the pages to Tim Arendt as he finished. Then he picked up the accompanying autopsy report.

"It's him, all right," Quinn said, voice impatient. "The bite mark, muffdiving, everything."

Amspoker nodded without looking up. He read on.

It was the second paragraph of the internal examination that stopped him.

The pelvis discloses a large uterus, averaging 13 to 15 cm. in diameter, which on opening presents a well-formed male fetus measuring 18 cm. from crown to rump and 19 cm. from crown to heel. (Approximate age of gestation 4-plus months.) There are no abnormalities of the placenta.

He felt the unaccustomed weight of tears in his eyes. He remembered the doctor walking toward him in a white coat down the hall—*click click click* on the tiled floor—and he knew before the hand grasped his arm. "I'm sorry. Your wife is fine, but I'm afraid the baby didn't make it." "What was it, doctor?" "A boy."

And then Maddie was pregnant again, locked in the bathroom. He heard her sudden cry from inside.

Maddie.

"So hot, it was so hot, Vic. It fell in my hand. My hand was cold and it was so hot. My God, Vic. I don't know what it was. Don't ask me. It was so tiny. I didn't know what to do. I flushed."

He looked up at the two men in front of his desk. Their faces were pale under the fluorescent light, eye sockets dark. *"Christ,"* he said. "We've got a repeater on our hands."

3:17 a.m.

In his basement room, Dalroi lay on the sheet-covered mattress staring up at the hanging bulb, mellow through its coating of dust. He could feel the change in himself. An iron bar once straight, and now bent. Flickers of pain behind the eyes. A vein that spasmed in his right calf. Something in his body wasn't right.

94

If only they would leave him alone.

Voices bricked the air around him, hot, edging closer, and no air.

He got up, carefully locked his door, climbed the three broken concrete steps to the sidewalk. From the outside the building looked silent and dark—a narrow four-story stone facade abutted by a semicircular tower. It was the tower that had attracted him, reminding him of his years in Inwood, where he had been a child—Manhattan's northernmost neighborhood with the medieval castle of the Cloisters bulking on the hill.

Eighty-second Street was dark and deserted, trash blowing in the gutter. He turned east toward West End Avenue, experiencing his glands and limbs, the pump of his heart. Something in his body wasn't right. He followed the street to the still, intermittent green of Central Park. Beneath the carbon arc lamps the dusty bare patches gleamed like the worn seats of jeans. The path was empty, leading up over the hill into darkness.

He followed, and he thought of Paige. The now-familiar knotting filled his stomach, wrenching higher and higher, crowding his throat. He swallowed. She was like Alexandra. He would follow her, approach her, he would give her the chance to ask for it. She gave it to everyone else, why not him? He was just another guy, trying to make out, getting in line.

Even though she thought she was better than he was, like Alexandra. She was hard, brittle, flippant. Her eyes mocked, like Alexandra's, and her voice. She walked toes out, knees stiff, chin stuck up in the air. And she thought she was beyond him, above his reach.

He wondered how much pubic hair she would have. And if the color matched her head.

He walked south through the urine-stained shell of the

underpass, emerging at the zoo. He stared into the quiet steel cages.

If only it was feeding time again. When into all the little mouths went things that crackled and crunched, protestingly. He liked to listen to the chop-licking and teeth-picking, and then the sound of small, moist breathing.

But feeding time, of course, was visiting time, when the crowds of hungry, curious, paunch-heavy people came to laugh and probe and tease. They stared and pointed and waggled a finger, entirely blind to the silent eye watchings that came back at them. They threw their candy scraps and ice-cream dribbles and cigarette butts on the floor and trampled them underfoot without even glancing down. They wiggled and tapped their fingers inside the cages, hoping for the rushed response of something within.

And after visiting time, the caretaker came to sweep up all the butts and papers and other human leavings. And when his radio wouldn't work or he was very bored, he probably wondered, Dalroi thought.

He probably wondered what would happen if he left a cage, just one cage, open some morning.

Chapter Four

Wednesday, August 10
11:41 a.m.

As the cab neared Eighty-first Street, Paige MacLeish looked out the window. Frank E. Campbell (The Funeral Chapel, Inc.) was an elegant four-story cocoa-colored stone building with white window boxes planted with red geraniums and ivy, the American flag fluttering on a pole above the door.

But it was the crowd she was staring at. Behind police barriers, several hundred onlookers lined the Madison Avenue entrance.

She should have expected it, she thought. But *why?* The main attraction was already dead. What was it these vultures hoped to see?

She looked across at her father, his face pale, flaccid above the charcoal-gray suit.

Willis MacLeish shrugged. "Human nature, honey. There were twenty thousand here for Judy Garland."

The cab braked at the curb.

She had watched it, she thought, so many times on TV: mafiosi, Charles Manson, John Mitchell walking the gauntlet between car door and building. Now it was her turn.

Uniformed policemen locked hands as Paige and her father stepped from the cab. Flashbulbs exploded. The round black mouths of minicams thrust toward them. A crowd of reporters, hydra-headed with wires and microphones, rushed to throttle their path.

Would the publicity ever get buried, along with the body?

PERVERT PURSUED ALEX, the *Post* had blared just this morning. It was no longer necessary to use her last name; her first was as well-known to readers as their own. And the shorthand served to skewer her girlishness, Paige thought. That was it: wave the sexual aspect on high, which was why everyone kept on buying the *Post*.

In fact, there was no fresh news, the "pervert" only an obscene caller who had dialed Alex at Gilbert, Levensky & Hane on five successive mornings in May. Alex had reported the incident to the personnel department, which lodged a complaint with the New York Telephone Company. But the calls weren't repeated and the matter ended there. Until some reporter's need for a headline broke it open again, Paige thought, like a goddamn scab off a wound.

Two black doormen in brass-buttoned burgundy uniforms opened the double doors.

The tumult was shut behind them.

Ahead, Paige could hear the muted thumping of an organ. The high-ceilinged entry was soft with the light from a brass chandelier and lamps on antique tables.

They were greeted by four men in conservative suits.

"I'm Mr. Hautzer, the family secretary," said the startlingly attractive young man. He held a pen poised over a clipboard. "And you're . . . ?"

"Willis MacLeish. And my daughter, Paige."

"Ah, yes. You may join the family in the family room. Mrs. Baskin has asked especially to include you there. She is looking forward to seeing you both." He glanced at the clipboard, then peered nearsightedly behind them. "And Mrs. MacLeish."

"My wife was very sorry not to attend," Willis MacLeish said. "She sends her deepest condolences."

Hautzer's eyebrow hitched upward. "Yes. Well, it is a busy season, isn't it?"

Busy with psychosomatic tics, Paige thought. Within twenty minutes of hearing of Alex's death, her mother had begun to see the "aura"—the flashing lights that preceded the migraine. *"Don't worry! It's not that! Less than one headache problem in ten thousand means a brain tumor." "But, Paige, you don't know how it feels."*

Oh, but she *did*. Bloodless by comparison.

No matter what she felt, her mother had always felt it faster, more intensely, for a longer period of time, and with more dramatic side effects, such as vomiting. It had made her, Paige thought, afraid of emotion, of involvement. She had followed the example of her father, retreating behind books, papers, theories. Intellectualism was a portable ivory tower, and feminism its headiest balcony. From its railing the whole of life and all its vagaries, including her lack of dates, could be explained in terms having nothing to do with personal insufficiency.

She felt her father's hand around her shoulder.

The small, thickly carpeted family room was crowded with people. Beneath a woven mural of horses, a row of middle-aged women in black perched on a velvet couch. Paige saw Francie standing beside a dark-haired young man with improbably lush eyelashes and a young woman with waist-length black hair.

Mrs. Baskin's face, smelling of powder, was suddenly in front of her, as shattered with lines as a dried streambed. Paige felt herself compressed against rock-hard breasts. She stared down past Mrs. Baskin's back into an ashtray heaped with long, scarcely smoked butts.

Mrs. Baskin stepped back, teetering on spike heels. The lids of her small brown eyes were red and puffed nearly shut. "Everyone," she said, turning to face the room, "I want you to meet Alex."

There was a sudden silence. The name lay on the air, visible as smoke. Mrs. Baskin looked around in confusion. "Why, what's the matter? Did I say something wrong?"

"Paige, my dear," Mr. Baskin cut in. She felt his fingers, hot and moist, grasping her arm. "Such a comfort to us that you've come."

There was another silence as beyond the closed door the organ music stopped. They could hear a man's voice: "Would everyone please rise?"

The door opened, and they were led through.

The chapel was white, carpeted in red. In front of a half-circle of columns stood the red-draped bier, on which lay the open casket. Summer wildflowers—tiger lilies, daisies, blue-bells, Queen Anne's lace ("the most chic, most modern choice," Paige imagined the director saying)—blanketed the top and spilled in huge pompoms down two pedestals.

Across the room, standing beneath a row of sconces that imitated candles, she could see the two detectives, Quinn and the one Francie insisted on liking—Amspoker—scanning the rows of faces. Macabre, but then, it was not unknown, the papers had said this morning, for a murderer to attend his own victim's funeral.

As Paige hesitated, a dour-faced usher approached. She took his black-gabardine arm, moving with him across the carpet. Heads turned, faces peering at her.

Dearly beloved, she thought. *We are gathered here today to join together in holy parody* . . . The organ, the flowers, the waiting rabbi—it was the wedding Alex would never have. Yet she lay dressed in white and waiting, Sleeping Beauty in her casket.

In the front pew Mrs. Baskin was sitting beside her husband, her small freckled hands tearing at a Kleenex.

Paige felt the red velvet cushion of the second pew slap up beneath her. She looked at Francie sitting beside her, face gone sallow under the lights.

The black-suited rabbi, a balding man with a well-trimmed mustache, walked toward the microphone. He peered out over the pews as the swells of coughing rolled toward him.

"Adonai maadam vatedaehu, ben enosh vat'chash'vehu. Adam lahevel dama, yamav k'tsel over . . . O Lord, what is man that You regard him, or the son of man that You take account of him? Man is like a breath, his days are like a passing shadow. You sweep men away. They are like a dream; like grass which is renewed in the morning. In the morning it flourishes and grows, but in the evening it fades and withers. . . ."

There followed a responsive reading of the Twenty-third Psalm, and then the eulogy.

"Monday last . . ." the rabbi began. He cleared his throat, the sound liquid from the loudspeakers. "Monday last, a young girl in the first fresh bloom of womanhood was taken from us. But we are here, yes, we are here to give thanks for the *life* of Andrea Elizabeth Baskin . . ."

Murmurs stirred through the pews.

"Andrea loved life. She was vital. She was vivacious. Andrea was—"

"*Alexandra!*" came a voice from the back.

"Thank you. Yes. Alexandra was a pleasure to her family and her friends."

"*El moley rachamim,*" the cantor was chanting, "*schochen bam'romin hamtzi m'nuchoh, n'chonoh b'tzel ka n'fey ha sh'chi noh . . .*"

When he had finished, the rabbi translated: "O God, full of compassion, Thou who dwellest on high, grant perfect rest beneath the sheltering wings of Thy presence, among the holy and pure who shine as the brightness on the heavens, unto the soul of Alexandra Elizabeth Baskin, who has gone unto eternity . . ."

And then the ceremony was over, and Paige felt shocked at the briefness, as she always had at weddings.

The rabbi led the way, and with a jerk the casket, closed now, followed. The pallbearers rolled it toward the side entrance, its wheels hidden beneath the red velvet drape. The doors opened, there was a noise from outside, and Alex went out to face the crowds.

"Come this way, won't you?" the funeral director was saying at their pew. They were escorted back to the family room.

"We'll just let the guests run interference for us," the director said. "The crowd is moving around to the side door. So we'll wait just a bit, comfortably here, and then we'll slip you out the front."

"Girls," Mrs. Baskin said to Paige and Francie. "I thought you might want to see something." She fumbled through a large, cluttered handbag, pulling out a folded page of note-

102

book paper. It was frayed around the edges. Her eyes pleaded.

Paige opened the sheet, Francie reading the familiar scrawl over her shoulder.

MY THOUGHT-THINKS
by Alexandra Baskin
Age 15 years, 3 months

1. Someday I will meet a man, and it will be all that I have imagined.
2. I long to be cultured and fastidious.
3. I am going to be superbly well-groomed and dressed.
4. I want to be creative, write poetry, stir young minds.
5. I have decided, variously, to live my life with intrigue and humor.
6. I'm going to get that nose job.

"Why?" Mrs. Baskin said. "That's what I keep on asking myself. "My God, *why?*"

"Come along, Mother," Mr. Baskin said, his thick fingers encircling her forearm.

"I want you girls to have it," she said. "You keep it. To remember how good my little Alex was. My baby. She was my baby."

Samuel Baskin's fingers moved to his wife's shoulders, turning her toward the door.

"You were her best friends," she said, looking back as her husband and the director started out of the family room. "You were the ones she really liked. Alex often told me so."

Francie's eyes remained fixed on the notepaper.

Quickly Paige folded it, fingers tightening back and forth along the crease.

103

Francie looked, she thought, like someone who had really lost her best friend. *But I'm your best friend. Alex was just one of our roommates. We're the ones who are really friends. Aren't we?*

"Francie, I don't care what you say, you're not going back to the hotel tonight. Okay? Will and Tessa want you to come out, you know that. Now you're coming with me."

Francie's face had the stubborn, suddenly rigid look. What was it, Paige thought, something in her that saw warmth as charity, something she didn't deserve, a debt she couldn't repay? Why? Because she didn't have her own home to offer, to retreat to?

"You're *what?*" Mrs. Baskin said. "Staying in the city—*alone?* I won't hear of this, young lady. Samuel, did you ever?"

"I'll be all right," Francie said. "I want to get out early tomorrow, start apartment-hunting. Keep busy. It's the best thing for me, really."

"I won't hear of it. Come along, dear. No back talk." Mrs. Baskin wedged Francie's hand beneath her arm, which was covered with raised brown moles and gold bangles. "We'll drive you all to Pinelawn. And then you—Miss-Francie-has-to-prove-how-brave-she-is—will stay cozy by us tonight. And that's final."

Francie looked at Paige. "But my stuff . . . it's at the Summit."

"We will just pick it up," Mrs. Baskin said, "on our way."

Surely Francie really was relieved, Paige thought. "I'll call you tonight, at the Baskins'," she said, nailing down the decision.

Outside the front door fifty people still waited, impatient to stare once more into the face of disaster. Paige saw a young father in cut-off jeans, his face squeezed between the thighs of his piggyback blond daughter, who brought her hands together, clapping with glee. Bored, another man broke from the fringes, peroxided hair above a walnut tan, wearing a turquoise T-shirt and denim jumpsuit. Gucci bag dangling from one hand, he signaled a cab with a cheroot in his other.

Then she saw him—a small figure in jeans and a sport jacket rounding the corner from the side entrance—the reporter who had touched her arm, had had the gall to phone them last night. Why? Because they were now freaks, goddamned curiosities, living witnesses to a titillating crime. His eyes were squinting at her through his glasses.

"Francine," someone called from the group behind him. "Look this way. Hey, Francine Francine Francine Francine."

Francie's face appeared at the window of the limousine, mouth opening mute as a fish behind the air-conditioning.

With her father's hand at her elbow, Paige climbed into the car behind. Mr. Baskin was already seated inside, opening down a built-in bar. Silver flasks and crystal gleamed.

As the limousine moved forward behind the police escort, Paige felt the pressure of his knee against hers.

"Libation, anyone?" Samuel Baskin said.

2:05 p.m.

He had just decided to drop in at Gilbert, Levensky & Hane on his lunch hour, Miles had told her.

Now he fed her his earnest-young-man smile. "Maybe you could just tell me a bit about the agency." (*Like, was it one of Alex's co-workers who killed her?*)

She looked at her watch. "Well, yes, I have a few seconds, Mr. Minton."

105

"Morton. It's Morton."

"Yes. Morton. That's what I said." She launched into a recitation of clients, millions billed, Clio awards won.

"I was particularly interested in working with Tibor Nagy," Miles said. "Quite a rep, you know."

Mrs. Lasker's face brightened, as if the praise were meant for her. "Yes, such a brilliant man. Been group creative head here for six years. He wrote *Madison Avenue and Me* in seventy-one, you know—such a *wicked* wit."

"An excellent book," Miles said. "An accomplishment for such a young man."

"Well, he's . . . I believe in his late forties, Mr. Minton. But that's not old today, hah-hah."

"If I worked for him . . . I mean, what's he like? Easy to get along with?"

"My, yes. So organized. Some people here think you can't be disciplined and creative at the same time, now isn't that just absurd?"

From his briefcase Miles drew out the first edition of Wednesday's *Post*, folded it back to the story on page two, pushed it across her desk.

FEAR STALKS
POSH EAST SIDE

by Miles K. Overby III

Hardware-store shelves are bare of locks, mailmen can't get apartment dwellers to open their doors for packages, and the ASPCA animal shelter on East 92nd Street reports a run on adoptions, at least of larger, fiercer dogs.

Such is the aftermath of Monday's

brutal sex slaying of brunette career
girl Alexandra Baskin, only daughter of real-estate investor Samuel R.
Baskin. . . .

Mrs. Lasker's gaze flicked up at Miles over her smudged half-lenses, eyes chilly.

"When I consider working here," Miles said, "I have to worry. Do you people think it's someone here at the agency?"

"Ridiculous! Since you're such a tabloid reader, Mr. Minton, you know we have offered five thousand dollars for information pertaining to that poor child's murderer. We hardly intend to pay it to ourselves. Thank you for stopping by. We'll keep your résumé on file."

"Thank you again, Mrs. . . . um . . . Linton."

Revenge, he thought, it was sweeter than cyclamates. He stood up, shook her hand. "May I use your restroom?"

"Down the hall to your left," she snapped. "And here. Take your newspaper."

As Miles turned, he saw his résumé descend toward the peeling walnut-grained wastebasket. He walked out past the personnel secretary, who was applying green polish to daggerlike nails. The sting of lacquer hung in the air.

"Terrific story on page two," he said, dropping the paper on her desk.

She gave him a conspiratorial smile, fluttering her nails in a good-bye.

Or, he thought, was it a drying pattern?

The hall was carpeted in green, fluorescent light burning above. Strongholds of personal expression rioted on each side. Radios were tuned to rock, plants of exotic shapes and spikes flourished, a poster argued in Day-Glo pink that A WOMAN NEEDS A MAN LIKE A FISH NEEDS A BICYCLE.

The slogan was depressing. Miles was standing at the

number-two urinal—as good a place as any, he thought, looking down, to take stock of one's prospects vis-à-vis women. He pressed the lever, producing a torrent of noise and water. "You want working urinals, work at an ad agency," Lowry had said when he complained that Eau de *Post* was adrift again.

He walked over to the sink, turned on the tap, and waited.

He had washed his hands through the passage of three conservative dark suits, one with pinstripes, when the door opened and in walked a young long-haired man. He looked cut sartorially in two: top half brown suit jacket with vest, bottom half jeans and Adidas green-and-white-striped running shoes.

Miles busied himself with the soap dispenser. "Any copy jobs around here?" he asked as the man unzipped.

"Sorry. Tighter'n a drum right now, man."

Miles waited until he had a captive audience, dick in hand.

"Hey, what's the scuttlebutt about that killer?" he said over the sound against the white porcelain.

The man looked over at Miles, bored face brightening. "Tell you, people are getting jittery around here. Cops have been, like, dropping in. They even questioned me, man."

"You knew her?"

"Oh, sure. Everyone knew Alex. No hour too late, no hour too early. If she was awake, she was alive. Count on her to goof, have fun, you know?"

"Go out with her yourself?"

"Me? I got a steady lady. Not that I wouldn't have, I got the chance, y'understand. I mean, man, she was . . . You ever get a load of her yourself?"

"One of life's pleasures I missed."

"See, Alex was . . . not just big knockers. She was really

one gorgeous, beautiful-looking woman. A hell of a damn shame, her going that way. Scary, you know?"

"She ever go out with Nagy?"

The man grimaced, bent down and peered under the stalls. "Don't know why she wasted quality merchandise on that SOB."

"So maybe he got a little overexcited, fit of despond, maybe?"

The man laughed. "Let's just put it this way. Cops come in and drag him off in irons, it couldn't happen to a nicer guy, we'd all say. But I'll tell ya, if you're really interested. Friday before, this guy comes around to pick Alex up. Sarah —she's the art director next to me—says he's Alex's new guy, she's crazy for him, Alex told her at lunch. Anyway, I'm in here for my afternoon defecation. Come out, he's at the sink. I say, 'You taking out Alex Baskin?'

" 'Yeah,' he says. 'What's it to ya?'

"So I say, 'Listen, is she really good in the sack?' He grabbed me, right around the throat. Crazy eyes, man. Then, when it happened, I thought for sure it's him. Because he had it bad for Baskin. And she could sure make you jealous enough to kill."

"What's his name, did Sarah mention?" Miles said.

"Dunno, some Greek foot-long thing."

"Xanthakis?"

"Yeah. How'd you know?"

"Read it in the papers. They're looking for him now. 'Wanted for Questioning,' you know. Say, is that art director Sarah Hanson? I know her from—"

"Nope. Salisbury. Well, nice talking to—"

"What was she *really* like? Alex, I mean."

The man's tongue clicked against the roof of his mouth. "Giving. Yeah. That's what I'd say. See, I got this ability to sum up a person, wrap 'em up in one word. Alex was a very giving lady. Saved my ass once. We got this client, and my word for him is 'Feet,' see, so I did a cartoon of him on pontoons. Then it got clipped in with all these roughs for a presentation, and the whole stack goes into the conference room where he's sitting. 'Alex, baby,' I says, 'could you go in there, suck him off if you have to, but get that fucking cartoon? I could lose my *job*.'

" 'I could lose *mine*,' she says. But she goes in and comes out with it, never did tell me how. See, that's what I mean about Alex, man. A giver. But all the world wanted to do with her was fucking *take*. I keep thinking. If I'd gone out with her, maybe none of this would have happened."

Miles nodded.

"Well, hope you get a job, man. Tough on the streets. Whyn't you try McCaffrey & McCall?"

"Sure thing," Miles said.

4:38 p.m.

"This isn't any heavy-duty thing, Tibor. We're just interested in finding out as much as we can about Miss Baskin, just trying to do our job, right?" Quinn said.

"My lack of interest in the exigencies of your job, gentlemen," Tibor Nagy said, "is exceeded only by my lack of time. Shall we get on with the matter at hand?"

It gave him, Amspoker thought, a private satisfaction to see Nagy at the table in the narrow cinder-block "interrogation" room. Despite his words, his arrogance had slipped a notch, removed from the high-backed swivel chair on the fortieth floor, where the carpet sank like moss, the view spread wide as what you paid for on top of the Empire State. There he had refused to answer questions—"Most unfortunate. IBM is in the conference room"—huge head, bristling with iron-gray hair, thrown back so that his pale eyes focused glassily down at them. "Then you can pay us a visit at the station house," Quinn had said. "Or tell it to the grand jury."

Gingerly Amspoker handed the hot mug of coffee toward him, holding it by the front rim, between thumb and forefinger. Nagy motioned him to set it down. He had a long nose with an upward dip at its end, and some variety of nervous disorder that caused a slight trembling of his head and barbered cheeks. He left the coffee, and the handle, untouched.

"As you wish," Quinn said. "How well did you know Miss Baskin?"

"She was employed as my secretary, as you know."

"Did you ever visit her apartment?"

"Certainly not. Why would I?"

"You didn't visit her there last Monday?"

"I have already informed you that the answer is negative."

"What were you doing on Monday?"

"I was in my office, where I am gainfully employed."

"Leave for lunch?" Amspoker said.

"Certainly. That lingering odor of food—I find it distasteful in an office."

"Where did you go?"

"I . . ." A faint glisten had broken out on his upper lip, and a cologne, damp and citrusy, drifted Amspoker's way.

"Orsini's. Yes, I believe it was Orsini's. I would, of course, have to consult my calendar."

"Two days ago and you can't remember?" Quinn said. "Anybody there who might remember *you*?"

"Yes. A reservation. Certainly. You might speak with Max, the maître d'."

111

"What about after five?" Quinn said.

"I had a few drinks. With one of my colleagues, Ian Meecham, at a spot called Runyan's Onion—one of the neighborhood watering holes. I believe then that I traveled directly home."

Home, Amspoker thought, was a large Tudor-style estate in Westport, Connecticut, with a wife, three children and a gray-and-white Old English sheepdog.

"How many drinks you have, Tibor?" Quinn said.

"How many? I believe five. I should say five martinis."

"You must have been fairly drunk."

"Let's not be naive."

"Was Miss Baskin attractive?" Amspoker said.

"You might say so, yes. A bit flashy. Not my type, most certainly not, you understand."

"You mean not like your girlfriend?" Quinn said.

"Monika?" Instantly he sensed his blunder, eyes hooding.

"Yes. What type was Monika?" Amspoker said.

"You leave her out of this. She knows nothing of this."

"Nothing of what?" Quinn said.

Nagy's fingers were trembling in gentle rhythm with his head. With an effort he brought his hands together, interlaced the thick, hair-covered fingers with their clear-polished nails, and placed the whole bundle firmly down upon the green table.

"We're all men here, am I correct in my assumption?" Nagy said with a smile. "But women are so irrationally jealous. I, uh, yes, I may have known Miss Baskin carnally, once or twice."

"Is that why you placed calls to her apartment from Pensacola, Florida?" Amspoker said.

Nagy's breathing quickened, but he maintained steady eye contact.

"Of course. I should have realized you would know all

112

that. I am most sorry to disappoint you. It was strictly business."

"Where did you go?" Quinn said. "To know her carnally, I mean?"

"I maintain an apartment on Fifth Avenue. The nature of my work is sometimes quite demanding, simply too fatiguing to commute every night."

Quinn leaned back in the folding chair, propping one foot up on the opposite knee. "Some women turn out to be real ball breakers, right, Tibor? From what I hear about Miss Baskin, she'd drive me right up the wall."

Nagy's head jiggled above his body—like a dried leaf, Amspoker thought, threatening to detach itself from a branch.

"I have not seen Alexandra, other than in her capacity as my secretary, since April. I don't see how I can be of further use to you, gentlemen." He stood up, buttoning his blond-linen jacket across the matching vest.

"Do you want to give us Monika's last name?" Quinn said. "Or should we call and ask your wife?"

The sidewalk had been freshly hosed. The chalky smell steamed upward as the two detectives paused before a turn-of-the-century building guarded by scrolled ironwork and columns. Above the door, stained glass glowed like a jewelry tray in the late-afternoon sun. Over each window a cornucopia bulged with stone fruit, framed in turn by a cord with stone tassels.

Twenty years ago, Amspoker thought, feeling the tiredness down his spine, they would have solved this case. Twenty years ago there were only three-hundred-some homicides. Last year: 1,622. Twenty years ago the clearance rate was in the nineties. Last year: 66 percent. Well, okay, but two-thirds arrested is still pretty good, right? Quinn had said. The figures had come in yesterday: 225,000 arrests last year, only 15,000 indictments. One out of ten felony cases went to trial. You measured the other cops lined up for morning coffee at Tony's, across Baxter Street from Criminal Court, knowing the wait in the complaint room could last until one the *next* morning, when your case would be a fallout from plea bargaining, dropped charges, failure of witnesses to show.

The black lacquered door was at the end of the hall. As Quinn pressed the buzzer, the sound of chimes echoed within.

The door opened. A pair of long hazel eyes appeared over the chain, coolly considering Quinn's badge. There was the scratching sound of the chain unhitching, then the door was pulled wide.

A drift of perfume, heavy with musk, enveloped them.

Monika Land had tangled beige hair and a profusion of breasts in a tight white blouse. Small gold rings glinted on her right hand as she swept the wave back from her forehead. Her eyes were brown, heavily mascaraed, her face marred only by a receding chin.

"What is this all about?" Her voice was precise, assured, as if asking a headwaiter.

"Routine check, Miss Land," Quinn said. "It's about the death of the secretary at Nagy's firm."

"The death?"

"The murder."

Her eyes widened, in their depths a precipitation of frost. "I got a call from a reporter already."

Amspoker threw a look at Quinn. *Christ*, the newshounds were scooping the cops.

"Just a few questions, if you don't mind," Quinn said. "Then we'll be on our way."

"Now, just a minute. I think you had better speak with my—"

Amspoker allowed an agonized look to pass over his face. "I . . . The bathroom, where is it?" His fingers clutched the roll of flab over his belt.

She stared at his fingers, then let out an exasperated sound.

"Enteritis," Quinn said. "Been like that for a week now."

Her full lower lip tightened, and she gave Amspoker a direct stare. He could see the moisture on her lip, its beveled center silk-smooth as the inside of a gun barrel. He thought of her mouth taking Nagy. The question was: why not Monday? Guilt? Lust already spent on a dead girl's body? Indigestion? Crotch itch?

"Isn't there a law"—she giggled—"against faking and entering?" Then she shrugged. "Come on, I've got nosy neighbors."

Amspoker watched her buttocks through the pale tweed slacks as she wheeled, pointing down the white-carpeted hallway. "Can's that way."

He wondered how much it took to afford such a woman. Monika Land's bathroom was papered with iridescent green and gold stripes. On a hanger above the bathtub, two scraps of triangular black lace dangled. He opened the medicine-cabinet door. Poor bitch. She seemed to have troubles with her functionings from head to toe. He took out his pen and began writing down the doctors' names from the prescription labels. He picked up a man's razor from the edge of the sink and unscrewed the blade. Hairs clung to the metal and dried cream, gray as Nagy's. But what use was it anyway? Even if it was him, they would never live long enough to see him behind bars.

He urinated, then flushed the toilet.

Monika was seated on the dark blue velvet couch, one foot tucked under her, clinking ice cubes in her glass. Across from her, balancing his stocky frame on a spindly chair, Quinn was nursing a Coke.

"You a boy scout too?" Monika said. Without waiting for an answer, she walked over to the pale birchwood bar, then handed him a Coke.

"Cheers," Amspoker said.

"So how long you known this non-boy-scout Nagy?" Quinn said.

"It isn't Nagy, that what you're thinking."

"You see him Monday night?"

"No."

"He ever drop over in the mornings, for lunch?"

"I work," she snapped. "A job, dig? I'm not some kept female." After a pause she added, "I'm in personnel now. Avon."

She was a typist, Amspoker thought. A typist who lived on the doorstep of Fifth Avenue, the only street in the whole fucking city without dogshit.

"Did you know Nagy's secretary?" Quinn said.

"That slut. I went to the Christmas party last year. With someone else, not Nagy of course, I won't say who. You could tell what she was just by looking at her."

"How could you tell?" Amspoker asked, curious.

"Women know."

The brazen women of the city, dead faces rouged to a semblance of life, crowded before his eyes. The Bed-Stuy two-dollar whores standing on glassine envelopes and hardened vomit. The shared property called Sweetlips and Cherry and Jugs, jiggling up to the patrol car, trailing you down the street, waiting outside the station house, drinking coffee at the cop diner and staring at you, eyes available, endlessly available as your wife's body began to sag. Her eyes said it too: available. Monika with a "k," like the Columbia hippies spelling it "Amerika." He remembered crumpling tinfoil behind his shield during the riots, to keep the numbers from standing out.

"Tell me about Tibor," Quinn said. "What's he like?"

"Tem-*per*. He beat me up once. Black eye and two broken ribs. Fact. Check the emergency room at New York Hospital, February twenty-first." Her face appeared proud.

"Why did he do that?" Quinn said.

"No reason for it, except he thought I was chipping around on him. Always thought that." She smiled. "Probably because I was."

"You file a complaint?" Quinn said.

"I had it coming. This is the third time, actually."

"He normal sexually?" Quinn said.

She shrugged. "So what's normal?"

"Any cunnilingus?"

"Say, you boys are educated. Yeah, oh, he dug that. Sure. Look, he may seem like a stuffed shirt to you. But ditch his clothes, he's a man like any other." Her eyes studied the melting ice cubes in her glass. She drained the martini, then speared the olive with a toothpick. The olive disappeared into her mouth. "Don't know why I'm going on like this," she said, putting the empty glass down. "You boys better go."

At the door she hesitated.

"You think he killed that bitch," she said, "you're wrong."

Behind her the room was silent, the white drapes billowing up from the air-conditioner vent.

She giggled. "You're *dead* wrong. He's hung up on me."

10:04 p.m.

She felt the presence of Alex all around her. She wondered if Alex would mind—if Alex could know, of course —this invasion of her room.

117

It was prim as a child's: ruffled white canopy over a white bed flounced with organdy tiers to the floor. Francie sat back on the quilted chaise longue, leaning against the stacks of pillows: a pink satin pig, a red velvet heart, a squashy blue terry-cloth telephone with red dial.

It was a disconcerting discovery. Alex had had everything: looks, money. Did she have to have character too? She had chosen to live with them in a ratty walk-up whose holes they plastered with Colgate. And Alex had been *rich*. Earlier that afternoon there had been the black Cadillac limousine, not hired for the occasion but owned. There had been the solid bronze casket, glittering heavily in the dirt, the woman behind her whispering, "Do they expect the mayor?" There were the sprawling flagstone wings of the house—mirrored walls, striped satin settees, oriental rugs.

Francie leaned toward the night table, turning on a lamp whose base was a white ceramic Kewpie doll. The blue glass eyes stared out above a Princess telephone. She thought about men calling Alex. Of course they had called. Alex had been just as beautiful at sixteen—pimples a foreign affliction, distant as leprosy. So many things a woman had to have, parts of bodies littered magazines: clear skin, firm breasts, shiny hair, flat belly, slim ankles, large eyes, straight nose, painted nails. Now, with *Hustler* magazine, even between your legs had to be pretty.

"Francie, will you quit being such a durf. Like, I'm in agony. Come on, now." Alex had pulled up her red kimono around her waist, bent forward, palms braced against her knees. She had looked expectantly back over her shoulder. Francie remembered the tweezers, the metal cold in her hand. She could see it—*"I see it, Alex"*—the sliver of wood halfway down Alex's right buttock, dark against the white below the bikini line. She had never realized you could see a woman's lips from the back, round and pursed between

Alex's thighs. Why, it looks pretty, she had thought, amazed as she thought it. She had often examined her own when she was thirteen, sitting on the floor with spread legs, mirror between her knees. But she had always stared with a mixture of curiosity and horror: it was so odd, so pink, so spiraled with hairs, so *ugly*. Except that Alex wasn't ashamed of hers at all, bending over unconcerned, sure that hers was unremarkable, acceptable, even pretty. And Alex's looked just like *hers*.

But then she remembered herself at sixteen, not pretty and never would be, the yellow school bus rattling, her profile arched down looking out the window into the sun, pretending her profile was Beverly's. Behind her Johnny Vaughn making rich farting noises. Because she didn't look like Beverly. And never would.

She had devoured all Beverly's fashion magazines but they only made it worse: "If the occasion arises when you have to run for something, such as a bus, keep the gazelle in mind, not the camel." And: "To be more beautiful you must find your type and, once you've found it, perfect it all through the year." The perfectibles listed were The Cool Beauty, The Outdoor Girl, The Ingenue, The Bold Adventurer.

The trouble was, at twenty-three she still didn't know which type she was.

Alex had known. Alex could go to a party, look across the room and say, "You. I choose *you*."

Francie got up from the chaise and unzipped her duffel bag. She pulled out the wrinkled plaid skirt and blouse, carried them over to the walk-in closet.

It looked like a department-store aisle. Dresses, coats, skirts, blouses, pants crowded on racks. Shoe boxes were stacked in unsteady pyramids against the shelves. The same spicy, flowery sachet Alex had used in their apartment lay heavy on the air.

Francie stepped forward. The first nightgown was the color of peaches, hanging limply on a padded white satin hanger. She ran her finger down the fabric, which felt cool and slightly damp.

She looked behind her, then let the plaid outfit fall to the floor. She unzipped the round-collared black dress she was wearing, pulled it off over her head, and removed her underwear.

The nightgown cascaded like water over her breasts, falling down and covering her toes. Holding the fabric bunched up at her knees, she found a pair of high-heeled slippers trimmed at the toe with a pouf of marabou. The feathers stirred outward with her breath.

The slippers clattered to the floor and she pushed her feet into them. They were too big. She crossed toward the dressing-table mirror, her toes clenching to keep the slippers on, the nightgown sliding heavy across her thighs.

She smiled at her reflection. One knee broke the fall of the peach silk as she posed, shifting her weight from foot to foot. She locked her hands behind her, threw back her head, arched her hips. The small, rounded hump of her pubis thrust forward through the silk.

Sex had never been something, she thought, that she yearned for. When she didn't have it, she didn't miss it. It had been a disappointment to discover that women too were supposed to move, that you didn't just get thrown across a bed. You were expected to learn, practice, to perform, to contort and flap like a speared fish, and to gasp like a beached fish. It was all so silly.

But *looking sexy* was something else again.

Looking, she saw her nipples rise.

"Francie? Francie, dear?"

It was Zohra Baskin's voice, followed by a quick rapping at the door.

"One minute! Just a minute!"

She raked the nightgown over her face, kicking it and the slippers beneath the bed. She was just buttoning her own striped cotton housecoat when the door opened.

"Thought you might like something nice and soothing," Mrs. Baskin said. She held a small bamboo tray on which stood a cup and a china teapot. "Won't keep you, dear, you're ready for bed. But this'll help your insomnia. It's poppyseed tea, works wonders. I've been using it myself, truth to tell. Every night since—"

"That's very thoughtful of you, Mrs. Baskin."

The older woman hesitated. Lipstick had bled up the lines above her upper lip, which was trembling.

Francie leaned toward her, kissed her on one tanned, leathery-feeling cheek. "Thanks, Mrs. Baskin. See you in the morning."

"This is a delightful room, isn't it, Francie, dear? We had it done when Alex was just fifteen. Prettiest room in the house, I always told... Well, it does me good to see a nice young girl like yourself here. I hate to see anything go to waste."

"Mrs. Baskin? May I ask you something? Why did Alex want to live in a ratty apartment like ours?"

"Oh! So independent, so I'll-do-it-my-way, my Alexandra. Nothing from us, her highness wouldn't take nothing from us, do it all on her own or not at all, she says. 'Then go on!' I told her. 'Right back down in the dirt, the cock-a-roaches running you crazy like they did your mother.' We wanted to give her the best. Everything. The *best*."

Mrs. Baskin walked over to the window. She held the sheer white curtains apart, staring down through the dark glass. Francie wondered how she looked—body light, face smooth—when Samuel Baskin married her. Now he called her "Mother."

"Of course!" Mrs. Baskin said. "You're skinny as Alexandra. Cheryl doesn't need them, I told Sammy. She's always spending Tommy's money on clothes. We'll give *you* Alex's things."

"Oh, no. I couldn't possibly. Really."

"But you can. And you will. I'll have them shortened up for you tomorrow, Francie, dear. I have a lovely seamstress. We'll have such fun doing it, like a party, just for us. Now, don't go spoil things and say no."

"All right. If you think it's okay. It's really kind of you."

"See you in the morning then, dear." Her voice had gone thin, as if dawn lay at the end of an exhausting labor.

Francie closed the door behind her. When the sound of footsteps had faded, she turned the round gold knob of the lock. She pulled the nightgown from under the bed, rubbing the silk against her cheek. Then she pulled off her housecoat, put the gown on once again and climbed into bed.

Alex's bed.

She imagined Alex lying in the bed, staring across the room into the Kewpie-doll eyes.

Francie sat up. Restless, she pulled out the drawer of the table beside the bed and rummaged inside. There was a collection of sore-throat lozenges, candy-bar wrappers, pens, a pair of sunglasses with a missing lens, and a white envelope. Francie picked up the envelope, drew out the card. On the front was a drawing of a white wedding cake, with a bride and bridegroom in blue jeans on the top. "Congratulations" was printed across the cake.

She opened the card. The handwriting was Alex's.

> Dear Ann,
> I wish you what I wish myself.
> Love that never stops, a long life,
> and happy babies.

There was no signature.

The thought that came frightened her. For the first time, she missed Alex.

She climbed down from the bed, retrieved her purse, took out the folded napkin on which the number was scrawled. The ink had bled into the nubby surface. She picked up the pink telephone, the numbers luminous in the dim room.

She felt an excitement move up along her body. *You. I choose you.*

She dialed.

"Hello. Miles?"

She had slept.

She must have slept: Because now, with a wrench, she was awake, staring at the ceiling, the peach nightgown dark with sweat along her body.

There was a sense of horror not quite remembered. She felt loose and rattling in her skin.

She tried to remember if she had swallowed the Dalmane, 30 milligrams, *h.s. (hora somni)*, at bedtime. She remembered the glass of water in Alex's lilac-papered bathroom. She tried to visualize the red-and-ivory capsule in her palm, then the dry plastic taste of it on her tongue, before the flood of water washed it down.

But she couldn't remember. If she took another, she might, like Marilyn Monroe, just never wake up. (And no glamour about it, you vomited even in a coma—she had read it in a magazine.)

She was remembering the two slides of rat brains in biology (the one class she had never cut). The brain on the left bulged firm in its walnut contours. But the brain on the right—of a rat kept alive through a coma—was foldless and formless as pudding.

DALMANE: Generic name Flurazepam hydrochloride. Estimated prescriptions 1975—11,558,000. Adverse reactions: dizziness, excessive drowsiness, staggering, loss of muscle coordination, falling (especially in the old and weak), lethargy, severe sedation, disorientation, coma. *And pudding brain?*

And then suddenly she remembered what the dream had been.

The door to the bedroom opened. Samuel Baskin walked through, a short terry-cloth robe tied around his waist. His eyes met hers—so dark the pupils didn't show, just like Alex's. His knee sagged the bed. Through the parted robe she saw his thigh, stubbled like a beard with short black hair. He pulled the peach nightgown up around her waist, quickly and painfully entering her. She felt the wave of pleasure begin, the wave that always began and then died to nothing but this time was sweeping harder up the center of her body. She raised her legs to stop it, to push him off, and felt a sudden blazing pinpointing rush of pleasure splitting her womb. "Daddy," she heard someone say.

3:27 a.m.

The lights of an oil barge sliced through the dark, and now he could see the broad prow pushing aside the sheets of dirty water.

Dalroi sat on the concrete wall of the overpass, beyond East End Avenue and Eighty-first Street. Ahead was the East River walkway—a narrow stretch of broken concrete, sagging wooden benches and trampled grass—while beneath rolled the noise of the few cars on the Franklin D. Roosevelt Drive.

A breeze came off the water, ruffling his hair with a salty dampness. Across the river in Queens the huge red neon sign was flashing: PEARL WICK HAMPERS, PEARL WICK HAMPERS. The barge surged up the west channel of the river, which was divided in two by the bulking shape of Roosevelt Island. The barge passed the small eight-sided building —the stair tower of the old New York Lunatic Asylum— and in its wake was the sharp taint of gasoline and rubber.

Dalroi walked down the steep stairs toward the walkway.

A young couple tangled on a bench. The male was sitting, the she's legs stretched out on the broken slats, shoulders curled upward in his lap as he bent over her, moving her violently up and down. His hand reached out, sank between her thighs.

Dalroi felt the erection spear outward in his slacks.

He wanted to laugh. He had been erect when he moved close to Paige at the funeral, but she didn't know him, had never seen him, could not suspect. He had even brushed her arm, with its white skin burred with faint gold hairs, had apologized and she had looked up, eyes meeting his. He could see the moisture on her upper lip, where there were more gold hairs, smell her smell, which was soft and powdery, as he smiled at her. He had imagined the loose powder spilling onto her bathmat as she dusted it down over her throat to her breasts.

And then the she had turned away.

Anger filled him. Instead of staying in the city, as he had planned, the she had driven out to her parents' home. He imagined her there, in her bed.

Fool, he thought. It would be isolated in New Jersey. It would make the whole thing easier, he would just follow her there.

He didn't want to hurt her. He loved her.

It was just that he wanted her dead.

Dalroi walked over to the bench, stood there until the young man raised his head. The she twisted around in his arms, startled, staring up. He could see the fear on both their faces.

"Don't want to break up your little party," he said. "But a lot of muggers around at this hour. Why don't you do this lady a favor and take her home?"

Chapter Five

"Where the fuck are you?"

The voice of Arnold Lowry, *Post* managing editor, had the projectile range, if not the breeding, of Sir Laurence Olivier.

Miles Overby yanked the receiver from his ear.

But that was no good. Past the telephone booth rolled the Brooklyn-Queens Expressway, upon which engines, horns, a cabbie bouncing a gas can off the hood of a stalled truck swamped Lowry's continuing harangue, any portion of which might require a response.

Miles clamped the earpiece back against his head.

". . . your ass up there," Lowry said.

"Arnie, will you listen? Arnie, I got through to him."

"Why, I even . . . Through to *who?*"

"Spyros Xanthakis' brother. I finally got him. On the phone. On my way now to talk to him. Xanthakis—what do you mean who? The Alex Baskin suspect that skipped, for Christ sake! Arnie, you read your own rag? It's your old dodge—Cain and Abel, right? Get to a man's brother and you're halfway home."

"Overby . . ."

When Lowry switched to last names, Miles thought, iron bowels danced. He dug into his jeans pocket for a Camel. Now he had a cigarette (crushed) and no match.

"What did the police sheet say this A.M., Overby? Or you lost the ability to read?"

"FALN bomb suspect Jose Colon, twenty-nine, Hispanic, found dead of gunshot in the Bronx." Miles found the matches, struck one, and inhaled. "Sir."

"Haul ass up there, then."

"Yes, sir."

"And, Overby."

"Yes, sir?"

"Lew Archer don't get paid by the *Post*."

Miles replaced the receiver, then checked his watch: 11:23. Scratch the second edition of the *Post* ("Wall Street —Today's Stocks"). No way the renowned Overby byline could make the last copy deadline of 11:30—either for the Puerto Rican terrorist or the Greek brother. The deadline for the next edition ("Wall Street—Latest Stocks") was 1:30. He could knock off the brother, drive the hell over to the Bronx, make it back with both stories. Two chances to brown Lowry and juggle his byline up front, past the small potatoes of pages four and five.

Miles gunned the dented navy Dodge Coronet toward the Ditmars Boulevard exit.

The diner Nicholaos Xanthakis had specified was a classic blue-and-silver-striped rectangle with a red neon sign. Placards advertised "Infrared Broiling" and "Vaculator Coffee." In the last of the ten vinyl booths a man in his midthirties was stirring a teaspoon in a cup. The metal clattered against china as he watched Miles walk toward him.

"Nick?" Miles said, extending his hand. "I'm Richie. Glad to meet you."

The man opposite was short and stocky, with dead-looking hair blown and sprayed into a puffy thatch. He was wearing a three-piece chalk-stripe black suit that looked, Miles thought, like the accountant he was. All his buttons were buttoned. Miles felt a strong and instant dislike. But then, Nick was undoubtedly feeling the same way toward him. He had read it once in high school: one-third of all people hate you on sight. It had struck him as the only complete truth he had ever heard, resulting in his stay in his room for a week afterward, pleading a gut ache of indeterminable origin. ("No, not there, Dr. Carlson, more to the left, down a bit, *ouch!*")

Miles sat down under the other's scrutiny, and when the waitress appeared, ordered a lemonade. Nothing more innocent than lemonade.

"You know, it ain't just that I still got that climbing gear of his, Nick. Hell, I figure whatever he run for, he must be scared. Needs a friend, you know?"

"Yeah."

"I mean, I would, I got dropped in his situation."

"How'd you come to meet him?" Nick said.

"Climbing, where else? But we didn't get real tight until

129

the time we got stuck—way over our ability—on bitchin' Cannon Cliff. It's up in New Hampshire."

"That's Spyros, all right. Always over his head, riding the edge. The more risk, the more he liked anything. Never could see it myself. So how'd he bungle this time?"

"We were on this two-day ascent up Fruit Cup Wall. It's rated five-eight overall, but five-ten's more like it," Miles said, repeating the description he had lifted from the Appalachian Mountain Club booklet. "It's getting dark, see. We're on the fourth pitch face climbing up this forty-foot wall. Suddenly I come loose, swing out hollering like a fool, bang my ankle back against the rock. Feels like it's busted. And I panic. Plain panic. Shaking so I can't hold the wall. Old Spyros starts talking nice and low, ten minutes, fifteen minutes. He gets me moving again, up five bolts and a mantle move when I'm perched on the top bolt. Then finally I pull over the edge of the bivi site—this huge flat ledge where we're bivouacking. Lay there soaking—and I'm not ashamed, crying."

Miles looked at the other man. "I want to tell you, Nick. He saved me. Your brother fucking saved my life."

Nick swallowed the last of his coffee. "He's such a hero, you tell me why he run like he did. My mother, my father, he's shamed them for good this time. They've worked forty years to own a decent house in a decent neighborhood. We're respected here. Then he gets himself blasted all over the papers. Stupid jerky kid. All he got to do is answer some questions, of course he didn't do it. But no, he runs. He runs and now they're all saying it. That he did it. Reporters are everywhere. My mother can't even go out, leave the house."

"That's a shame."

"And you can tell him when you see him we don't want him home no more. You got that? We don't want to see him. We don't want to hear from him. Dad's written him off. You tell him that."

"Yeah, okay, Nick. But where do I find him to tell him?"

Nick studied his face.

Okay, Miles thought, so he was a shit. A lousy, dirty, shitty shit. But then, the whole business of journalism was a shit. After the U. of Missouri, with all the reporters coming out of the woodwork, he'd been unable to get a job, had to crawl home. Local boy doesn't make good. Judge Miles K. Overby Jr. intervened with the editor of the *Commercial Appeal*, who was a personal friend of his. But then, half the town's gray eminences were personal friends of the judge. Then had come his first murder: the black woman in the hallway, the pool of blood, bits of white later identified as the crown of a tooth. He had rushed to his desk, written the story, handed it in. *"Son, now, is this poor woman, you should pardon my French, of the coon persuasion? Uh-huh. You got a passel to learn, Miles, my boy. We'll start with Rule One: cheap people, cheap stories."*

Miles looked back at Nicholaos Xanthakis.

"You can trust me," he said.

"He's in New Paltz, that's what he told Grandma. You know, hippieville."

2:24 p.m.

"Paranoid psychosis encapsulated, schizophrenic reaction with paranoid overtones, neurotic personality with a psychotic core ... Hell, Chuck," Frank Quinn said. "We've heard everything about this killer except something *useful.*"

A dry rustle forced itself from the chest of Charles J.

Batchelder, M.D., Ph.D. Only when the sound had lain on the air for a minute did Victor Amspoker realize it was a laugh. Batchelder picked up the color photographs—of a bedroom and of dunes—fanning them out like cards across the brown felt blotter. His lips pursed in study. As he bent forward under the lamp, his round bald spot gleamed like ivory. His pen scratched notes in the silence.

Amspoker shifted in the leather chair. More damned horses' asses per square mile in psychiatry than any other profession. Pompous dunderheads spouting professor talk and theories, theories, theories. Which had nothing to do with reality. Had they ever come up with a name, an address? Now Quinn was wasting still another hour with Batchelder—one of his John Jay profs he'd talked up to the lieutenant.

Batchelder looked up, steepling his plump fingers. "So, I take it, you want to hear more than that he's a white male in his late teens or early twenties, a loner, with low self-esteem, an inability to form meaningful affectionate or sexual relationships, who feels a raging need to establish his masculinity and retaliate for a past rejection by a female."

Quinn laughed. "On the nose. But at least the profile's now unanimous."

"But fits ten thousand men in this city," Amspoker said, "who *don't* go out and kill."

Behind the q⁣artz-thick lenses, Batchelder's eyes closed. He brought his fingertips to his lips. Then his eyes opened, looking down at his notes. "All right. We will go beyond such superficial prescriptions. The murder of two young women—in such a manner as this—it is a form of self-expression. Now, what is this self like? He is not a paranoid schizophrenic. He shows few symptoms of any known psychosis. He probably has no record of mental illness or criminal acts. He is the type of killer hardest to spot, even for a trained professional. Fortunately for us, in this country he comes along only every few years."

"All right," Quinn said. "Make with the jargon. What do you boys call him?"

"A sadistic sociopathic killer. He tortures, mutilates and kills in order to reach an orgasm. Because of the orgasm, he is the killer most likely to repeat himself."

"You mean like that giant out in Santa Cruz in seventy-three?" Amspoker said. "What was his name—Kenter?"

"Edmund Emil Kemper III. Big Ed, almost seven feet tall. Within eleven months he beheaded and mutilated eight women, raping them after death in his own bed, with his mother in the house. He even ate several, raw and cooked in casseroles."

"I remember that case," Amspoker said. "Because at the same time two psychiatrists were examining him, giving him a clean bill of health, a girl's head was outside in the parking lot in the trunk of his car."

"We're not infallible," Batchelder said. "And of all killers, the sex murderer is least likely to foam and have red eyes. Two types of murderers, you see: the undercontrolled and the overcontrolled. The sex murderer appears to be the overcontrolled type—rigid, polite, bland, often puritanical, allowing no outlets in his life for normal aggression. To friends and relatives he is the model father, former boy scout, churchgoer, too good to be true. The aggression builds. And finally it's too much and explodes. Unfortunately, he makes few mistakes, leaves no clues—which is part of his control over himself."

Batchelder sat back, a gentle smile revealing yellow incisors as he watched the frantic scribbling.

"Now," he continued. "This matter of the biting of the breast. . . . In the unconscious mind, of course, the infant we once were lives on." He tapped the photographs. "When this man attacks, his unconscious mind rips open. He is again the child at the breast. *But the child wants to kill his mother.* Kemper, for example, killed all those young hitch-hiking coeds in rehearsal, as it were. His real target, which he finally got around to, was his mother. After killing her, he gave himself up."

"Hold on a minute," Amspoker said, ignoring Quinn's look. "Isn't that way out in left field? Maybe the guy we're looking for hates his *father*."

"The point is," Batchelder said, "as infants we *all* wanted to kill our mothers. Yes, Mr. Amspoker. When the teeth erupt, we get our first weapon. We enter what the Freudians call the oral-sadistic, or cannibalistic, stage, in which we bite whatever is handy—nipple, mug, toy, sibling—with all our strength. And though there's the Good Mother, who lets you suck her milk, there is also the Bad Mother, who takes the breast away. Who leaves you to cry yourself hoarse in a dark crib. The mother is both a monster and a siren. Therefore the infant is ambivalent—both sadistic and loving. In actual fact, the real mother could be harsh, domineering and cruel. Or, on the contrary, sweet, gentle, even seductive. The point is, let's let the mothers off the hook. It's not really what they do or don't do. Cruel mothers can bring up loving children, loving mothers can bring up psychopaths. It's the child's terrifying *fantasies* that cause the harm—fantasies of killing the mother, of being killed by her, of sleeping with her. Some children are apparently hypersensitive, can't deal with these fantasies in a normal way.

"Matter of fact, some adults can't either. In his years as a prison psychiatrist, Robert Lindner noticed there was one expletive that even among hardened cons could get a man killed. Karl Menninger later confirmed it."

"What expletive was that?" Quinn asked.

"Motherfucker," Batchelder said.

134

The new apartment living room was a bare white rectangle fronted by a single window, shuttered now behind venetian blinds. Sunlight limned the edges of the slats. The floor was blond hardwood, planked precise as graph paper. The air was hot, heavy with the smell of cheap paint inexpertly smeared on the walls in a shade as thin, as blue-white as skim milk.

On the bare floor in the center of the room, tethered by a black cord, the telephone was ringing.

Startled, Francie Perry hipped the door shut, set down the grocery bag, and threw the two bolts. But their new number was unlisted, as Detective Amspoker had suggested. Only Paige, their families, the Baskins, or the police could be on the other end. She could pick up the receiver, separated as she was by telephone wires, two doormen, an entrance video surveillance system, and two new locks. She felt like a chrysalis, surrounded and safe.

"Hello?"

"Miss Perry? Detective Amspoker here. Just wanted to find out how you two girls are doing."

"It's nice of you to call. We're okay, I guess."

"Wanted to tell you I checked out the Regency employees. You never know. Some of these buildings have doormen, porters with records. But the Regency's clean. Far as we know, you're in good hands there. Change the locks like I said?"

"Oh, sure. And added one. First thing we did."

"I also wanted to give you my number at home. Unlisted. You or Paige need anything, questions, whatever, you give me a call, okay?"

"Thanks. We appreciate it, really." She heard in her voice a kind of excessive gratitude, as when her father turned to look at her, take some notice.

"Miss Perry. Are you all right?"

"It's silly, I know. But I keep thinking about it. And I have trouble sleeping. Paige and I have talked about it. We feel . . . afraid, I guess."

"Miss Perry?"

"Yes?"

"We're going to catch him, you know."

She replaced the receiver. She crossed to the window, opened the blinds, peered out and then up toward the sliver of sky. It was like living in steerage. Above you the penthouses sailed in fresh winds beneath stars. Below, your window opened onto another apartment wall.

She pressed the switch on the air-conditioner. Soot blew up from the raised slats into her face. She sat on the floor, cross-legged in her jeans, pressing her back against the cool plaster. Through the wall, from apartment 31, came an intermittent thumping noise. The occupants, two gay men and a harlequin Great Dane, had clinched their choice of floors. "What could be safer?" Paige had said, loud enough for the super to hear. "Two women in fag heaven."

It was ironic, really, all those comments about how isolated people live in New York City. In reality, you heard the rhythm of headboards assaulting walls, flushings, groanings, laughter and curses. If you were very *un*lucky, you heard, saw, or even smelled someone die.

"Orange cupcakes," she remembered telling Paige, sniffing the air in the foyer. The scent had even made her salivate—like the tart peel of lemon in espresso. But through the locked inner door and down the hall the scent blossomed, grew oppressive like a mass of flowers just starting to decay. The door to apartment 12 was ajar. A patrolman sat inside on a wooden chair, his hands hanging between his knees. "What is it?" she had whispered to Paige as they climbed the stairs. "I remember now," Paige had said. "Went to a funeral home when I was ten, and

136

there was that same—orange cupcakes. Some chemical they use to cover up the stink."

The doorbell rang once, twice, jarring her thoughts.

"Hope you like wine," Miles Overby said, his chin wedged down onto two overflowing grocery bags.

"Did you find a place to park on the street?" she said, starting to unpack the bags.

"Yeah. Only mashed the *front* bumper to get in." He looked around. "When's all your Picassos arrive?"

"Believe it or not, not till this weekend. They *think*. They've got this sign stretched over the door: 'Crime Scene Search Area. Stop. No Admittance.'"

"You know, you got a pretty nice pad here, Francie." Miles was looking through the door into the large rectangular bedroom. Two foam mattresses were stacked against the wall. He pulled one out into the living room. "What's it cost?"

"Two-oh-five. We got it through Mr. Baskin, he arranged the whole thing. And no way that's the regular rent."

"Nice. You like Niersteiner Dommethal?" He pulled a bottle of wine from its corrugated wrapping.

"Oh, sure, yeah. If it's a good year."

He laughed.

They sat together on the foam mattress, backs against the wall, his arm around her. The wine was white, dry and flinty, the way she liked it. She quickly drank several glassfuls.

"You know . . ." She twirled the empty glass, staring down into its reflection. "I keep on wondering. If it could have been someone I knew. Someone out for me, who got Alex instead. Someone I maybe insulted without knowing —I have been known to do that."

"That's crazy, Francie. How can you even think that? Alex wasn't responsible. No one's responsible."

"Like dominoes. Like I was the first one to tumble over,

137

and Alex was the one I knocked down. Someone who saw me withdraw money Friday at the bank. Someone who saw me once, followed me home. Someone who found out there were three women living in our apartment. Maybe he stood around that morning, saw us leave, knew Alex was up there alone . . ."

Miles pulled her down beside him on the mattress. His breath near her smelled of tobacco and the flowery wine and the creamy, dark, molasses-tasting beer they had drunk after the wine was gone. She wondered when Paige was coming home.

"Want me to sing to you?" he said.

She nodded, her head tucked down on his chest, and he began to sing "Greensleeves."

His voice was surprising, a baritone that resonated in his chest, burrowing up along her cheek. His sweat smelled young and green and not unpleasant at all.

> Alas, my love, you do me wrong
> To cast me off discourteously,
> And I have lovèd you so long,
> Delighting in your company.

When he turned to kiss her, his face was so close she couldn't really see, she thought, that he wasn't attractive to her at all.

Then he was lying on top of her, and she felt his erection pressing into her abdomen and his hands rasping up along the sides of her thighs. She remembered the first time she had kissed Spy, on a trip in his ancient car through the mist, his friend J.R. driving. On the radio: "I'd Like to Get to Know You." The car stopping, Spy taking her hand. And then they were running back into the mist where J.R. couldn't see them, Spy's tongue hot against her cold, mist-wet face, his erection hard against her jeaned belly for the first time and the two of them staring at each other, both knowing it was love for the first time.

"No," she said. "Miles. The blinds are open. Someone can see."

They both looked across to the end of the room.

Miles got up and clicked off the overhead light. Through the open slats and across the narrow space a figure stood silhouetted in a window. The man, as one-dimensional as a cardboard cutout, was staring down at them.

Miles snapped the blinds shut. Then, "You going back to work tomorrow?"

The afternoon, she realized, was over. She had failed to make him like her, to establish that bond that would make him see her again.

"I quit my job at *Nebula*. Oh, not because of this whole thing. It just wasn't working out anyway, boss problems and all. I applied for Alex's job."

"You what?"

"I got it, too."

He was staring at her.

"I don't know why I did it. Spur-of-the-moment thing, I guess."

He took her hand, his fingers warm around hers, opening them out. She had always hated her hands, she thought, very stubby and with nails that never grew.

"True?" he said.

"True. Well, sort of. Alex is gone and I have to..."
Have to what? "I have to find out..."

"Find out what, Francie?"

"I don't know."

Find out why Alex died. Alex was gone, but she wasn't gone without a reason. There had to be a reason. Something that made sense of it.

Didn't there?

She smelled it again—the thick sweetness of raw cabbage. It was pungent but pleasantly rural after the smoke and smells of the oil refineries along the twelve-lane New Jersey Turnpike.

Paige MacLeish glanced out the open Volkswagen window at the cabbage field whose chalky blue heads marched unevenly up a hill. Highway 571 West was a two-laner that cut through rolling brown-clay farmland planted with corn, soybeans, and wheat.

The car passed wooded stands of scrub pine and birches, climbing on toward Princeton, where it followed a black Mercedes-Benz through the center of town. The university's ivy-covered brick buildings bulked comfortingly up ahead.

It would be five days tomorrow, Paige thought. But still it was bones she was thinking about. Alex under the ground. Will MacLeish's drawers and drawers of bones neatly labeled "tibia," "fibula," "clavicle" in his workroom on the anthropology floor of Green Hall. Herself seven years old, pulling the drawers out, staring down at the porous, spongy-looking but brittle knob ends of bones lacquered yellow-brown with preservative, the smell of more preservative where her father was working at his table, hair pale as he bent forward under the metal lamp.

Diogenes asked Plato, "What is Man?" Plato: "Man is a two-legged animal without feathers." Diogenes plucked a rooster and said, "Here is Plato's man." "To an anthropologist," her father had said, "man is a two-legged animal without feathers and possessing flat nails."

Paige turned onto the narrow local road out of Princeton, accelerating past Cedar Grove, impatient suddenly to get to Hopewell.

Where everything might somehow get right again.

It was after dinner when the words she had been expecting arrived.

"We want you to stay, Paige. Permanently. It's as simple as that." Tessa was pouring coffee into the Royal Doulton cups that had been Grandmother Anson's wedding gift. Her hand trembled and the coffee spilled.

Paige looked at her mother across the plates, shiny from the baked Virginia ham and sweet potatoes glazed with honey.

She had eaten too much again, Paige thought. She could feel the too-tight crotch of her slacks, the fabric strangling her upper thighs. But Tessa always cooked her favorite foods when she came home. To refuse would be a slight of love.

"Can't work at a better place than the university, Paige," Will said. "Doesn't cost anything to ask. An instructor's job, perhaps."

"I just don't know."

"Don't know what?" Tessa said. "Whether you want to be *alive* at this time next year?"

"Please, mouse," Will said.

"More than four murders a day in the city. And what was that—what they called 'stranger murders.' It was in the *Times*, Will. How the city ranks first for that kind of murder—where the victim doesn't know her killer."

"*For Christ sake, Mother,*" Paige said.

There was a sudden silence. The name, rusty with disuse, seemed to hang in the air with a palpable odor.

"What do you want me to do? Lock myself away in here? Never go outside? The spinster daughter, getting fatter and fatter up on the second floor, grayer and grayer, reading Jane Austen and looking out at the rain? *Shit!*"

"You could commute. And don't use that word," Tessa said.

"*Shit.*"

"Paige, now let's be rational...." Her father's eyes seemed to shrink behind the squares of glass.

"I want to tell you something. Both of you. *I have a right to use the world.* I wanted to camp out that summer I read *Walden*—alone, with nature, remember, Will? But you said I had to take your pistol, no, it was too dangerous entirely on second thought, men might come. I wanted to have a drink in the sun at a table at Les Deux Magots like Hemingway. But I couldn't sit down anywhere in Paris, even inside Chartres, without some pervert after me babbling in French, trailing after me while I walk up and down on my corns. It doesn't do any good to run. I'm not going to run *anymore.*"

"Oh, my God," Tessa said. "My baby. My poor baby." She rose and bent over Paige's chair.

Paige buried her face against her mother's white blouse, which smelled of sun and a hot iron. She wanted to cry. She felt the tears come drop by drop, harsh and unrelieving.

"The truth is..." Paige wiped angrily at her face. "It's more than just my job. I feel less safe here than I do in the city. In an apartment there are so few entrances, ways for someone to get at you. But you've got nothing like that here. You're like on an island—all these houses—like islands made of Swiss cheese. Doors, windows everywhere, and right on ground level. Somebody could be screaming on another island and you'd never even hear."

"You still seeing Aurelia?" Will said.

"Yes. Twice a week. You know that. You get the bills."

"Well, keep on, then. Maybe longer sessions would be a bigger help. I don't see how you can accomplish anything in thirty minutes."

Paige thought about Aurelia-the-shrink, whose main advice so far was that time was needed, time would heal, in time she would forget or at least accept, knead Alex's murder into her life like a bitter spoiled fruit and go on.

Outside, a smell of rain lay on the still-warm air, carried on a breeze which shivered her bare arms. The night was black around her.

She climbed into the front seat of the Volkswagen.

"We love you, Paige."

It was her mother's voice. Both her parents were standing on the round, columned porch. The hair in the V of her father's shirt was white under the light.

Why, he's got *old*, she thought. And then: *I could still go back. Turn off the ignition, get out, run back.* But you couldn't just run from something. You had to run to something, too.

"Good night," she said.

She released the handbrake. As the small red car nosed slowly down the driveway, she looked into the rearview mirror. Her parents were framed there, distant as a daguerreotype. Severe as a Grant Wood painting.

No, she thought. It was one of the captioned photographs in *The Family of Man:* "We two form a multitude."

She saw her father put his arm around her mother.

It was like a circle, closing her out.

3:14 a.m.

He felt the strong wind passing through his body, quivering like a thin leaf. He felt thin-skinned and veinous, like dry reptile wings, now discarded.

He paused beneath the shadow of the tree. The bark was dark gray. Its flat-topped ridges rasped his fingertips, which probed between to the diamond-shaped depressions. His fingers rode the bark.

It was an elm. An American elm, *Ulmus americana*. He had not been an Eagle Scout for nothing.

Four-leaf clovers, and he had never found one.

Dalroi looked out at the expanse of manicured lawn. His shoes lifted, glinting with dew through the grass. His white socks were peppered with the brown pronged sticktight seeds from the woods through which he had walked.

The seeds rode with him, scratching hornlike through his socks.

The dark square of window was open at the top. His fingertips settled lightly into the dust, urging the top pane down.

He peered within.

Slowly his eyes adjusted, gray shapes bulking toward him out of the blackness.

There was no one in the single bed. *Her* bed.

Paige MacLeish's bed.

Dalroi felt the trembling begin. He was not wrong. This was her room. He had been in the house, through the house while its occupants were gone that afternoon.

On the square night table, illuminated digital numbers flipped upward in a clock.

It was 3:17 A.M.

The *she* had cheated him.

The *she* should have been here. Here in her parents' fancy house in her bed, the long heavy body lying inert, asleep by now.

He felt his shoulders rise, crack tauter, and then sag.

His heart thudded out into the room.

Like that mongrel, he thought. The one he had owned who threw himself toward dinner against the screen door, white chest hairs splayed against metal—again and again.

144

Dalroi jerked his head out of the window as the rain began to fall. He turned his face upward, searching for the warm spaces between the spattering drops. Clouds scudded in rags, and he could hear the click of crickets, monotonous as machinery.

He thought about Tessa MacLeish.

But she was too old.

Frustration rose, prickles of heat out of every pore. Every hair on his body stiffened out of its follicle on end.

Dalroi unzipped his pants, pulled out his penis, on which the chill rain dropped.

He sent the hot urine arcing across the lawn, steam dancing behind.

Chapter Six

Friday, August 12
8:56 a.m.

The Gilbert, Levensky & Hane reception area on the fortieth floor was crowded with seven-year-old boys and their mothers. The boys had freckles, red or blond hair, and were reading comic books, legs over the armrests of brass-studded leather chairs. The mothers sat upright, clutching purses in their laps.

Francie Perry walked to the reception desk, which was

unattended. Red waxy-looking anthers with drooping pistils (or was it stamens?) were in a vase on the embossed leather top.

The carpet was green as money.

The paging bell chimed its code: once, three times, two times—soft as a harpsichord, she thought. Or was the sound more reminiscent of Macy's?

She had just decided to navigate her own way down the hall when a tall man in his late thirties pushed through the glass doors. He wore a well-worn green corduroy jacket, khaki slacks, and pointed-toe cowboy boots. His hair was black, and his face was pitted with the healed ravages of acne, which gave him a battered but rakish look. His eyes moved down Alex's shortened white suit, which she was wearing with one of Alex's tight black silk blouses.

"Going my way?" he said.

"I'm trying to find ... that is ... Mr. Nagy's office. I'm his new secretary."

"Ward Yates. Welcome aboard. And if you just take ten baby steps, or scissors steps, or any kind of steps *at all* to your right, you'll see his name on the door."

"Thanks." She turned, feeling his eyes on her back.

"But just don't trip."

She looked back. "What?"

"Should you get horizontal, it'd be all over." He winked at her, his fingers scratching his chest between the shirt buttons.

She felt herself redden, and then she smiled back.

The ten steps took her to a large open space washed with blue-white fluorescence. Offices formed the outer perimeters, but most of the brown-lacquered doors were still closed. Before each office stood a gray metal desk manned with a typewriter and telephone. A variety of young women in their twenties were opening up shop for the day, uncover-

147

ing typewriters and Styrofoam cups, unwrapping toasted corn muffins, chatting with familiar ease.

Francie felt back in first grade, wondering if anyone would like her or even talk to her.

"Hi, there. *Je suis* Kandis," said a familiar-sounding contralto behind her. It was the voice from last Monday, the voice that had started it all.

Francie turned to see a tall woman in her late twenties with ash-blond hair through which ran an improbable variety of streaks. She looked aggressively well-groomed, as though she douched every day.

"I'm Francie Perry. The new—"

"I know, I know. Nagy's newest slave. I saw him directing you out after your interview. Welcome aboard, as they say."

"Thanks." She was beginning to think she had embarked on a cruise. "I feel a little nervous, I guess."

"Oh, Nagy's really a sweetie. A bit of the old 'You vill *type* ze letters and you vill *enjoy* it!' Just to warn you. But you'll like him. Me, I work for Pete Heimer. Keeps me twice as busy as Nagy'll do you. But Pete's single, you know. You sit right over here," she said, patting a metal desktop. "And I'm right behind you in the caboose. Oh, hi, Mare."

A small girl with ripe-olive eyes was walking down the aisle. She was wearing a T-shirt that read "Here Today— Gone To Maui."

"This is Mary Sills. Francie, the new secretary."

"Oh, you're working for *him*," Mary said, eyes fastening on Nagy's brushed-brass nameplate. "He's only brilliant. Travels half the time, too, so you won't even be that busy. You're her roommate. I mean, was, aren't you? Alex's roommate?"

"Mare," Kandis said in mock despair.

"Yes."

"Awful," Mary said. "I just couldn't believe it. Still can't."

"It must be painful to talk about it," Kandis said, frowning at Mary.

"Good morning, girls," said a voice marbled with European undertones. "I see you have introduced yourselves."

"Good morning, Mr. Nagy," Francie said as he unlocked his office and walked inside. Soft lights flickered on.

She looked up at Kandis and Mary with a little nervous shrug.

"See you for lunch?" Kandis said, *sotto voce.*

"Love it."

The two women turned to their desks. Francie picked up a printed sheet from her In box. "Red is fading as the top packaging color," it read, "and being replaced by green, blue, black, and some pastels."

"You can come in now, Francine," came Nagy's voice.

For a reason she couldn't name, she felt a thrill of dislike go through her. She picked up her steno pad and walked in.

Tibor Nagy, whom she had met for just five minutes during her interview, was seated behind a walnut table supported by chrome legs. His swivel chair was turned toward the window, through which loomed gray slabs graphed with glass.

As Francie entered, he turned the chair toward her. His head jiggled above his body. She tried not to notice, to focus steadily on his eyes, but the effort made her dizzy.

"I hope you will be happy here," he said. His voice was professorial. "And that we may perhaps help you forget that most . . . unfortunate occurrence. Please, have a seat."

She was staring down at the desk, on which stood a foot-long porcelain sculpture of a lion pursuing a zebra. The lion rose off its right hind foot, its claws extended above the zebra's contorted rump.

"Exquisite, isn't it?" he said as she sat down in the padded black chair in front of his desk. "I'm afraid I have quite a pile of correspondence to get out this morning, Francine.

These temps, you know ... Oh, a point of information. My girls never drink coffee at their desk. Sooner or later, you know, you'll spill it all over important papers."

Back at Alex's desk—*my* desk, she corrected—Francie began typing the first of the pages covered with shorthand. Almost immediately she made two mistakes. She opened the center drawer, looking for a bottle of correction fluid. Except for a pile of pencil shavings, it was completely bare. Someone had cleaned it out—spare her the sad relics, perhaps.

The top two side drawers were also empty. But in the bottom of the third drawer she found a crumpled newspaper clipping. She picked it up, flattening it out on top of the desk.

PUBLIC NOTICES
TREASURE Expedition Spanish galleon pinpointed equal split gold bullion coins jewels 105-foot fully equipped salvage vessel sailing for Central/South America room for 2 more in crew no experience necessary share expenses.

Why didn't you go, Alex? she thought. Why didn't you just *go?*

2:57 p.m.

Paige MacLeish stared at the heart-shaped leaves of the philodendron on her desk. The green had gone sick, edged and marbled with a spreading yellow. (Alice in Wonderland: "We're painting the roses *yellow*. We're painting the roses *yellow*." Alex's roses yellow.)

It was Alex she was seeing—moving down the stairs one last time to the street, clothed only in the stretcher's rough white canvas. Alex remained—like a quick-frozen specimen under the microscope. She remained, like the hot hiss of the heater against her leg when the principal burst into class: "*The President's been shot.*"

Alex living, and now Alex dying, had detonated their lives like a stone dropped in a pond. The splash, and then the ripples spreading out and out.

But she was handling it all better than Francie.

It was so obvious, Francie's guilt for asking Alex to move out. The unadmitted part of her that wanted to be sexy and free like Alex (as if anyone was ever free in sex and love).

But why was that so bad? Everyone had parts of themselves capable of everything.

And now Francie had taken Alex's job.

Which could only make things worse.

At Hornblower this morning, everyone had stared at her, looked away, then stared again, as if she were a celebrity (or a criminal?), memorizing her expression to relate to lunch-mates and spouses.

Or they had not looked and sidled away. As if she were diseased, murder of a roommate somehow catching.

The worst of it, she thought, was that she—the grind of Sarah Lawrence, to whom work was the ultimate solace—didn't care if she never worked again. Her desk was piled with Xeroxes, graphs, magazine clippings, yellowing news-paper columns. Her notebook was filled with data on con-sumer electronics. But the idea of knitting the parts to-gether made her feel physically ill.

Maybe her mother had been right; she had come back to work too soon. (Stay home until you are without symptoms or fever for twenty-four hours.)

But the only thing that could help was to forget, resume just as things had been, work harder than ever so there wouldn't even be *time* to remember.

Except that she felt so afraid.

She thought about the peace of Sarah Lawrence—thirty acres up in Yonkers, lawns, trees, ivy-covered dons. Bates Cafeteria *and* the health-food bar. The sign she had pasted on the dorm refrigerator: "Abandon All Hope Ye Who Enter Here." Always someone in the lounge at three A.M., typewriter and small tin ashtray on the table, bare feet or in bright blue fake-fur slippers. She remembered typing her own thesis: "The Childbirth Metaphor in Sir Philip Sidney's *Astrophel and Stella*." It was a sonnet sequence of over a hundred English Renaissance poems interspersed with songs, and she had slept with them, talked to them, carried them around with her for over a year.

Now all that seemed as charmed, as innocent, as distant as hopscotch.

She felt so afraid.

But it's over, you dumb-ass. No, Alex's expressions were much more precise: *schtunk* (rat fink with nebbish undertones), *wimp, nerd,* and of course her favorite pejorative, *durf.* It's over, you durf. Like getting robbed, you know now at least the percentages are in your favor, lightning doesn't strike twice, et cetera.

Schtunk, you believe in statistics and numbers and odds, don't you? Well, don't you?

The downdraft from the air-conditioning vent was suddenly apparent.

Paige got up, closed the door to her office, then dialed the operator.

"The number for Public Information, the Police Department," she said.

"Officer O'Brien speaking," the low, rather nasal man's voice said a few moments later.

"Um, I wanted to know—that is, the most recent figure you might have for how many rape-murders there are in the city. I'm working on a thesis, college thesis."

152

"The breakdown we have is for homicides involving sex, not necessarily rape."

"That would be fine."

"May I have your name and number? I'll get the figures for you, call you back."

Paige began picking the mealybugs from the undersides of the philodendron leaves, her hand starting when the telephone buzzed.

"Miss Brown? I have those figures for you."

"Oh. Thank you."

"These are for nineteen-seventy-six. New York City, all boroughs, there were forty sexually oriented homicides."

"Forty."

"Of which twenty-one were female, nineteen male. For seventy-five, now, the figure is eighteen total, eleven male victims and seven female."

"Officer, may I ask you a personal question?"

"Yes. Shoot."

"Don't those figures seem very low to you?"

"As a matter of fact, yes. I checked them twice. But the preceding years are close to those numbers, too."

"What would you have thought they'd be?"

"In the hundreds. Definitely."

("Five percent," Francie had guessed Tuesday night, voice coming thin from the other bed. "Five hundred thousand, maybe.")

Paige hung up and pulled down her almanac from the sagging shelves. The 1970 Census reported 4,191,507 females, all ages (but infant girls, octogenarians were raped) in New York City.

She pressed the On button of her calculator, punching rapidly on the keys.

So. As of 1976, she had one chance in 199,596 of being murdered by a sexual pervert in New York City.

Feel better, *durf?*

153

Strangely enough, she thought, she felt worse.

But the scare stories, the headlines, the fear that cramped you into certain buildings, routes, neighborhoods, hours, that rode you down every grimy street, were all out of proportion, totally out of whack with how often it happened.

As a crime, it was *rare*.

Thank you, Mrs. Trowbridge, she thought. You *schtunk*. The actress had known how to mesmerize her little-girl audience (her daughter and Paige and Bonnie Farr). She had served them Velveeta on white bread with pickle relish and mayonnaise, along with stories to curdle their blood.

They had believed them, of course.

When you're twelve, adults are to be believed. It wasn't until she was seventeen that she realized too many blood-curdlings had happened to Mrs. Trowbridge.

There was The Night Mrs. Trowbridge (then Nancy Rusk) Was Parked with Her Boyfriend.

"Frank turned the radio on—some music, romantic, you know. The song was only *halfway* through—it was 'Crocodile Tears'—when this ominous *voice* cuts in. 'Special Bulletin! Be on the alert! A *sex* murderer, believed armed and *dangerous,* has escaped from the Mid-Hudson State Prison for the Criminally *Insane*. He can be recognized by the following: his right hand is missing. And he wears a *hook!*' "

Paige remembered the urge to wet her pants, which always seized her at just this moment, prickling desperately.

"Anyone want more Velveeta?"

"*No!*" three childish voices had shrilled.

"So Frank says to me, 'Give us a kiss.' I scream, 'Frank! We got to get out of here! Now!'

" 'So all right,' he says. And we drove off.

"At my house he got out, went around to open my door (men did that then). But he didn't open it, just stood there staring down.

154

" 'What *is* it?' I said, rolling the window down.

"He pointed. Stuck in the door handle right there on *my side* was—*a hook!*"

It would be laughable, Paige thought, if only it hadn't had such long-term effects. Like mercury poisoning, incremental daily amounts entering her bloodstream, years later warping her responses.

Her "sexual dysfunction," as Aurelia-the-shrink had put it. Oh, screw sex.

Paige crossed to the door, opened it, then stared down the hall. Hank Blaise's office door—his *vacated* office door, she corrected—was open. The light inside was on.

She walked past. Seated behind the large walnut desk, sorting through a stack of papers on which the sun from the corner windows fell, was a tall, thin young man with glasses and prematurely gray hair. He looked up, gave her a pinched smile.

Anal retentive, she thought. But what was he doing in there?

She walked on down the hall.

Max Dornbush, director of research, was a small man given to too-tight plaid suits, one of which he was now wearing.

"Come in, Paige. Come in. And close the door, would you?"

Like her father, Paige thought. Like the principal. Like every time you've been bad or the blow was coming.

"I suppose you want to know who the new import is, am I right?"

Paige nodded, shook out a cigarette and lit it. She felt the trembling begin already in her chest.

"You know we're very pleased with your work, Paige, why you got that raise in April. You're one of our brightest young talents. But look, dear. Knuth's been on me about this consumer electronics report. You know how important it is. Jack Beaham out there was recommended to Knuth by some Yalie friend—the good-ole-boy network —so I gave him the nod for senior associate. And he'll be helping you out with this electronics thing, give you a chance for a breather now and again. You look like you might be able to use it."

"What do you mean, 'help me out'?"

"Well, supervise, actually. Now, Paige. I'm on the seventh floor and Knuth is up on ten. What can I tell you?"

"Did you at least *suggest* me for the spot?"

"No. No, I didn't. And I'm not about to now. It's a fait accompli. Look, I'm very sorry about this. I think we can see our way clear to boosting you another twenty-five dollars in October."

"It's not the money, Max."

"Well, I thought, too, this was a bad time for you. What with that terrible . . . thing. I know you said you'd be in, but I didn't expect you to. Didn't expect you'd be able to work for another week, maybe two. And Knuth was on me about that damned report, has to be upstairs next Wednesday, he says. You know how he is."

Hobbes, *Leviathan*: "Is any social unit held together by justice or power?" Paige wondered whether she was actually going to cry. You can't take it with you. But Alex *had.* Alex had taken everything with her.

She stood up. She made her voice hard, to still the trembling. "I thought I would at least have gotten the sympathy vote."

4:09 p.m.

"Fourth Zone Homicide Squad Detective Amspoker may I help you. Hold on, slow down, slow down, madam, I can't understand . . . The strangling? What particular case, madam? Alexandra Baskin, all right now, yes, yes, may I have your name? Mrs. Willa—would you spell that?— G-r-e-e-n-e-w-a-l-t. Now, what is the information you have? The man across from you has no bathroom curtains? Yes. I see. And he wears women's pantyhose. Yes, the victim was strangled with pantyhose, but— Uh, yes, exactly where were you in relation to this, um, sighting? What time of day was it? Um-hm. Was it well-lit? Um-hm. Were you wearing glasses? I see, let me write this down, he uses Head and Shoulders, you can read the label. Now, Mrs. Greenewalt, forgive me for asking this next question, but it is necessary. Are you a woman who is prone to drink? Well, no, no . . . um-hm. Have you ever been a witness to anything before? May I have your phone number? Thank you very much for your help. No. No, I'm sorry to say I didn't think about Jesus today. Yes, I will, good-bye ma'am. Good day now. Yes, certainly, um-hm, good-bye."

Victor Amspoker replaced the receiver with an exasperated noise. "If this keeps up, the next call will be from Judas Iscariot saying it's Jesus H. Christ."

From the desk in front, Frank Quinn laughed. "New York nuts. But one of those fuckers just might be—"

"That's the problem."

Amspoker began thumbing through the "Chronic Calls" list, but Mrs. Greenewalt had not yet made it. Well, give the old bat another week.

"I like the one says it's a UFO," Quinn said, turning around to look back.

Amspoker knew he was studying the gray pallor that had edged up beneath his skin, pooling beneath his eyes. Care, oh sure, you were supposed to work through the night, care like hell about your job. But not give a damn about the victim. That was not objective. No, that would be get-

157

ting personal, dangerously overinvolved. Hindered your work, sent it off on skews out of your own troubled mind.

But always one case or another came along that grabbed your mind, blasted objectivity all to hell.

This time it had grabbed the whole city's mind.

This time it was Alexandra Baskin.

Amspoker picked up the coffee, tasting the paper, damp and shredded, at the container's edge. What could you do, all the cups were dirty. "It's like roaches on a crumb, Frank. Every damn drunked-up, wacked-out, hopheaded loony in the city is getting off on this one."

The publicized special number had not stopped ringing twenty-four hours a day. There had been numerous phoned-in "confessions," three of the callers so insistent they had had to be arrested and charged with harassment.

So many letters had poured in—typewritten on letter-head, scrawled in shaky pencil on pieces of brown paper bags—they had had to hire a graphologist and questioned-documents expert, Dr. Helene Untermeyer, to separate the nuts from the reasonably balanced citizens.

But that was it. Somewhere in the calls, cryptic notes, paranoia, might lie a reasonably balanced clue, might even be a message from the perpetrator himself.

Amspoker thought about the two roommates, anxiety twisting in his gut. He had had to warn them not to open any envelopes whose sender they didn't recognize. He had had to see their eyes go wide, startled with fear. They were instructed to forward such mail to the Fourth Zone Homicide Squad, where paid public servants would read the public's dirt.

It was the one thing he hated about being a cop: it was like living in a toilet.

He had smelled what the "shitters" left beside safes, on the middle of beds, in jewelry boxes after breaking and entering. He had slipped in junkie shit, vomit, urine and blood, which flowed down tenement halls as cheap as Thunderbird wine.

He couldn't help it; he held it against them, he hated them for the garbage of their lives.

He stared down at the bulging folders on the desk in front of him: the five-hundred-odd sheets of official forms, photostats, tape transcriptions, typed interviews, reinterviews, third interviews—the subjects hostile now, and frightened—the piles of photographs that made you want to cry.

"Oh, no. You can take it. Here, take this one too." Mrs. Baskin had been more than willing to give them the photographs they needed; she had pressed on them more. "Just look at this one, did you ever? Lovely, wasn't she? A real picture. I always said it, didn't I, Sammy? Someday there'd be Alexandra Elizabeth dolls and Alexandra Elizabeth everything. . . ."

Amspoker picked the photo out of the folder. It was of no conceivable use for their purposes. It showed seventeen nine-year-old girls lined up at the practice bar at the American Ballet Theater School. They wore scooped-neck black leotards and white tights with wrinkles at the knees and ankles, one toe pointing outward, small hand curling for grace. Third from the front, dark hair parted in the middle, with a serious frown on her face, stood Alex Baskin.

She had, Amspoker had learned, taken ballet lessons, tennis lessons, piano lessons, and horseback (English style) lessons. She had gone away to expensive summer girls' camps with names like Sea Spray East.

He remembered Ninette's hand in his at the start of the church day camp—down in the church cellar rec room with boiler pipes overhead. Her blue eyes gone wide and milky and frightened at the door. The smell of faded corduroy and graham crackers. And then, when he picked her up, found her red-eyed and crying because the excitement and games and three glasses of cherry Kool-Aid had come together in their inevitable result.

He picked out the most recent photograph, placed it beside the small dancer with the plump thighs. At twenty-one, Alex's hair had grown darker and very thick. It was cut Chinese style, with long bangs and straight sides. Beneath the bangs her eyes, he noticed for the first time, were not quite in line. One stared boldly into the camera, while the other flirted warily off toward the side. It was a flaw, tiny but disconcerting, an asymmetry that drew you back.

"We're missing something, Vic," Frank said. "Not picking up on someone. Read over that goddamn fucking list again."

Amspoker put the photographs back in the folder. "Xanthakis, I still think he's the one. Served three months at Goshen, assault with a deadly weapon. Drew a knife on a fellow student, claimed self-defense, judge didn't buy it —twelve years ago. Joined SDS at City College in sixty-nine. Parents live in Astoria, claim they don't know where he is." Amspoker winced. He could still feel the broom crashing down on his head, Xanthakis' grandmother screaming in Greek on the concrete stoop. Nothing there, Greeks were tight as fists about family.

"Two, of course," he said, reading from the list, "is Dalroi."

"*Dalroi*," Frank said. "What the hell kind of a faggy name is that?"

"Not in the nickname file. Or any of the city phone books, we checked all boroughs."

"Pet name, maybe? For Xanthakis, maybe?"

"Bill's still making the rounds of all the florists," Amspoker said. "Problem is, all these guys selling roses out of pails on the corner. That card he could have picked up anywhere."

"Let's scratch Xanthakis and Nagy too for the moment," Frank said. "Been over them enough. Let's go on from there." There was a loud crunching noise as he chewed up a diet peppermint candy.

"Okay. Decedent's brother, Thomas R. Baskin. Age twenty-eight. Married. Works for father. Picked up in nineteen-seventy-one for exhibiting to small boys. Under psychiatric care, dad did some tinkering, charges dropped. He says he was at work all day Monday the eighth, but secretary says no, he went out for lunch."

"Incest, maybe?" Frank said, picking a piece of candy from a lower back molar. "A thing with his sister dating back? Homicidal jealousy?"

"Then we got Ian Meecham, TV producer at the agency. Married, but plenty of 'business' trips not for business. Credit-card bills for hotels, dinners. Get this: one thousand three hundred thirty-five big ones for a diamond bracelet. Wife has no such bracelet. Known to have dated decedent for two months, ending March this year. August eighth out for lunch—alone—between twelve and two-thirty. Right in the target time."

"Go on," Frank said.

"Ward Yates. Art supervisor at the agency. Married, Westport, two kids. Boss says he's been drinking heavily. Womanizer. Girlfriend Jeri Sue Anspach says he's talked about nothing but Alex since the murder, goes in for biting and muff-diving, she says, only she calls it 'head.' And get this. Didn't come to work until one on the eighth."

"Where'd he say he was?" Frank said.

"Jeri's apartment. She denies. But this is after he dropped her for another broad."

"And . . ." Frank said wearily.

"Cesar Rosario—son of wealthy Mexican banker. Decedent met him at party Saturday, August six. Spent Sunday, her last living night, at his place—Fifth Avenue, big posh place."

"Yeah, I like him," Frank said. "What was he doing on Monday again?"

"Quote: 'For any information, I think you should see my lawyer.' We got Spence and Dan on surveillance now."

The two men looked up. In the doorway Detective Second Grade Ron Diamond was holding an envelope and a sheet of paper.

"Just got the fingerprints off this," he said. "Look at this bugger. Last name St. Gryphon. First name *Dalroi*."

9:10 p.m.

The curtains were open, twilight dampening the still-warm breeze. Beyond the circle of the desk lamp, the high-ceilinged room on upper Central Park West was in shadow. Dr. Helene Untermeyer—graphologist and document examiner, accepted as an expert in the New York courts of law—held the sheet of white paper under the fluorescent arc. Cinnamon freckles stood out against the blue-lined whiteness of her hand. Down the inside of her arm tracked more blue lines, which had faded from blue-black to a washed-out denim. The edges had blurred, but still formed a readable four-digit number.

She opened the way—letting the specimen's appearance fall upon her conscious and unconscious mind, just as it had been written, by a conscious and unconscious mind. She felt her heart begin to move faster. The corners of her lips trembled. Her cheek muscles began to twitch.

Slowly she felt the brain behind the writing surface toward her. But she hesitated—not quite yet—to grasp at the elusive gleam.

No. Let it swim nearer, show itself more boldly.

She looked out the window at the darkening sky. "Brain writing," Dr. Wilhelm Preyer, a physiologist, had termed it—the hand transcribing what the brain designs. He had taken as his subject a quadriplegic forced to learn to write with his mouth. After the learning was complete, the two samples—handwriting and mouth writing—were compared. With minor differences only, they were twins.

She smoothed the letter with her fingers. She raised her hand, writing and rewriting his strokes across the air.

And the brain leaped free of the page.

She stared at the brain as she had stared at the tall, dignified man with the cane—the "Angel of Auschwitz" they had called him—waving some to the right. And without hesitation, some to the left.

The two detectives were staring at her. She nodded at them, sat forward at her desk, opening the balding brown leather case. Inside, in custom-shaped pockets lined with green felt, lay two magnifying glasses. She drew out the $4\times$ lens.

Under magnification the letters leaped up at her—thick and knotty, freeform as Rorschach blots. Their margins peeled scaly with the movements of the writer's pen.

Her eye followed the lens across the lines.

Dear Mr. Quinn, sir,
　It is no use for you to look for me now. . . . Don't trouble yourself about me until I return, witch will not be very long. . . . I like the work too much to leave it alone. . . . It was a good job the last one. . . . I had plenty of time to do it properly in. . . . Now the hole world is mine!

You poor stupid fucking bastard.... When I have done another one you can try and catch me again.

Good-bye and good night, dear Boss, till I return. ...

Your faithful serpent,
Dalroi St. Gryphon

P.S. Don't worry about the girls.... They are in good spirits.

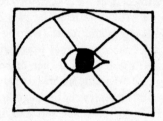

"That block printing give you any trouble, Mrs. Untermeyer?" the chubby, balding detective asked, smoothing his mustache.

"Not at all. Printing is a fairly common masking device used by anonymous-letter senders. I studied one letter printed by a right-handed man using his left hand and forming the letters upside down. His personality traits were no less apparent."

"And what are the traits you see here?" the tall detective said.

"He is extremely dangerous. I say 'he,' although there is no unequivocal data that the writer is not a woman."

She saw the tall detective direct a resigned look at his feet, and began to speak more quickly. " 'He,' then, is young, between seventeen and twenty-three, is intelligent but his thinking process is not the fastest one. However, he can be very thorough in producing logical sequences. He can be very methodical when method is called for. He completed high school but his education went no further. His early background was rigidly religious—Catholic, I should venture. He is emotionally immature, with a violent sense of anxiety and inferiority. He is a practicing heterosexual much given to strong sensual pursuits, although he shows signs of leanings toward his own sex—something he could never admit to himself. Physically he is large and strong. The size of the letters, the pressure with which he writes, indicate considerable manual dexterity. You might look for someone who works with his hands for pay or as a hobby—a carpenter, perhaps, or a cabinetmaker."

"How in the world do you get that?" the tall man said.

"A hand when writing makes the same gestures it is accustomed to make. And this writer forms his letters, his strokes, very hard, sharp, rigid, straight. Back and forth, up and down—like the zigzags a carpenter makes while planing. And look at the whole page: there is a geometry here. All those right angles—like a construction, a fence or bars. They also suggest quick slashings, knife marks. You might look for someone good with knives, because this man writes with daggers."

"*Hamlet*," the one with the mustache said. "In that speech to his mother, right? 'I . . .' Let's see, what is it? 'I . . .'"

"'I will speak daggers to her,'" Helene Untermeyer said. She felt a sudden sense of warmth toward him. "Daggers to her, or to a female. There is a marked sexual abnormality in this letter. You see? Among all these straight strokes, look here. His *w*'s are rounded, like a woman's breasts."

"What about that crazy gizmo at the bottom?" the tall one said. "Mark of Zorro, whatever it is."

"Yes, quite remarkable. The circle is the first drawing made by little children. The four limbs are added shortly after. Perhaps for this reason the circle associated with four elements, such as Mr. St. Gryphon's circle in a square here, is found in all cultures. Jung referred to it as the mandala, or magic circle. In all its appearances it represents a protective or spellbinding wholeness, and is the traditional antidote for disordered states of mind. Psychotics in hospitals draw them, Tibetan Buddhists draw them—both for the same purpose. To achieve a state of order and calm."

"Uh-huh," the tall detective said.

His partner tossed him a look, crossing his leg at the knee. The tight fabric of his trousers strained across his thigh. "What I would like to find out, Mrs. Untermeyer, is what that name might tell you. It's outlandish, made up, we have to assume. But why *that* name?"

She felt as blank as the time her childhood friend in Mannheim asked for a demonstration, pulling an envelope at random from his father's drawer. The handwriting was her mother's.

"Reminds me," the other man said, "of the stuff you see in those sword-and-sorcery mags."

"Sword and what?"

"Frank, you never read them? Small-size mags on the newsstand. Fourteen-year-olds buy them. Always about a young prince in search of his grail, knights saving damsels, running around poking dragons with magic swords. Good and evil and heroes beating the evil. Nice upbeat endings."

"Arthurian trappings," Helene Untermeyer said. "That is quite interesting. A gryphon, after all, is a mythological kind of dragon: half-eagle, half-lion."

"Yeah, I like it," the plump detective said, sitting forward, hands on knees. "We'll trace subscribers to the mags."

"Kids buy them, Frank. Not the type that writes out checks for subscriptions. And even if our boy read them, it must've been a while ago. He's got the story ass-backwards

166

—I beg your pardon, Mrs. Untermeyer. But he's slaying damsels, not the dragons."

She smiled. "The damsels *are* the dragons, gentlemen."

10:08 p.m.

Just like people, there were apartments that you immediately liked.

Miles Kendrick Overby III's apartment, on Park Avenue and Thirty-fourth Street, had a working fireplace, an overstuffed couch, two rattan rocking chairs with fat green pillows, a sheepskin rug, a striped Navajo rug, and a battered piano whose bench was draped with what appeared to be the skin of a coyote. On the coffee table were recent copies of *The New Yorker* and *Field and Stream*.

Francie Perry glanced at the bedroom on her way to the bathroom. The king-size brass bed was covered with a fake-fur throw whose matted beige fibers stuck straight up in clumps. In the bathroom the towel racks were heated.

She came back out and sat down on the couch. On the opposite wall was a huge oil painting—one of those modernistic mishmashes of red and yellow that appeared to take as its subject detached portions of human anatomy.

"Nice, huh? I got it at the Washington Square art show," Miles said. "Want a beer?"

She nodded, although she wondered how it would react with the Dubonnet, wine, pasta, zabaglione, espresso, and brandy they had already consumed.

As domestic sounds issued from the kitchen, she wandered around the living room, hearing Paige's voice again as she had that afternoon.

"Are you out of your mind? He's just a goddamn opportunist."

"Why is it so impossible he might *like* me?"

"He's a reporter."

"They take girls to dinner, too, you know."

"I'm telling you, he's after you for a story. Don't go making a fool out of yourself."

"But there's something wrong with every man I meet, according to you."

"I just don't want to see you get hurt."

"I like him. I don't know why. I just want to be with someone. I don't want to be alone."

"I see you've found my knife collection," Miles said. "Lovely little devils, ain't they?"

She had been staring into a glass case mounted on the wall. Eight knives were held by brackets, steel blades glittering, points downward. Each had a gracefully curved handle with brass fittings.

"What do you *do* with them?" Francie took the beer, gulped through the foam to the cold liquid beneath.

"I'm a backpacker from way back. Always take one along —cuts rope, skins fish. But I just collect them, really. You know, everything today is mass-produced, schlock quality. But these little doggies are all handcrafted by a guy in Aiken, South Carolina."

Miles opened the case and lifted a four-and-a-half-inch blade from its pronged holder. He laid the knife across his palm. "This is as much art as the painting. It's one-fifty-four CM steel—so hard it's difficult to sharpen, but the edge you get'll last a long time. And the handle—get the heft of that—it's stag horn. Go on, give it a try."

Francie picked it up by the handle, feeling the cold circles of the brass rivets against her palm. It was surprisingly heavy.

She laid it back across his hand. Holding her beer tightly,

she crossed to the couch. She sat down, pressing her neck back against the faded, scratchy material.

"You don't think this looks like a mammary-magazine set, do you?" Miles said. "The apartment, I mean."

She opened her eyes. "Not till you mentioned it." Then she laughed. "No, I like it, Miles. Honest."

"I like you. Do you know how few nice, honest, straight-forward people there are to like in this city?" He sat down on the couch beside her. The cushions sagged.

"And I would like to get to know you better," he said.

She felt his lips on her throat, and then on her mouth. His tongue thrust possessively within.

Then he pulled back from her, looking down at her face. "Hey. You don't really need to do that."

"Do what?"

"Make that little sound, propitiatory noise, like a dog on his back before a bigger dog. I ain't exactly threatening, you know."

She felt the rush of shame. "I didn't know I—"

His mouth was on hers again. She felt his hand behind her neck, pulling her harder against him. He took her palm, and she felt him guiding it down past his belt. His fingers closed her fingers around his erection, which through his slacks felt as hard-edged as the knife. She let her hand remain there, passively, without moving.

She remembered the man brushing up against her on Lexington Avenue: "*Uptight broad,*" he had said.

Miles kissed her again, and a hot tingling moved up along her body, almost as it had felt in the dream. What would it be like to do as Alex had done? To make love—no, to have sex. To screw. *To fuck.* And have it casual and manageable. A simple pleasurable act. Something without the terrible hurt and vulnerability, the betrayal that came when they left.

169

So he would put his . . . penis, *cock* inside her. What was the big deal anyway?

She felt his hands on her ankles, swinging her legs up beneath him on the couch.

She felt herself sandwiched between his shirt and the couch. And then it came back: a crushing wave of fear, depression, and passivity. She felt like a specimen pinned to the couch.

She thought: The horse that gets ridden often gets thrown. She heard the litany of parents, friends, magazines: "He wants to go to bed with you, not much else. Your object is to get from the beginning to the middle, where they start to care for you, unscathed. Delay the moment of truth in the Amour Derby."

But then: *Why not?* she thought. *Alex did this all the time.*

As he struggled her skirt up, she thought how lucky it was she was wearing the red bikinis, not the frayed white ones turned gray in last week's wash. And then she felt inexplicable tears starting up, tasted the salt running down onto her lips.

"Don't worry, darling," Miles was saying into her ear. His lips followed back along the streaks of tears to her eyes. "You're in good hands, my darling. Don't worry."

She felt her bikini slide over her knees and across her cold toes. He was back across her body, but he didn't enter her.

And still he didn't enter her.

And then she felt the softness of him fall against her thigh.

Francie turned her face into the back of the couch. The fabric was dusty, rough against her nose. She breathed in the dry, mildewed smell.

He let her go in the silence, and she heard the flare of his lighter, the sucking pop as he drew on a cigarette. It made her feel part of a ritual, like coffee after dinner. Then his sinewy arm, which was surprisingly strong, pulled her back against his abdomen, cupping like spoons.

"I'm sorry," he said. "Sometimes I'm like this at first with a new girl."

Francie closed her eyes. She wished she could think of something sympathetic, understanding to say. But there was nothing. She felt his skin warm and moist against her, slice curved to slice, making a whole? She doubted it. Besides, as her biology professor had pointed out, that particular cavity was not really *inside* the body. No, it was outside, merely an infolding of the body's exterior margins.

And Miles was not the man she had always planned on meeting. He was certainly not Spy Xanthakis. As long as she kept that in perspective, knew he would not really enter her inner life and mind, everything might still be okay.

"Come on," Miles said when she emerged fully clothed from the bathroom. "Let's go out, huh? We need some air."

His face looked young, hair rumpled. She wondered if she might dare to like him again.

"Okay. I need some fresh air. My head feels stuffy, like a cold coming on. I took some Dristan."

"What Dristan?" His voice was sharp. He swung his feet around to the floor, sitting up. Like Alex, he had no apparent modesty. Below his boyish face, his body was surprisingly male, adult and muscular. Reddish hair gleamed damply down the midline of his body. His penis had shrunk like a wrinkled accordion beneath the thick, dark brown growth.

"The Dristan in the bottle. In the medicine chest," she said.

"How many you take, Francie?"

"Two. Why?"

"They're not Dristan. No harm, I guess. But don't take any other drug tonight."

"What is it?"

"Elavil. Antidepressant." He studied her face. "I hope you're not one of these pharmacological Calvinists, thinking all us poor slobs can make it on willpower alone."

"No, of course not."

"Depression is a chemical imbalance in the brain."

"Yes."

"Now, let's get outside."

Soft rain was falling, slate-gray lightening to silver under the lampposts. Miles took off his shirt and they held it up over their heads and went stumbling and hip-jostling along the wet sidewalks. And as the rain dampened down through the thin cloth and touched their faces and silvered the edges of his no-color hair, he leaned to kiss her. His lips felt cold on the outside, warm as he opened them against hers.

She thought: Studies show that fifty percent of all men have potency difficulties at least occasionally. It's not that he thinks I'm ugly.

"I feel something special about you," Miles said. His eyes stared at her, dark in the space between the streetlamps.

" 'In Oberlin, Ohio,' " she said, " 'if I give you dark eyes, baby, please don't turn me down.' "

"What?" He laughed.

"A poem a kid wrote back at college. Thought of it for some reason." She was suddenly overwhelmed by a feeling of sadness.

"Promise me," he said.

"What?"

"Promise me you'll let me make you happy."

She wondered why she felt so afraid.

In the damp heat that followed the rain, mist clouded upward across the glass front of the Food Fair grocery. Already the pyramids of fruit—red, yellow, orange just inside the window—were disappearing into a pastel smear.

Had he waited too long?

The mist was edging higher. In the darkened doorway of the men's clothing store across the street, Dalroi strained to follow the bright spot of red hair as the she walked up the narrow aisle, scanning the shelves.

He had been more than patient. He had followed the she from work on foot, sat in the row behind in the Carnegie Hall Cinema while the she watched *Baby Doll* and *A Face in the Crowd,* waited while the she ate a hot pretzel from the tinfoil-lined pan on the pushcart, waited while the she smiled at the sneakered juggler with his five white rubber rings in front of the Plaza Hotel, waited while the she went up to another pushcart—Marino's Real Italian Ices—debating over Lemon Orange Cherry Pineapple Chocolate Grape, and then her mouth engulfing the round purple dome in the white paper cup. On around the south edge of Central Park, the sun gone now, the she eating a Sabrett hot dog, tapping her foot to the chanting, swaying, long cotton billowings of the shaven devotees aboard the orange-and-yellow-draped truck with the huge sign: SOCIETY FOR KRISHNA CONSCIOUSNESS.

And then the rain, the she opening her umbrella, quickening her steps home. The rain fell upon the wilting white chrysanthemums in the creased green paper, trickling over his wrist as he followed.

The she stood suddenly in the Food Fair doorway, eyes seeming to find him in the opposite doorway. His lungs struggled for breath. The she settled the brown paper bag

173

on her hip, and without another glance his way, began moving up the sidewalk.

He felt the immediacy come upon him, wrapping tight as leather. His heart vibrated his body. His shoes reached off the curb as he started to cross the street.

"Paige!"

The voice was calling from the open window of the yellow cab as it swerved over beside the she. Two people were within. The door hung open and the she disappeared inside.

Laughter and smiles.

Dalroi watched the cab accelerate, turning the corner. A fullness expanded in his chest, burning up into his throat. His fingers convulsed through the rubbery strength of the stems until he heard the snap. He threw the flowers into the gutter.

There was still the game.

He walked to his car, which he had parked on York Avenue, in readiness, half a block south of the she's apartment.

He would play the game he played sometimes when he drove, looking for a she walking, a she alone.

It was only for fun.

There was one up ahead, walking on the sidewalk. *If the she turns right,* he thought, choosing arbitrarily. His heart accelerated as the car neared her. But the she turned left, vanishing into a carpeted lobby.

But there was another she—there, up ahead. But this she was accompanied by a man protector. Smiles, the man's fingers feeling she flesh, wrapped around the she's waist.

Tight and smiles.

Frustration rose. His car moved south, then west, following Eleventh Street toward the Hudson River, the buildings shortening to tenements and warehouses, darkened windows blocked with tin. The area was without movement until his headlights fell upon a she, back to him, walking a small tan dog.

He thought of entering, the inadequacy, the terror of feeling forward within the giant cave. And then the hard knob up at the end of her that would fall down on him, hammer down again and again because the she would love it riding on him hammering down on him the she couldn't get enough.

It was so strange—the orgasm. You would choose to die rather than not have it. Afterward, of course, you would prefer to live.

Dalroi accelerated until he was opposite. The she turned her head, eyes wide, staring. "Miss," he said, leaning across to open the passenger door, letting her see the gun.

"What do you want?"

"Just get in."

"Here, take it. Twenty dollars in here. Please just don't hurt me."

He raised the gun. "You won't get hurt if you do what I say. Now, get in."

"What are you going to do?"

Shut up shut up shut up shut up.

"Please, I can't do anything, the doctor says no."

"Drop that leash and get in."

The she looked down at the dog, who was watching them with eager eyes, terrier ears pricked forward.

"No, please. He'll get lost, run off, please. You can do what you want, I won't say anything, won't go to the cops—"

He felt the slim circle of her wrist in his palm and she was suddenly beside him, the gun barrel jammed into the firmness of her neck. The dog was barking. The heat, the scent of her, sharp as earth, filled the front seat. The she was very short, with thick curly brown hair that fell down her back, in a sleeveless blue blouse, white slacks and white sneakers. As the car pulled away the she turned to look back. The dog's bark was hollow in the stillness.

Pier 48 stretched the length of several blocks over the Hudson River: an abandoned structure of rusting metal and rotting timbers. A sign announced PROPERTY OF THE CITY OF NEW YORK, NO TRESPASSING, VIOLATORS WILL BE PROSECUTED. Dalroi pulled the she from the car. The river lapped against the pilings in rainbowed oily swirls. The breeze was cool, at once fresh and yet heavy, organic with decay.

Inside through the gloom he could see broken windows, archways, deserted loading platforms. Rooms and cubby-holes branched on all sides. Stairs led up to unrailed landings, empty space gaping beyond. There were holes in the floor, the sound of water sucking beneath. The corners were piled with rubble and dust, the color of pepper. A rat's tail gleamed palely, flickered and was lost down a ramp toward the water. Dalroi listened to the swimming sounds.

He hesitated, the piece of rope coarse in his hands. He saw his own face reflected in her eye, like a stuck square of film, playing again and again. Her face was split white with the gag. He could feel the blood pulsing out into his spread fingertips and he saw the cry on her face, unable to reach her lips as the rope tightened. She thrashed beneath him and he could feel the heaving wetness of her terror as the rope bit through and he could feel her neck give there was a sound but it wasn't a live thing at all it felt soft and hollow as a rubber doll.

Don't you do that stop it don't do that I hate that it's dirty filthy stop it stop it.

He had to shut the box up at both ends.

Chapter Seven

Saturday, August 13
8:46 a.m.

"Who would want me? You son of a bitch, you lying bastard, who would want me?"

It was an original defense, Victor Amspoker thought, his eyes averted from the fierce red circle of his wife's face. He felt a certain admiration for her, for her willingness to go this far—savage herself. But still it was not enough. Not enough to deflect from the discoveries: the new black lace lingerie, the Avon bills, her hair no longer silvered mouse brown. No, now it was fox red.

He could not let her, his own wife, make an utter fool of him.

But the momentum of what he had nudged into motion frightened him. This time she hadn't responded as the unspoken agreement between them dictated. Always before she had met his anger with her arms out, with her love. She had understood what no one had ever understood —that his anger with her was always fear. Fear that she had stopped, withdrawn, didn't love him anymore.

All he wanted, all he had ever wanted, was assurance that this time too she still cared.

But this time she had met his anger with anger.

She shrieked.

He looked back at her. She had pulled her dress above her waist. He felt a wave of revulsion, of shame as she forked her pants down with two fingers to the edge of dark hair.

"Get a good look at this gorgeous quiff, you bastard. Who did it to me?"

He looked at the loose bulge of her abdomen, stretch marks like a platinum web. "Maddie, please. Don't. Please don't do this."

She shrieked again.

Now it was the back of her thighs, her legs spread apart, lumped like cottage cheese and almost as white. Her flesh, he thought, looked as dead as their love.

He remembered the man on the subway—white skin, bald scalp, fine black hairs on his hands and arms. He sat hunched forward on the seat, head bowed, hands clenched. Beside him the short, dark-woman kept sharply, impatiently crossing one leg, then the other at the knee, scolding on and on and on in some unknown language.

You always saw it like that, the bracketing of love, beginnings and endings, on the subway. The loving, body-hugging start of relationships (usually teenagers). And then this: the tag end, the burnt-out finish. How did they go lurching from beginning to end so quickly?

He looked back at her thighs as she turned to face him. It was the shame at finding her unattractive that goaded his anger. "Don't lie to me, Maddie." He was ready, he realized, to scrape the bottom, take what had been off-limits for his arsenal. "I found his shirt."

"*Shirt?* What shirt?"

He tried to read her face. "It's in the closet where you got careless and put it."

"Will you tell me *what shirt?*"

He walked over, jerked open the closet door. His fingers grasped the red-and-green plaid. Every day he had had to look at it, kept hoping she would remember, remove it without him having to say a word. But every day it had hung there, taunting on the hanger.

He bunched it in his fist, tore it off the wire. There was the sound of shredding fabric, cutting through his mind. He threw the shirt on the floor.

She stared down at it. "What do you mean? That's yours, Vic."

"Don't try to pull that on me."

"What are *you* trying to pull? You bought it, you liar, you—"

His hand caught her across the mouth. Her mouth fell open, tongue reaching on her lip for the single drop of blood.

Oh, my God, he thought. Forgive me.

The telephone shrilled into the room.

"Don't answer it!" Maddie was at his side, hands wrenching down on his arm. He felt the stab of pain as her nails

179

bit in. "Please don't answer it. We're talking now at least, we—"

"May be business. Important, Maddie, you know that." The violence he had felt had drained from his body. He felt without emotion.

"What's important, me or the work? We're talking, Vic. We're really talking for once. We got to—"

"Get a grip on yourself, will you?"

The telephone kept ringing.

"Please, Vic, don't answer it."

"Don't make me choose, Maddie." He crossed to the telephone on the nightstand, picked up the receiver. "No, not at all, Frank. Be glad to talk to her, I was just on my way in."

He reached for his jacket, then turned to face his wife. "Look, I'm sorry. It's this case—I've got to go in. What can I tell you?"

"You care more about that dead girl, that *Alex*, than you do your own wife."

He opened the bedroom door. Down the hall he could hear the sound of Ninette's crying.

"Okay, Miss Perry. Shoot. I'm here to help, you just tell me how."

She looked up. Across the coffee-shop table, her face was tired and drawn. On the plate in front of her, the eggs were congealing in an orange-yellow mass.

Victims, he thought. They were all victims, not just the one who died. All the friends, mothers, fathers, acquaintances; even the people who just read about it in the papers, went out and bought a new lock and prayed it wouldn't happen to them—they were victims too.

Francie Perry had beautiful eyes. Must be attractive when she smiled. He realized he had never seen her smile.

"I hate to take up your time like this, I—"

"No. Not at all. I'm here to help you if I can, okay?"

"I guess I just need someone to talk to about it. I don't sleep right anymore. You know, you never think about how you get to sleep until something goes wrong with it. I wake up in the middle of the night, and then that's it. No more sleep that night. I don't think I can sleep until you find . . . him. I get so angry when I think of . . . him. Out there. Still walking around."

He was remembering the night that he didn't sleep at all—in the first year of his marriage—how he had lain tense beside Maddie until the first light-sifted hours. And then packing a silent car in the dawn and driving, the two of them, with that ringing sound of tension in his ears. And then stopping for lunch, the radio tower across the grass, and they were running, racing to see who could get to it first, climb it first. And they had met again at the top of the tower, breathless, and he had kissed her, knowing that what had forced its way between them was gone again.

It seemed like a very long time ago.

He combed his fingers back through his hair, sliding his hand down his neck. His fingers kneaded the pinched tension.

"I'll tell you something, Miss Perry, I've never told anyone. My wife lost our first baby. It was a son. After that . . . it was the end of sleeping for a while. I would wake up and the bed was empty, night after night. She would go out in the living room, sit with her knees up in a chair."

"I'm sorry. It must be so really sad to lose a baby. How did your wife get over it?"

"It took us a while, but she got pregnant again. Laurel. She's nine now. What I'm saying is, fill your life, replace what's missing is the only way. You lost a friend you really cared about. Go on now and make new friends."

She nodded, but her eyes studied her plate, her hands moving the napkin, creasing and recreasing it.

"Take my advice, you'll get married and go home."

She smiled—a very wan smile. "Marry who? Go home where?"

"I'm sorry." Damn. He always blundered. He'd forgotten they had lost their farm.

"Do you have any real idea yet? About who did it?"

"Leads, yes. But nothing provable, even indictable."

"But what do you think?"

On an investigation every guy had his favorite: one suspect who became a personal obsession. But could he tell her that his was Xanthakis? That they had asked the P.O. to slap a mail cover on the homes of his relatives, had tried the special-delivery ruse? That his name had gone out on the teletype, police circulars and journals, the FBI bulletin, the wanted card at the local and state BCI, even a notice in the monthly bulletin of the American Hotel Association?

"We think he's in her address book. We've talked to every name we could locate. And they're a rather unsavory bunch, for the most part. But that's one man's opinion."

"Unsavory like what?" Francie said.

"Oh, call it executive dirt. I mean all those guys at the ad agency she worked with." His gaze narrowed, focusing beyond her shoulder. "Never met so many men with so much to hide."

"Hide? Hide what?"

"Sorry, Miss Perry. I can't go into that. But it makes me sore just to think of them. All that money, and not one has done an honest day's work in his life."

"That sounds like you're not exactly the son of Rockefeller."

"My father was on the force too. Died young chasing two punks down an alley. No, no hero stuff, they didn't shoot him. A heart attack dropped him. Just like that. He was forty-seven."

"It seems you'd want to be anything but a cop, after your father . . ."

"No. You see, Dad was all right. A really good man. He honored my mother. And when everyone else was on the take, he kept clean. I was just raised to look up to him, admire him. When he got wasted, it seemed the best thing was to try to fill his place. Not that I could be what he was."

"Are you happy? I mean, that you chose being a cop?"

Happy—it was all over his house. Ceramic and plastic figurines and paper and cloth hangings whose subject would have been appropriate on the buckboard of a covered wagon: a small girl in ankle-length print dress, white apron, sunbonnet, snub nose heavy with freckles, with legends reading BE HAPPY, THINK HAPPY, and just SMILE! In the kitchen Maddie had hung a painting of orange and yellow flowers rooted on a brown horizon of words: HAPPY HAPPY HAPPY HAPPY HAPPY.

"Happy?" he said. "I don't know. Don't have time to think about whether I am or not."

1:05 p.m.

The sign read DINO'S MALTEDS SANDWICHES CIGARS FOUNTAIN LUNCHEONETTE, decorated at each end by a red-and-white Coca-Cola rosette. The plate-glass window advised of the availability of TABLE SERVICE and WE DELIVIR.

Above, the second-story window said DONORS PAID BLOOD BANK DONORS PAID.

Miles Overby felt his missed-lunch hunger depart as he

followed the perspiring shirt and sunburned ears of Emmanuel Gold into Dino's.

"Great blueberry pie," Gold said as they sat down at a small formica table by the window. Miles stared out at passersby who looked in need of the receiving end of the bloodline, through RIVILED EW. The rich smell of coffee clouded from a stainless-steel urn and mingled with frying hamburgers.

"So what's new with the boy reporter?" Manny said after they had ordered. "Other than your pandering headlines."

"Up yours, Goldbrick. Actually I have contrived to meet a girl. Possibly, it should be considered, The Girl."

"Yeh? What happened to old 'Good-in-Bed-and-No-Strings-Attached'?"

."The way of all flesh," Miles said. "Good-in-Bed" had been Volume Eleven in an encyclopedia of fictions.

"So what's this sweet young thing like? Stacked?"

"Not exactly. But she's . . . attractive. I like her. What can I tell you?"

"Another Julie?"

"Hell, no, not another Julie."

"You're so full of shit," Manny said as their orders arrived, "it's backed up to your eyeballs."

"That another of your wise saws in modern instances?" He was watching Manny's fork sink through khaki pie crust into navy filling. The fork disappeared between his full red lips. Manny chewed rapidly, his moving tongue staining blue. He looked across at Miles and grinned, large teeth blued despite a washing of coffee.

"You know," Miles said, "ever since this bite-mark business, it's like I'm aware of teeth for the first time. My teeth, man-on-the-street teeth, Polident-ad teeth. I turned on the tube last night at two-ten A.M., there's Doris Day's big white ones in *On Moonlight Bay*, snapping into an apple. I'm the first man in America to fall in love with Doris Day's *teeth*."

"And should she prove false, you'll still love her Polident. Hell, Miles, I'm toothdom's biggest fan. I love all one hundred sixty surfaces. But let me tell you—about teeth, people are weird. As I should know, trying to get the assholes to let me pull 'em."

"How do you mean?"

"Losing a tooth, people get upset out of all proportion. I finally added it up—the emotional baggage. The teeth are in the mouth, right? And we use the mouth to eat and breathe, talk, smile, kiss, give head, all the really important stuff. I was reading about a case where a girl had all her teeth out and then, blammo—she went psychotic. Which reminds me of this case in Crystal Lake, Illinois. This woman was strangled with venetian-blind cord. Deep bite wounds on her breast. Police finally located a suspect, but the bugger'd had all his teeth pulled. It took months to find the oral surgeon who took 'em out, but he still had the dental records, which—you guessed it—matched the bite marks."

"And I used to be scared just of getting dog-bit," Miles said. "This big Airedale lived up the street."

Manny pureed pie crumbs between his fork tines, then licked the fork. "At least with a dog bite you'd have the smarts to go to a doctor, right? But with human bites, people don't go until it's giving them trouble—infected, whatever. Most human bites are on the hand, from fights. And because of complications, ten percent of victims lose their hands. Whack-off. Amputation."

"Always count on you," Miles said, "for a pleasant meal. Anyway, Goldbrick, I need your advice about something."

"Shoot. Advice, I'm full of it."

"It's about the Baskin case. There's this suspect—her boyfriend, Xanthakis—that skipped town."

"Yeh. I read it."

"I got talking with his brother and he spilled a few of the wrong beans."

"Like?"

"Like where the brother is. Uh-uh, I'm not gonna tell you. I haven't written anything up, told anyone so far. I'm not sure I should."

"Xanthakis skipped. He was innocent, why run?"

"Maybe that's what his brother wonders. The guy's got a record for assault, and he's listed in the Subject File of the Civil Disturbance System—antiwar demonstration in sixty-nine. Typical long-hair troublemaker. Dropped out of City College with flunking grades. Been supporting himself with odd jobs of carpentry—loft beds, bookshelves. His best friend was supposed to be Scott Eckley—"

"The Weatherman?" Manny said.

"Yeah. There's a fed fugitive warrant still out for Eckley. Mob action and aggravated battery. But story is Xanthakis split with Eckley because Eckley was a bomb freak. And Xanthakis wanted to work above ground. You know, change the system, fuck the coeds."

"Yeh, what about the coeds?"

"Definitely a swordsman."

He, Nicholas Adams, could have what he wanted because of something in him. It was a Hemingway story, and Miles remembered the knowing of it, that he didn't have what Nick had, would never have what Nick had, the knowledge of women that put Nick with Kate naked on the blankets in the woods, Nick in Kate from the front and then, rolling over, from behind. Because Nick did what men did, "persuading, and taking chances, and never frightening, and assuming about the other person, and always taking never asking." But he, Miles—inches was more like it—with his bottle of Cornhuskers Lotion and sperm-stiffened sheets, had never wanted to take without asking. No, he wanted to be asked, to be assured he was wanted, before he took.

"So what's the question?" Manny said, draining a second cup of coffee and eyeing the round plastic pie holder on the counter.

"I went to the place the brother said, and it was simple. Got the paper from the week before—it's a weekly—followed up on all the 'For Rent' ads. He's got an assumed name, of course. Now his address is burning a hell of a hole in my pocket."

"So you're wondering whether to write it up?"

"No. He'd just skip again, vanish. But if I tip off the cops, I could be there with a photog and get an exclusive on the capture."

"So where's the problem?"

"The responsibility, I guess. Nobody wants to think of himself as a stoolie."

"Do I detect the faint gleam of morality in your eye? Hell, Miles, no reason for him to run unless he did it. *It*, don't forget. Murder. That's what I keep coming back to."

3:45 p.m.

"Don't you like it?" Francie said.

Paige stared as her roommate emerged in a cloud of steam from the bathroom—wearing a strapless pink terry-cloth wrapper and her new haircut.

"It's so much cooler," Francie said. "Off my neck this way. Don't you like it?"

"My God."

"Can't be that bad." Francie twirled in front of the mirror, her hair lifting outward in a solid curtain. As she stopped, facing the mirror, her arms pressed against her sides, bulging the curve of her small breasts above the elastic top. The hair swirled over her face and then parted, revealing a straight Chinese-style cut with long eyebrow-brushing bangs. Her face was flushed as she stared into the mirror.

"You've never looked prettier. But you know what's wrong as well as me."

"No, I don't. What's wrong now?"

"For God's sake, Francie."

"*What?*"

"It's *hers*. It's *her* hair."

Francie turned to face the mirror. Her eyes studied her reflection, smeared with condensation from the shower. "You're wrong. Alex's didn't look a thing like this. I always wanted to try this style." She reached for a lipstick brush, began to stroke on the new bronze shade that had replaced the pale pink, her little finger propped on her chin.

The buzzer from the lobby sounded. The lipstick brush clattered onto the dresser top, blotting brown against the blond formica.

"Okay, Carlos," Paige called into the intercom to the lobby. "It's Miles," she said, walking back into the bedroom. "He's coming up." She watched as Francie ran to the closet, on the door of which hung an expensive red matte jersey halter and pants that had belonged to Alex. In the silence the snaps of the wrapper exploded. The terry dropped to the floor.

Something about her now, Paige thought as she watched Francie struggle into the jersey. She looked thinner, darker, her eyes different—harder, maybe. Well, we've both been through hell, have to change some way. Maybe it was just that she looked sexier in Alex's clothes. She had offered Paige first choice among them. The *last* thing I would do, Paige thought. Wear a dead person's clothes.

The doorbell buzzed.

Paige headed for the kitchen as Miles pulled Francie into a bearhug. To paraphrase Rousseau, she thought, "To live is not merely to breathe, it is to eat." She opened the door of the refrigerator. On the top shelf were three covered plastic dishes containing Eggplant Orleans, Zucchini Casserole and Hi-Protein Soybean Casserole. She withdrew a can of Budweiser, took out a glass, carefully poured the beer down the side to minimize the head.

"Hey, your hair," she could hear Miles saying. "It's different. It really looks great."

Paige waited until the thin line of foam at the top of the glass had flattened, then poured the remainder of the beer through the middle. She upended the can, allowing the last few creamy drops to slide onto her tongue. Her tongue probed the sharp metal edge of the opening.

"Paige?" Francie was standing in the kitchen doorway. "You don't feel bad tonight—staying here alone?"

"Don't be a sil. I'm going to watch *Agronsky and Company*—hate to miss that. Sorry about the hair thing. You do look great."

"Thanks, Paige." Francie's voice lowered. "Look, come out in the living room, why don't you? I think it embarrasses Miles. Every time he comes over, you go charging out of the room."

"Sure," Paige said.

Francie preceded her out of the kitchen.

"Hi, Miles," Paige said, eyes down on the brimming glass as she carried it across the rug.

Miles was smoking his usual acrid cigarette in the overstuffed chair—*my* chair, Paige thought—one chino-clad leg draped over the arm, sand-colored desert boot swinging. It was amazing how a foot could look so insolent.

Where the pants legs met, the bulge was clearly defined.

"How's the scribbling?" Paige said, sitting on the couch.

"Doctor said come by Monday it doesn't clear up," Miles said.

Francie laughed. In the thin red jersey halter her breasts swam up like jellyfish. The halter was like the rest of Alex's clothes, Paige thought, like the slit gowns in *The Story of O* —designed to maximize female accessibility. Pull aside a slice of fabric and you were nude.

Paige set the beer down on the coffee table. "Well, go on, you two, run along. You don't have to stick around and entertain me."

She picked up the beer, touched it against her lips, then set it back down.

"Say, how's about joining us for the movie at least?" Miles said, swinging his leg off the arm of the chair, the sole of his boot scuffing the pale green fabric.

"No, really. But thanks." Paige got up and headed toward the kitchen. "Forgot the coaster," she called.

She was holding the wooden disk in her hand when she saw Francie precede Miles out the front door, speeded by a possessive whack on the butt.

"See you later, Paige," Francie said, voice trailing back from the hall.

In the pig's eye, see you later. Francie wouldn't be back at all—or why tuck a pair of bikini pants in an envelope in her purse? What did she see in that goddamn opportunistic little twerp? He was, as Alex would have said, very *nerdy*. Okay, it was none of her business. Who was she to talk, never great shakes in the men department herself. But how could Francie *possibly* go to bed with Miles? Unless it was an act of charity—Francie Nightingale spreads her wings among the unloved, unwashed, unwanted. Uncircumcised, undoubtedly. Miles looked like the type that finished in two thrusts.

Paige switched on the television. The white pinprick swelled across the black screen.

Always one roommate stuck at home. At college, in New York, no matter what combination of women, there was always someone without a date. So it had been her for a couple of years. There had been Michael at college.

But instead of the television screen, in her mind she was seeing a graph labeled "Copulatory Sequence." Successive mounts were indicated along the base line, the number of thrusts along the vertical axis. *Intromission achieved. Male dismounts. Intromission terminated.*

Anthropology 101, she thought, had been a good introductory to life. Even at the age of eighteen, while reading about the female baboon and the male macaque monkey, she knew she was seeing life as it really was, behind the phony veneer of romance.

The young couple had mated the minute they were caged together, with (it was noted) much lip-smacking and general gusto. But with the passage of time, greater and greater amounts of "precopulatory stimulation" were required. Frequency plummeted. Then "Timmy" was introduced into an adjoining cage with a new female, and lo, copulation was again vigorous and immediate. ("Grace" lured her rival to the wire netting and poked her in the eye.)

Then she was remembering the high-school party. Drunk and come to behind the chair and a strange guy's humping you. Still feel that—prickles of ice with each thrust, like a foot that went to sleep and now you're running on it.

But that was a long time ago.

Everyone has problems, hell of a lot of problems worse than mine. Real problems.

But why the whole shitload of mine suddenly back now, stinging like a torn scab?

Because of Alex.

The trouble was, it all looked downhill from here. Just a few backwaters to enjoy along the way. But maybe that was the trouble. Try to enjoy something for once, stop worrying where all the streams terminate, where all the springs originate. Fuck Aurelia and analysis. Fuck men instead, like Francie. Whoopee.

She had the distinct feeling, in fact she *knew* that she had to get her head in order and control some of her worst traits. When you got out of the habit of doing something, it was more or less easy to resist temptation. The mind comes back to that old escape, in times of need, but finds the opening plugged up.

Then she gave up and called the pizza takeout.

4:05 p.m.

As James Diefendorfer MacKenzie stared down into the bilious currents of the Hudson River, he was surprised by a cramp of . . . well, not exactly fear, of course. No, call it a cautious, prudent sense of unease.

Which was only reasonable.

It was his first assignment as the rookie of the Underwater Recovery Team, the elite seven-man diving unit of the New York Harbor Patrol.

Only one certified scuba diver for every thirty survived the required physical and even-more-rigorous mental hurdles. On the other hand (so said the old-timers, grizzled salts well into their thirties), you had to be full-out crazy to *want* the job.

Last year the team had logged three hundred assignments, fishing up a smorgasbord of dead human bodies, guns, car licenses and occasionally the cars they were attached to. All this while disporting in sixty-foot depths, with a visibility of six inches, through an unseen landscape of wire, glass, rusted fenders, boulders, staved-in shopping carts, stoves, chemicals, raw sewage, and the occasional eel. The story went about the champion diver all primed to show his hot-shit balls. Then he swam blind into a sunken phone booth and shit his wet suit.

But today, James reminded himself—a day bright and sunny above the midnight water—looked as uneventful as they could get: simple gun recovery, position known. Some junkie nut had shot up the cashier at a Chinese takeout, then tossed the .38 revolver off the old Pennsy Railroad pier, number fifty, at the foot of Bethune Street.

The deck of the patrol launch rose and fell beneath his feet. The sensation lumped unsteadily beneath his ribs, James decided, was only the sardine-and-mustard sandwich packed by his wife, the former Charlotte Diefendorfer, whose name on the Lord & Taylor charge card read Diefendorfer *hyphen* MacKenzie. He, however, had taken his cue from John Ono (no hyphen) Lennon, who knew a man had to draw the line somewhere.

Out in the little motor dinghy Charlie Albright was heaving the orange buoy over into the water. It popped up, the red flag that signaled "Divers Below" taking the breeze. Then the grapnels bombed the surface and sank, taking with them the ropes they would hang on to, to keep the ten-mph current from ripping them downstream.

James shifted his weight from one heavy black rubber flipper to another. Behind him he heard the scrape of steel as Vinnie DiBenedetto, his diving partner, lifted the forty-pound air tank.

"Upsy fucking daisy."

This from Vinnie. And he felt the tank collide against his back, and then Vinnie was strapping him in.

"Baptism time, hey, Jimbo?" Vinnie said, whacking him on the butt, which was armored with red rubber beneath which he was greased with sweat.

Weight belt on. Molded red rubber hood. Face mask. Mouthpiece (always that taste like machine oil, you couldn't rinse the river out). Check. Black rubber gloves with gauntlets halfway to his elbows, fingertips pitted with tarry wear. Serl Dive Light, on-off, on-off. Check.

(*The 33-foot no-decompression limit may fail—working dives to 25 feet or less have caused bends.*) Oh, hell. Here we go.

He clamped his mouthpiece in with one hand, the flashlight in the other, let himself fall backward into the water.

Click. The flashlight illuminated about as much as a one-eyed headlight in a black snowstorm. The susurrant rush of his breathing filled his ears—in and out, in and out. The current tugged at his legs and his gloved right hand tightened on the rope.

Flash of light. Vinnie's face appeared, his goggled eyes moving froglike nearer, then winking out as he motioned downward.

James descended to the bottom, which was so thick with mud every move you made stirred up silt. Like swimming through syrup. Too bad it was the Hudson and not the East River, he thought, hand groping along the bottom.

Gun barrel? No, a rusty pipe.

The East River, now, its bottom was hard and graveled, boulders looming big as cars. Helluva current through Hell Gate, but anything was better than fucking mud.

Now, where had that junkie bastard ditched his gun?

Or was he just a talker stalling the cops for time?

James Diefendorfer MacKenzie started. In his ears he heard his breath spurt from jog to run. Something was holding, tangling, sliding around his legs. He resisted the urge to grab at it. (*"Don't put your head or hand anywhere you can't see into first."*) He hung still and limp, brought his light down to focus on the obstruction.

Film, for Christ's sake. Movie film. Like octopus tentacles, hundreds of feet of transparent squares entangled him from ankles to knees.

He kicked loose, peeling the film down over his flippers, then again, shaking himself like a water rat as he felt more film slide across the top of his head.

He looked up.

Brown seaweed that was not brown seaweed beat up and down, swirling on the current.

He raised his light. He heard his breath gasp into the mouthpiece.

The nude girl rotated slowly nearer, arms bent up at the waist, fingers curled, reaching. In her open eyes there was a question he knew he couldn't answer.

7:42 p.m.

The Indian restaurant was called Nirvana.

At another time, Francie thought, it might have been.

Through the fourteenth-floor terrace windows, Central Park floated like a green island in concrete. Above the tables, tapestries winking with tiny mirrors were gathered to form a tent. The music of a sitar, played by a cross-legged Indian man on a rug, shivered across the brass plates.

"It's called *lassi*," Miles Overby said as the two foaming glasses arrived. "Yogurt and rose water. Elton John liked it so much when he was here, he took a jar home."

Francie took a tentative sip through the foam. It tasted good but smelled like cold cream.

195

At an adjoining table a balding man was conducting a monologue. His red-haired girlfriend was picking bits of lamb off his plate. His *wife*, Francie thought. Only married people ate off each other's plates, invading the other's territory with unquestioned ownership rights.

The thought made her feel lonely.

"Miles, I don't know beans about Indian food. You order for me and I'll visit the ladies' room."

When she came back through the arched doorway he was replacing something in her handbag.

"What are you *doing?*"

"For true?" he said.

"True."

"Sit down first, okay? Look, I'm an insecure guy, Francie. I wanted to know whether you'd chucked that photo of Xanthakis. I wanted to know he didn't mean anything to you anymore. Hell, plain jealous, I guess."

"I took it out," she said, sitting down, "and cut it up and put it down the incinerator. Okay?"

The plates of fried vegetable fritters, centered by a *poori*—a giant hot-air balloon of flaky pastry—arrived.

"I think you'll like this wine," Miles said as the Indian waiter poured. "Alsatian Gewürztraminer. Only wine I think complements curry."

Francie drained half her glass, hoping the languorous bold warmth she was feeling would stay. She leaned forward in the red halter, elbows on the table, as his eyes moved where she wanted them, onto her breasts.

"Just curious, I guess," Miles said, "but this constant Shirley Temple stuff everyone says about Alex—she was so sweet and so on. It makes me wonder: didn't she have any vices at all?"

"Living with Alex was like being the only clothed person at a nudist camp."

"Oh, yeah?"

"It was hard to get used to. She even exercised nude, right in the living room."

Miles laughed and refilled her glass.

She was on her fourth glass, detailing some of Alex's exploits, when he said, "You know, I wanted to know if you still cared about Xanthakis, because I found out something about him today. It's just as well you've forgotten him."

"What do you mean?"

"Did you know he was arrested at fourteen?"

The bubbles of winy headiness winked out, were utterly gone. "How did you find that out?"

"Guy up at Goshen tipped the police off. Anonymously. The record's sealed because of his age."

"What is Goshen?"

"The state secure facility for juveniles."

"It was a frame-up," Francie cut in. "A cop grabbed him to search for marijuana. He didn't have any, but the cop beat him up anyway. Then charged Spy with assault."

Miles was staring at her over the cooling lamb curry. His eyes moved out to the park, north toward the haze of Harlem. "That what Xanthakis told you?"

"Of course. That's what happened."

"Record shows he cut a fellow student with a knife."

"*No!*"

The red-haired wife was looking at her.

"Hey." Miles took her hand, pressed her stiff fingers against his throat, unrolled them, kissed the pads of her fingers. "Francie, sorry, really. I get too wound up in this thing, worry about it. You don't think I'm using you in any way, do you? I worry about it because of you."

"You think he did it, too, don't you? Because he ran. He went to prison, Miles, for something he didn't do, do you hear? He was *framed*. He told me these men tried to rape him in prison. I knew the way he said it that they raped him. He told me he would never let the cops get hold of him again."

"Francie, let's forget about it. Dammit all, I'm sorry. I shouldn't go talking shop all the time. Maybe I hide behind the work, I don't know. I had an unhappy suffering Southern-fried childhood. To my father I was one big disappointment, with the horrifying result you see across from you."

"Not so horrifying. Anyway, aren't all childhoods unhappy?"

Miles spooned more chutney onto her plate. She bit down into a spiced, pale green mango, which felt furred like a peach against her lips.

"You know," he said after a time, "I see myself sometimes—myself at seven—running toward me, eyes all squinted up in the sun. The way I looked then: curly hair, this long, misshapen, ugly little monkey face, bony knees going every which way, covered with scabs. Big horn-rimmed glasses even then. I see him running and running toward me, like he's running from something, his arms reach out. And I wonder, why didn't they love him? Why? He wasn't that bad. He at least deserved to be loved. I would have loved him."

His face seemed to have narrowed, sucked inward along the ridge of his nose, tight at the nostrils.

"Well, I do," Francie said.

"Do what?"

It wasn't true, she thought. But it was like having a long oar in a rowboat. You had to reach out with it to a drowning man.

"I love him," she said.

When they stood in the narrow carpeted hallway at her

apartment door, Miles pressed her suddenly against the wall. She felt his erection hard between them.

"For true?" he said.

"True."

"I've been wanting to jump on you all night. Let's hop a cab. Back to my place."

"It's late, Miles."

"I'm climbing the walls." His lips covered hers. He ground his erection against her. "Come on, huh? What do you say?"

"No, Miles. Really."

She turned in his embrace. He nuzzled the splay of hair from her nape as she opened the three locks and pushed the door inward. The living room beyond was dark, filled with the fluid rush of the air-conditioner.

"Paige asleep?" he said.

"I guess so."

"Let me see you safely inside. Shhh." He motioned toward the closed bedroom door. "Let's let sleeping Paiges lie."

The wine was back. She giggled.

He took her wrist, and she felt her pulse jump beneath his fingers. He pulled her up against his body, bending her backward. It was so black in the room that he could have been anyone. The thought was oddly exciting.

He pulled her shoulders toward the couch, but she resisted, holding herself stiff. His face moved down onto her breasts. She felt his tongue arch against the nipple through the thin cloth. His breath was warm and damp, now on her bare skin. The nipple rose.

"No," she said. "Paige will hear."

His mouth came back up to hers. He lifted her in his arms. She felt his muscles trembling as he carried her into the kitchen. She felt the linoleum tiles press up cool beneath her thighs. Then he was closing the kitchen door and turning toward her, his face illuminated by the streetlight below.

It was obvious and yet no one had ever pointed it out, she thought. The fact that New York's cobra-necked streetlights looked just like the death rays in *War of the Worlds*.

Miles was staring down at her, face naked without the glasses, his fingers tugging at his belt. His slacks dropped as if several sizes too large.

He was no longer impotent.

She felt the cool air skate across her bare thighs.

It was the first time she had ever undressed, not waiting to *be* undressed.

"No," he said into her ear as he entered her. "We can't. Paige will hear."

She stared at the ceiling while the sound rubbed and rubbed.

She had heard the sound before. Like sand in a shoe, it had annoyed her awake. She had sat up in bed, eyes straining toward the living room through the closed bedroom door. "Harder. Harder." The voice was Alex's, of course.

In the kitchen the rubbing sound moved faster.

Francie felt the hot rush of pleasure seize her body, break from her pores.

"Harder. *Harder*."

Obediently the rubbing sound moved faster.

She heard a cry hang in the air. For a moment she wondered whose it was.

From the other bed came a light, bumbling snore. She turned her head: Paige was asleep, mouth open.

Francie stared back up at the ceiling. The wash of sweat down her body felt like grease. Again. The waking. When would it stop? She tried to remember the tiredness of physical exertion that made you drop off and not wake till the alarm jangled across the room. She tried to remember the get-in-the-corn tiredness—the never-stopping that lasted a month, racing the winds that could topple the ear-heavy stalks and make them impossible to harvest by machine.

Instead she remembered walking down Thirteenth Street, crossing to the tiny used bookstore. Inside was dust on old covers of stacks of books. She had stood staring at the row of paperbacks, true-crime tales printed in the fifties. *The Girl in the Stateroom*, *The Girl in the Death Cell*, *The Girl in Lover's Lane*, *The Girl in Poison Cottage*, *The Girl in the House of Hate*, *The Girl with the Scarlet Brand*, *The Girl in the Red Velvet Swing*, *The Girls in Nightmare House*, *The Girl on the Lonely Beach*, *The Girl in Murder Flat*. "They found her naked and dead in the dusty belfry!" read the cover line for *The Girl in the Belfry*.

"Very popular, that Gold Medal series," the proprietor had said over steel-rimmed half-glasses. "Only time I see them is when some collector croaks. You want them, better grab. Sell out fast as I get them in."

She had continued staring at the cover illustrations—photos and drawings of blondes, brunettes, redheads sprawled on their backs with limp upflung arms, closed eyes, scarlet slashes of mouths.

"Do you take checks?" she had said.

12:02 a.m.

The sporadic blows of the typewriter keys seemed to penetrate, separately and painfully, into the front of his head.

Victor Amspoker paused, hunched his shoulders up and

down to shake off the ache, and typed on. When he pulled the last sheet out, the memory of the girl's nude body dampened his sense of accomplishment. It was like a brand, that bite mark: coral on the gray-looking flesh of her left breast. The same young, white victim, this one in her early thirties—Rita, her name was, Rita Sue Viseltear, a social worker who just wanted to do good. Her husband had had to be sedated.

But worse than the body dragged staring from the river was the pile of clothes. They had searched through the area's abandoned buildings north of where she had been fished out. He remembered their shoes stirring up puffs of dust as they entered Pier 48, through the broken windows the setting sun filtering orange and rose. His own shoes coming to rest in the dust as he stared down at the little heap of garments. "Frank," he had called. There was something wrong with his voice.

He began to read over the sheets he had typed from his notes.

EXAMINATION OF EVIDENCE

1. A sleeveless, button-type, blue-colored "Acrylic Fiber" blouse.
   Several hairs removed for examination.
   Examination: Human, 17″ in length, dark brown in color, fine texture, fragmented, missing and continuous medulla. (Refer Evid. #3 and #7.)
   Several animal hairs from canine family also present.
   Several red-colored stains found present—identified as rust stains.
2. A soiled white brassiere labeled "Forever Yours."
   Left side of brassiere is torn.
   Trace amount of blood found present—quantity insufficient to determine origin or grouping.
   Nothing of further significance noted.

3. A soiled white panty girdle labeled "Formaid Pick Ups."
   Blue-colored male and female sex symbols on girdle.
   Front portion is extensively ripped and torn.
   One hair removed for examination—identified as human, 1⅜″ in length, med. brown in color, coarse texture, missing medulla. (Refer Evid. #7.)
   No bloodstains or spermatozoa found present.
   Nothing of further significance noted.
4. Beige-colored panties, no manufacturer's label.
   Garment is extensively ripped and torn.
   No bloodstains or seminal stains found present.
   Nothing of further significance noted.
5. White slacks, labeled "Cotton."
   Slacks are damp and present a musty odor.
   Middle rear waistband area is ripped and torn.
   No bloodstains or seminal stains found present.
   Several hairs removed for examination.
   Examination: Human, 15″ in length, dark brown in color, fine texture, fragmented, missing and continuous medulla. (Refer Evid. #7.) Several animal hairs, from canine family, also found present.
6. One pair of soiled low-cut white sneakers, labeled "98430."
   Gray-colored residue present on sole area of both sneakers—identified as soil—quantity insufficient for further analysis.
7. Plastic box labeled "Known Hair—Specimen from Deceased."
   Examination: Human, 15″ to 17″ in length, dark brown in color, fine texture, fragmented, missing and continuous medulla.
   These hairs are similar in color and physical characteristics to the hairs in Evidences #1 and #5, but not to the hair in Evid. #3.

Whoopee, Amspoker thought. So now they know the psycho had at least one hair on his head 1⅜ inches in length, medium brown in color, texture: coarse.

Unless it was a pubic hair.

1:27 a.m.

Inside the Muriel cigar box the watch lay beating.

Dalroi smiled.

He sat back in the chair, an unsteady office relic on casters, tattered brown leather crisscrossed with cracks. He had rescued it from a sidewalk of rusted file cabinets awaiting the sanitation trucks.

He exhaled sharply. He felt good and clean and pleased. He put his feet up on the seat, arms locking around his knees. The movement rolled the chair backward, bumping across the dirty linoleum of the basement room.

He laughed. He put one foot down and propelled the chair back toward the Muriel box, which sat on a small round table that listed on a broken leg.

He lifted the Muriel lid.

Yes, it was a beautiful watch. He liked the way it belonged beside the gold clip and the red sash. He knew they would all get along. The band was fine gold mesh, soft to the touch. The face was a green oval—a tender pale green beneath the hard glass.

He was having the most wonderful time of his life. The watch played its music in the box.

But they had been pale green too.

No.

Yes they were too.

The camp latrine phosphorescent peeling white boards in the dark, the urine smell and disinfectant smells, rows of covered holes empty in the middle of the night, the concrete cold beneath his bare feet, which numbed and rooted him to the cold as he stared at the electric bulb and the wall.

The wall was green, soft and furry, moving in waves, flittering pieces that soared and fell and nested back covering the wall covering each other, suffocating covering smothering, covering him with thousands of green luna moths thousands thick in the air beating the air with his scream.

Dalroi stared down from the huddled height of the chair. Below on the brown linoleum the watch lay faceup, glass shattered.

Chapter Eight

Sunday, August 14
9:06 a.m.

The *Daily News* had beaten them to it, the headline covering half the page: STRANGLER CLAIMS HIS THIRD.

"Where the fucking hell have you guys been?" Lowry said, volume well above the conversational level.

Silence followed.

Into it Miles had heard his own voice, naked with excitement, spilling out Xanthakis' address.

Now they were sitting around, over, and partly in the

holes in the seats of his Dodge Coronet, parked down the street from the antiseptic pile of cinder blocks that called itself the Twentieth Precinct Station House.

Just past nine, Miles had phoned in· the tip from the corner booth, wedging the door open with his foot because —oh, *Christ*—someone had pitched in the corner.

It was 9:32 before Detective Frank Quinn's metallic blue Mercury pulled up at the station house. The passenger door swung open. Detective Victor Amspoker—looking, Miles thought, like a bear with poached eyes—studied the gutter for a spot free of the 150,000 pounds of turds deposited daily by New York's dogs. Then he stepped down and climbed within.

As the Mercury threaded north toward the Tappan Zee Bridge, Miles kept well behind. He knew where the cops were going, of course. The important thing was to arrive when they did, in time for a banner-making, byline-starring, photogenic capture.

On the seat beside him, the top *Post* photographer, Bart Newell, his thin, sinewy neck hung with the paraphernalia of his trade, was finishing a container of extremely bad coffee. In the back seat, his soiled stocking feet pressed against the side window, police reporter Tony Rosell was making his usual wisecracks. Rosell was an expert at graphic . on-the-scene descriptions, having covered some twelve thousand sudden deaths in his career, including one by toilet-tank cover. Lowry, the managing editor, had amputated Rosell from another story to "flesh out the coverage. But your byline'll come first," he had assured Miles.

Team reporting was all very efficient, but it whacked the hell, Miles thought, out of journalistic initiative.

"Hey, Miles," Rosell said. "Heard you got yourself a new little honey. Gettin' any off of her?"

"She offered her honor," Newell said, "he honored her offer."

"And all night long," the two sang, "it was honor and offer!"

"Fuck, you married boys're all jealous."

The blue Mercury six cars ahead of them turned north, accelerating onto the concrete plain of the New York State Thruway. As his Dodge followed, settling into the stream of traffic, Miles felt the doubts return.

But Francie didn't care about Xanthakis anymore. She had incinerated his picture, right? And even if she *did* still care, even after last night, she would certainly want to see the one responsible behind bars, right? And anyway, maybe Spyros Xanthakis had finally smartened up. Maybe he had packed up and lit out for someplace else, this time *not* telling his grandmother, for God's sake.

Would a murderer tell his grandmother where he was going?

The thought came, slipping like a thin blade into the center of his unease. He tried to imagine what his feelings would be on getting there, finding Xanthakis gone.

Disappointment or relief?

10:25 a.m.

The Shawangunk Mountains arched above the river valley like a Brontosaurean spine. The sheer white cliffs rose from downward-tumbled boulders and surrounding woods thick with pine, dogwood, rhododendron, and huckleberries.

At Exit 18, the two detectives turned west toward the ridge, following Highway 299 into New Paltz.

Frank, Victor Amspoker noticed, had switched again to

an ankle holster, his short boot unzipped to accommodate the two-inch leather band lined with felt, the fancy embossed holster laced against his shin. About his piece, Amspoker thought, Frank was as vain as a girl. But then, he had a love affair with guns in general, calling it "sacrilege" to dispose of confiscated guns the way they did it now: melting them down to make manhole covers.

Amspoker was remembering the past summer's shooting cycle at Rodman's Neck, near Orchard Beach in the North Bronx. The department's shooting range was down a dirt road and 150 lanes wide, with dirt-covered hills of cantaloupe rinds for the backstop. They had signed in, had their guns checked out, fidgeted through lectures, fired fifty sweaty rounds, fidgeted again, fired again. Quinn had qualified as an expert shot, one of only five members of the police department so designated.

"For his sake, let's hope to hell Xanthakis comes peaceable," Amspoker said as they entered the village on a street bordered with trees and seventeenth-century Huguenot stone houses. They were met at the small headquarters building by Police Chief Sewell Hoskins, two green-looking members of his force, and three Ulster County deputy sheriffs.

Hoskins was a short gray-haired man whose buttons strained to encompass a basketball belly. "You boys want to come in for a swig of coffee first?"

"I want to nail this SOB," Quinn said, "get him cuffed. And then we'll see about it."

"Sure thing. I'll ride with you, show you where. We got two men out there now keeping tabs. Hell, I'm glad to help you boys. And 'tween you and me, I'm glad to see him go."

"He cause trouble?" Amspoker said as Hoskins climbed into the back seat.

"Not him particular. But see, all these street people drifting in giving us a problem. 'The Situation on Main Street,' people are calling it. The college is closed for the summer, see, but this town stays wide open. Drugs, long-hairs, crazies, rock climbers, health-food nuts. Stoned lost kids going back to nature in a poison-ivy patch. Hotheads getting into fights about gay lib, women's lib, ever' kind of lib. Hell, now people are screaming for walking patrols on Main Street because this nut wearing ice skates, buffalo horns and a gorilla suit picked a fight with a shop owner."

The Mercury stopped for a light. A young man with a blond ponytail, his body sliding naked beneath an over-sized workman's bib overall, crossed the street. He glanced in their window, eyes milky blue and vague.

It was a good place for Spyros Xanthakis, Amspoker thought as they passed a store advertising soy hamburgers, countless windows crowded with needlework, pottery, baskets, macrame, and leather. One more long-haired radical ex-student with no job was about as noticeable here as a clam in the ocean.

They crossed the Wallkill River and followed Mountain Rest Road out of town. The vertical rock face of the ridge bulged ahead. Amspoker felt the tension knot his stomach, twist higher. Hoskins blithering on, and they were so close. So close to ending it. *If Xanthakis did it.*

"Turn right up here," Hoskins said.

The Mercury swerved onto Canaan Road.

"Just a little piece down the way here," Hoskins said. "You boys like to fish? Island Pond in Harriman tops all. Great trout, mostly brookies. Nice fighters. You get a rainbow now and again. There's a cold channel in there a hundred feet deep for the trout, but you also get the warm-water babies—bass, pickerel, perch."

Would he ever shut up?

"Dip 'em in cornmeal and fry 'em up. Pure eatin' gold. Here we are."

The house was a mile out of town—a tiny, white-frame square badly in need of paint, its sagging front disappearing into uncut grass, yellow dandelions and white clover. In the driveway stood an equally dilapidated van, its sides painted with vistas of mountains.

As the three men stepped from the car, Amspoker tapped the hard gun butt between the open buttons of his shirt. He could hear the sound of insects, the sound of his heart.

They waited until the other men joined them, Hoskins motioning two toward the rear of the house.

On the porch stood two wooden rocking chairs, one occupied by a white cat that regarded them with unblinking topaz gaze. As Amspoker reached the porch flooring, he extended his hand toward it. The cat leaped without a sound, disappearing between two broken boards beneath the porch.

The rusted screen door shook in its frame at Quinn's knock. There was no response from within. Quinn tested the door: it was unlocked. Quinn motioned Hoskins and the others to remain. Then, drawing their guns, the two detectives stepped inside.

The tiny living room was dark, white curtains drawn against the sun. A huge couch, gray stuffing sprouting from its flowered cover, was the only furniture. A damp, rotting smell lay heavy on the air. Sleeping bags and a tent trailing leaves were stacked against one wall.

To the right was a small kitchen, to the left a bathroom, both of which were empty.

Down the unlit hall they could see the door to the last remaining room. It was closed.

Amspoker pressed his ear against the peeling white paint on the door. No sound came from within. Quinn raised his gun as Amspoker flattened himself against the wall, barrel across his chest, muzzle pointing at the door.

Quinn thrust the door wide into the room. *"Police. Freeze."*

From a mattress in the center of the floor came an explosion of movement. A female voice screamed. A naked girl, pendulous breasts swinging, flung herself back against the wall. An equally naked man trailing a white sheet ran toward the rear door.

"Freeze or I'll shoot," Quinn said.

The door was wrenched open, a bar of white light beyond into which flashed the tanned back and white buttocks. The man held a dark compact object in his right hand.

Amspoker heard the sound split the air, swallowing the girl's scream.

The man dropped, as if his legs had been kicked from under him.

On the surface of his palm, Amspoker felt the hot, stinging impact of the gun's discharge. He stared down, saw the powder from the cylinder flash.

The girl screamed again, voice high and ragged. "Don't shoot me! Don't shoot!"

The two detectives stepped cautiously past her. The man lay on his back, his feet with long ragged toenails stretched out to the edge of sunlight through the open door.

"Spyros Xanthakis?" Quinn said.

The man did not respond.

"You have the right to remain silent," Quinn said. "Anything you say can be used against you in a court of law. You have the right to the presence of an attorney. If you can't afford an attorney, one will be appointed for you prior to any questioning if you so desire."

The man lay motionless, his shoulder-length hair spread in crisp red-brown waves, blood pooling out from beneath his back. His eyes under straight black brows stared at the ceiling.

His right hand had fallen open.

Beyond his fingers lay a dark blue six-by-four-inch hardbound book, its title stamped in faded gold: *Wilderness, A Journal of Quiet Adventure in Alaska,* by Rockwell Kent.

Victor Amspoker knelt beside the man. The eyes moved, caught at his face.

"Spyros Xanthakis?" Amspoker said.

"I can't move. Help me, man. I can't feel."

Then the flashbulbs went off.

6:14 p.m.

"... two thoracic vertebrae—T 11 and 12—were completely shattered," said the precise, high-pitched man's voice. "The spinal cord was severely damaged by the pressure from the surrounding bones. Now the paralysis of both legs and the lower portion of the body results from the fact that, like a damaged telephone cord, a damaged spinal cord can no longer carry messages."

"Dr. Raskind, will he walk again?"

"While we do not believe at this point that he will achieve ambulation—that is, walking with braces and crutches—our prognosis is guardedly optimistic until further tests can be completed."

"Thank you, doctor. We have just been speaking with Dr. Lorimer Raskind, chief physiatrist at the Institute of Rehabilitation Medicine, who has just examined the strangler suspect Spyros Xanthakis, wanted for questioning in the murders of three New York women. Xanthakis was shot and wounded this morning by police while resisting arrest in a house outside New Paltz, New York. From New York University Medical Center, this is Adam Jultek reporting."

The television screen switched back to the bland face of the anchorman.

Paige MacLeish, alone in their new apartment, got up from the couch. She felt a sharpness of horror that in the next moment was blotted by an overwhelming release.

It was over.

They had got him, caught him, captured him and shot him. The system still worked, after all. Rapists and killers were caught, they were punished. Eye for an eye. Two legs for a life.

Her mind moved numbly over the remembered features of Spyros Xanthakis. She had thought it absurd at first that the Spyros she had known could be a suspect. And yet day after day the papers had hammered out his name in bold black type. HUNT BOYFRIEND OF SLAIN BRUNETTE... ALEX SUSPECT MEMBER OF SDS. Seventy-three percent of murders, the papers also reported, were committed by assailants *known* to their victims. One in every six female murder victims was killed by her lover. Jealousy, old evergreen green eyes, was the most common motive of all.

And Spy had clinched it, hadn't he? Left town, run away, hidden out, and now resisted arrest. It just proved you couldn't trust anyone.

And that other thing, then, it had been after all just her imagination. That feeling of being followed. Of looking back, seeing no one, only the preoccupied crowds. She was glad now that she had told no one. Hysterical female, they would say. Obviously just a fledgling case of paranoia, "raging hormonal influences," fear grabbing her imagination like a mugger's hand in the dark.

It was over.

She wanted to rush from the apartment, run through

the streets, find Francie wherever it was she was meeting that girl, Kandis, from the office. She wanted to be the one to tell her, to shake her by the shoulders and yell, "It's over."

But why hadn't one of the detectives—Quinn, perhaps, or Amspoker—called to give the good news? She felt almost like a winner snubbed by lottery officials.

Paige pulled open the drawer of the walnut-grained pasteboard telephone table. She took out the white card whose blue-and-gold shield depicted a farmer, an Indian, and the scales of justice, and dialed the number.

She could hear the voices of a number of men while she waited for Detective Amspoker to reach the phone.

"Miss MacLeish," he said, "how are you?"

"I heard about Spyros on the news...wanted to congratulate you. I mean, you got him, it's over now, isn't it?"

She heard an exhalation of breath, thinned through the wires.

"His alibi for Monday checks out, Miss MacLeish. Two friends say he was with them all day the eighth."

"Then they're lying!"

"Also his blood type differs from what we know to be the perpetrator's."

"But how can that be? Spyros ran, didn't he? The TV said he resisted arrest?"

"We found two one-gram packets of cocaine on the premises. Other than that, we don't know. He told us he left the city because he didn't want to be hassled. "

"Is it true—that he'll be crippled?"

"I'm afraid it is true, Miss MacLeish."

"Does this mean," she said carefully, "that you're . . . that we're all of us back to zero? No new leads? No closer than you were *six days* ago?"

"Miss MacLeish, I assure you we do have some leads,

some new ones that look very promising. We're working on them now. As soon as anything definite shows up, we'll let you know."

Six days. Almost a week. Maybe what Francie had told her was right, even if Overby *was* the source. Maybe Quinn, Amspoker, all of them had already written Alex off, turned their attention to the next killing. Or the next. They had to, didn't they? They couldn't hold the backlog at bay forever.

A stream jammed with bodies filled her mind.

"You've got to find him," Paige said. "You've got to."

"Miss MacLeish, please understand. We're as anxious to find him as you are. We're doing everything we can, you have my word on it."

"Maybe everything isn't enough," Paige said.

"It's *got* to be," he said. But the line was already dead.

6:31 p.m.

At his desk, Victor Amspoker sat with his hand on the telephone. It was the eyes he kept seeing. The eyes staring at the ceiling, then moving wounded to his face, like that shepherd he had found on the highway at ten, its hind legs a black-and-gray smear, its life spiraling out in blood dark as the wetted concrete.

Only this time *he* had crushed its legs. And still its eyes sought his face for help. As if he were innocent. Not guilty.

The inquiry had already begun. Was the shooting justified or unjustified? And what about this defendant, Amspoker? What did his fellow officers think, rumor, make up, dislike about him? Had he ever been disciplined, chronically late, unwanted as a partner in the patrol car? Was his hair too

216

long, salary garnisheed, DD-5's incorrectly filled out? Had he ever stopped off the beat for an egg cream without signing? Did he screw around, drink too much, get off-duty hand injuries that suggested brawls? Had his wife ever called the commanding officer? Had he shot off his lip or his gun too much?

Because the object in the hand of Spyros Xanthakis—fleeing homicide suspect—had proven to be a book, not a gun, the shooflies from the Internal Affairs Division were fanning out from 72 Poplar Street. Because this time it was pages, not bullets, the hunters from headquarters were pulling his file, judging whether he would join the fifteen hundred other cops who wound up every year getting their heads shrunk at the Psychological Services Unit, or their livers thumped by the alcoholism group.

Criminal charges could follow, and removal of his guns, transfer to desk Siberia, a departmental trial, "wrongful injury," dismissal from the force, deprivation of pension, even imprisonment.

And yet he, Victor Amspoker, had logged twenty years in the gutters, alleys, tenements and on the roofs without firing his gun until this morning. Despite being called a honky motherfucker, being spat upon, hit with lighted cigarettes and filled soda-pop bottles. Despite facing guns and fearing guns, afraid like anyone else, and yet having to make on-the-spot decisions while wondering how it feels to get your gut split like a watermelon with a blast from behind the door. Despite knowing, while you're wondering, that in this country in the last ten years, 786 police officers on duty got blown away—414 while attempting an arrest.

But that was it. His judges were goddamn limousine bleeding hearts, SOB's living white as slugs behind their desks, miles above the street. They weren't the ones who felt the pain the leadlike overcoat stabbed through your shoulders every start of winter, or heard the electronic gore pour over you on the patrol-car seat, sprung from ten different drivers a week. They weren't the new minority: refused service in a restaurant because the uniforms "might upset customers." They weren't the ones who never made it home for Christmas, birthdays, anniversaries, school plays, confirmations, whose wives took to drinking or whoring around.

No, his judges were not the ones who found dead babies stuffed in trash cans, or tried to comfort four-year-old girls with cigarette burns on their crotches.

They had never stared down into the face of a strangled, once-beautiful girl.

They were beyond all that, and beyond the understanding. And they, God help him, would be his judges.

Amspoker picked up the receiver, began to dial.

"Yes?" Her voice was high, tense with a guarded edge. He was surprised at how girlish she sounded.

"Maddie."

"Oh." Her voice dropped, like a diver off a cliff. "Hello, Vic." The sound of his name was like a deep warm pool. As if the anger had never been. He realized how afraid he was of her anger. How much he wanted the warmth.

"How're the kids?"

"Fine." Up again, tense again. "If you came home once in a while you wouldn't have to ask."

"You think I like it in this frigging dormitory? You think I like working thirty hours a day? I'm sorry, Maddie. But I kill myself down here for you. You and the girls, that's all. You know that."

"Ninny was asking for you."

Guilt. It came needling in all his pores like a dash of ice water. "Look, I'll try to get back tonight. But I don't know. All hell's broken out here, do you have the radio on? We thought we had the guy and he was going out this door, running with a gun in his hand, and I let some go at him, Maddie. I just went pop. They could hand me my head on a tray over this, d'you understand? Hell of it is we're back to ground zero because he didn't check out anyway. So I don't know, I'll try to get back."

"It's okay, Vic. You don't have to come home tonight." Neutral now, as if she didn't care.

"Maddie, for Christ sake I want to. Don't you understand? I want to be with you and the girls very much, but I can't."

"You don't have to explain. Perfectly all right, okay?"

"I mean, you knew I was a cop when you married me."

"Yes."

"Okay, then. Just so you understand. I . . ." It was so hard, impossible to say. "I need your understanding."

Silence.

"Maddie?"

"I'm just tired, Vic. Just tired, that's all."

"I'll let you go, then. Say good night to the girls for me, will you? I'll try to get home tomorrow night."

"Don't break your neck on my account."

Click.

He stared down at the round mouth of the receiver. But at least he knew one thing. He didn't care what she had done, he wanted her, he wanted his family back.

The question was, did she still want him?

6:55 p.m.

Runyan's Onion was a grounded bar car for commuters anxious to delay the trip.

Yet even now, on a Sunday night, it was crowded.

Francie took a breath: peanuts, talc-dusted sweat. She was

sitting beside Kandis under an imitation Tiffany lamp that seemed to sway in a fog of smoke.

"Are you joinable, ladies?"

Ward Yates's black eyes were staring directly into hers, and she felt her nervous system jump. He was wearing the kind of jeans you sent to the dry cleaners, a brown-and-black-plaid shirt, and on a thin gold chain around his neck a tiny ivory hand with the thumb sticking up between the fingers. At this close range his features looked too small for his face, as if designed for a much shorter man.

"*Very* joinable," Kandis said.

Francie picked up her glass. The lime slice, backed by two ice cubes, crashed against her teeth.

Ward sat down beside her, fingers clutching a highball glass, which he raised unsteadily to his lips. "Kandis," he said, running the rim along his lip, "whyn't you run along home and leave me to get to know our new friend here?"

"Because," Francie said, "I'm supposed to meet a friend at seven-thirty and I'll be late already. In fact, I'd better call now."

"What are you, the White Rabbit?" Ward said. "I'm late, I'm late, I'm late?"

She slid out of the booth and pushed through the crowd toward the wall phone. The mirrored wall behind the bar was crowded with bottles, between which she could see the backs of heads as the men turned to look.

She tried his apartment, but no one answered.

"New York *Post*," the operator said.

"Miles Overby, please." She twisted the curled black cord. "Miles, it's me. I'm feeling really low. Wondered if we could maybe—"

"Speak up! Where are ya? Sounds like Times Square."

"Just a bar."

"Ah-hah. Din of iniquity. Look, Francie, I'd love to see

220

you but we're going bananas over here. Bombing in another
Chase branch. Be a bomb under me if I don't get this copy
in."

"Oh. I'm sorry, I didn't know."

"Go home. Get into bed. Alone. And take two aspirins.
I'll call you in the morning. And, Francie."

"Yes?"

"Love ya."

She replaced the receiver very gently on the hook.

Love ya. But did that mean the same as "I love you"?

She turned around. The booth in the back room seemed
suddenly far away, a porthole seen through the wrong end
of a telescope, across a shifting deck. She could see the
tanned disk of Ward's face as he raised another drink to
his lips. His roughened skin, scarred by acne, was shiny over
the rim. Why did such men hold a lure, an erotic glamour
that a genuinely nice person like Miles could never have?

She waved good-bye, but Kandis was laughing, leaning
close as Ward whispered into her ear.

The street outside was empty, the night wind sweeping
rubbish and a damp chill before it. She rubbed her arms,
bare in Alex's thin sundress, looking for the yellow of a cab
with the bright, glowing On sign above.

The cab was pulling up in front of her apartment building when through the metal partition the radio crackled out
the news: "Completely paralyzed from the waist down,
Xanthakis is . . ."

11:58 p.m.

The black skin felt grainy under his fingertips, as though
from a permanent case of goose bumps.

Miles drew her to him, her jutting breasts brushing his

221

chest. His tongue touched her closely cropped skull. The taste was raw, reminding him of turnips.

She pulled away. When she emerged from the bathroom she was completely naked, a white towel over her arm—a parody of a waiter.

Forget that. Forget that, you fuck. Forget Xanthakis and just get into it.

"Let's get us a little wash," she said. "Okay, honey?"

Her ministrations were nurselike, ruthless in their efficiency.

She walked over to the narrow bed, which was covered with a drooping, pebbly chenille spread. The light clicked off, leaving the room dim between the sporadic neon of the Times Square signs.

Two key things that everything comes down to. Survival and money.

She lay on the sheet beneath his gaze. Suddenly her legs forked apart and upward, bent at the knees. She clutched her hands together beneath her knees.

"Come on now, honey," she said.

What is omnipotent and omniscient besides God? Pattern. The existence of pattern.

He forced himself to stare down at her, seeking something, some suggestion of grace or animal crudity that could excite him. She was young and not unattractive, although her belly, now that she had removed the rayon print mini-dress, was thickened. He wondered if she was pregnant.

Her pubic hair dotted blacker against the surrounding skin, the tight kinks spiraling independently upward. The folds hung glistening pink, the puckered kernel below an absolute black.

A circle of men rules the country: from Ivy League universities to foundations to government posts to law firms and around again.

He lay on top of her, ground his hips against her, but still there was nothing. The turnip smell rose into his eyes.

The wall in his mind crumbled. He was staring again at the naked body on the wooden floor, toenails reaching out, just into the sun.

"Goin' havta hurry," she said. "Ain't got no hour, you know. You cryin'?"

2:11 a.m.

Pig. Piggie. Pig pig pig.

Stupid fat-assed fools.

He could do anything he wanted to any *she* in the city and the cops couldn't touch him.

Pig-brained bastards with guns for balls.

They were two thousand miles off on all the wrong tracks. When who he was so obvious.

Dalroi searched, sponging among his emotions for the satisfaction. But it had dried up, was gone.

He walked faster, turning south on First Avenue, passing the glassed slab, the sharp fence of the United Nations.

The enjoyment was gone.

He should have waited, that was all. It was the she who had been wrong. She was a stranger, not like the others, whom he loved.

He did still.

You took the time with someone you loved.

The other shes he had followed, crossed in front of, walked them home. He had looked at their names beside the buzzer, pressed their numbers. Light and young, hollow with echo, their voices had talked to him: "Yes? Who is this? Who's there?" He had learned their routines, their paths to and from, smelled their perfume waiting for a streetlight and a bus.

Yes, it was just that the she had been wrong.

He wouldn't feel like this with Paige MacLeish.

In the night air above him, still warm and dense, an electronic whir sounded. He started, looked up. The Twenty-eighth Street light blinked from green to red.

Beside him were derricks and cranes and mud, the sheared-off guts of a building. They were starting to tear down the old Bellevue Hospital complex, amputating the worst wards, peeling corridors, sooted bricks.

The streetlamp whirred to green. Dalroi didn't move.

At his grandmother's he had hunched down into chairs and over against walls and behind doors. At his grandmother's she had pulled him out, up into her broad lap. But then the wrecker had come, booms and smoke and lumber stripped from the framework, leaving a latticed suggestion of the remaining walls. And then there they were—all his special things exposed to view and the sun, all the places he had stuffed with secrets now opened up to any passing eye. The rooms where he had learned to laugh, briefly sketched in by a few doorframes.

And after the rubble and the hall toilet and the white floor tiles zigzag-bordered in pale blue had been hauled away, the reverse procedure began. The bare-bone scraps of the new building were set up, the outlines of rooms and walls and glassless windowframes, the tracings of floors. There were new rents his grandmother couldn't pay. *Even could we find one, she couldn't manage a new place, you know that, a pity, they said. Not with her hip, and did you see the price of bread?*

She was gone.

And he had watched them from the sidewalk, trying to fix what they had done. He had stared at the unmet corners

224

and rain-filled, cement-bag-slung rooms, where people would soon feel warm and enclosed. They would feel safe in clothed walls and down against overstuffed sofas and over in the darker corners.

The thought that their lives could be sent scattering out as easily as the debris of a wrecked building would scarcely cross their minds.

Chapter Nine

Monday, August 15
9:05 a.m.

Victor Amspoker felt the tiredness ride him like a hunchback into the coffee room. He shook the restaurant-sized glass sugar jar to bury the rattling lump, then upended it over his mug.

He drank. Well, at least it was hot.

When he walked back to his desk, the room was dim, the sunlight shuttered behind the closed blinds. Daytime, nighttime, the passage of days and dates had become one coagulation of work. And yet they were no closer than two file drawers of diligently pursued, diligently checked-out dead ends.

He sat down. In the wire basket on the corner of his desk lay a legal-sized white envelope, its spidery black script addressed to him.

He ran his finger under the flap.

My dear Mr. Amspoker:

I am a Roman Catholic priest and, of course, I am not free to break the seal of the confessional. Yet in the past week I have found myself much torn between my pledge of silence and my obligation to protect the lives of innocent people.

Certain information has come into my possession that is of the greatest importance to the police.

I am writing to you now because my dilemma has been resolved by a fortuitous circumstance, enabling me to tell you some of the particulars.

A penitent of mine, who calls himself Dalroi St. Gryphon, visited me recently. I am not free to reveal what was said in the confessional box. But I can tell you that he was unable to make a firm purpose of amendment, and consequently, although tormented in my mind, I was forced to refuse him absolution.

In the event, he returned last night in an agitated state, at three A.M., and sought my advice. I was very relieved that we were able to have the conversation in the parlor in a counseling situation. Under such circumstance, I feel no longer bound to secrecy, insofar as revealing the content of that particular conversation.

Mr. St. Gryphon is consumed by an increasing urge to kill an innocent young woman.

I of course counseled him to go immediately to the police, to turn himself in, but his fear is that he may not possess sufficient will to do so. Neither can he attest that he will be able to avoid the enactment of his urge.

I lay the matter now in your hands, and in the hands of the Almighty. I myself can do no more, save to point the way. The individual of whom I speak is a member of the police force of New York City.

I hesitate to sign my own name lest I be pressured to break the seal of the confessional. In deepest appreciation for your attention to this matter, I remain

> Sincerely yours,
> Cognitor

Chief of Detectives John J. Donoghue laid the letter back down on his polished dining-room table. The thump of his fingers against wood jarred the silence.

"A priest," Detective Bill Szkotak said. "Think of it. A fuckin' killer confessing to his *priest*. Sweet God in heaven."

Donoghue traced his finger along the edge of the letter. "God's not the problem. The problem is what this damn thing says—accusing a cop. Undoubtedly nothing to it, but ... More coffee? Can't take the credit, it's this Colombian blend I get ground up for myself."

There was something inexplicably but definitely wrong with the taste. Slowly Victor Amspoker pushed his cup forward, followed by Lieutenant Jimmy Reid, Sergeant Brune Corolla, and Frank Quinn—who was nursing a reopened peptic ulcer and had been limiting himself to skim milk.

Deputy Chief Inspector Andrew Halle sat with thick arms stretched out on the table in front of him, hooded eyes fixed on the sheet of expensive white bond. "We could be running off half-cocked here. There's no evidence this priest's for real."

"No evidence he's not," Amspoker cut in.

"We showed the letter to the monsignor," Donoghue said, referring to the septuagenarian in the Chaplains' Unit. "He says it looks like the real article."

With a flick of his eyelids Halle turned his attention from Amspoker to Donoghue. "Any fingerprints, we should be so lucky?"

"Zero. Priority one is we find this cop the priest refers to. Whether he did it or just likes to mouth off in the confessional we'll worry later. If there *is* this cop, which I seriously doubt. Priority two is we clamp the lid on. Why you're here now. Can't tip our hand or we'll blow the whole thing. We'll meet here odd hours, and just don't run off about it in your sleep or to some lovely, understood?"

"What in hell does that name mean?" Brune Corolla said. " 'Cognitor'?"

"It's Latin for 'The Knower,'" Quinn said. " 'One who knows.' "

"Okay, now," Donoghue said. "Jimmy, first I want you to go personally to Shafer and dig through the bad-apple barrel with him."

Heads nodded. It was rumored the director of the Psychological Services Unit had hundreds of names.

"Now, most of the guys on the force, as you all know, are Catholic," Donoghue continued. "The most religious we can figure are in the line organizations, right? Biggest is the Holy Name Society—annual communion breakfast pulls four thousand cops. Quinn, I want you to hit the line organizations—get us a list of all names. We'll start there. The rest of you, paste your ears on the ground and see what the locker-room scuttlebutt says, who's having problems, and so on."

Inspector Halle leaned forward, his massive shoulders straining the white stitching on his brown jacket. "I have the six-month IAD records here," he said. He drew a sheet from the folder. "Seventy-two cops in hot water so far this year. Thirty-six arrested, same number suspended or put on modified assignment. That's eleven more total than the first half of last year."

Donoghue's eyes narrowed as they ran down the list of names. "Fine. I'll check these out personal. It'll be a pleasure."

"We also got three thousand seven hundred thirty-eight names from the Civilian Complaint Review Board," Quinn said. "Working those up now."

"Jimmy, you pull as many men as you need to cover this," Donoghue told the lieutenant. "You got thirty thousand cops to check over. But it's gotta be done neat. No loose ends. No talkers, you got that?"

"Right," the lieutenant said.

"Point is . . ." Halle said, slipping the band off a large gray-green cigar. He lit up, into air already blue with smoke. "Point is, this could put us on the political hot seat, what with the PBA locking horns with the commissioner over every little piece of business."

Heads nodded. The Patrolmen's Benevolent Association had nineteen thousand members and a Committee on Political Education that was backed up by a computer. The cops, the PBA president was saying, were going to be militant as the other public-employee unions—the sanitation men, the teachers, the transit workers. You went after one cop, he said, and they all got hurt.

"Agreed," Donoghue said. "Too many fuckin' eyes down on us already. First the Knapp Commission, now the PBA. Remember the field day the papers had with those two city ex-detectives—that hit scheme on the Denver businessman? One convicted of homicide, the other conspiracy? We get hit enough ourselves from the outside. Let's not go giving 'em any free ammunition."

"Let's look on the bright side," Quinn said. "This letter's

the break we've been waiting for on this case. This is pay dirt, fresh as hell, I can smell it."

"You better do more than smell it, you goddamn better get the animal dropped it," Halle said. "And that's straight from the commissioner, buddy."

"Could be any cop, uniform or not," Amspoker said. "Hell, we all know at least one guy should retire tomorrow. The important thing here is we follow this where it leads, even if it goes to the top."

"What make you think this bird's at the top?" Halle said, voice arctic.

"I didn't say that. Just that we can't justify digging at the bottom when the dirt may be anywhere."

"You made your point, Vic," the lieutenant said.

"Whatever we do," Quinn said, "we better do it fast. According to this letter, he's planning to hit another girl."

3:22 p.m.

He was watching the muscular globes of Kirsten Ray's ass as she maneuvered the rows of dirty-beige, olive-green, turquoise, and gray typewriters over to the *Webster's Unabridged,* whose page edges were completely blackened by inky fingers.

She was a blonde given to leaning against desks, tilting her pelvis in the direction of any nearby male. She reminded him, Miles Overby thought, of the girls reclining in daisy fields in cigarette ads, graffitied with bubbles that read "Fuck me, baby."

He stubbed out his cigarette and looked down at the take of copy rolled into the carriage.

STRANGLER SPURS CALLS

by Miles K. Overby III

"Could I be next?" That is what many women who live alone or whose husbands work at night are asking themselves, in the wake of last week's sex slaying of two Manhattan career girls. A third victim, from Montauk, Long Island, has been linked to the case.

Hundreds of frightened women callers from across the city are dialing the seventeenth floor of 1 Police Plaza, where two policewomen dispense reassurance and calm.

"You're not a reporter, you're an alarmist," Julie had said.

He ripped the paper from the machine, crumpled it with one hand and tossed it toward the wastebasket. *Jump shot. Overby puts it in and . . .*

It hit the lip and bounced on the floor.

Caring, he thought, is a vestigial organ. A way of behaving that once was useful but is no longer.

He squinted his eye to avoid the smoke, rolled a fresh copy book into the typewriter.

But the trouble was that the singles life—the touted armies of "Good-in-Bed-and-No-Strings-Attached"—just didn't *exist*. Everyone, male and female, was just too fucked up. There were too many spillovers, great tidal waves of neurosis that crashed down on the bed. It was ingress, egress, *regress* every time.

Miles leafed through the folder marked ALEX. There was an idea, had to be a hook for a story in there. Her last night, he thought. She had spent it with the only son of a rich

Mexican, eating two frozen Celeste ("Everything you like and plenty of it!") sausage pizzas, watching Channel 9, *Boris Karloff Presents—The Lethal Ladies*, followed by Channel 13, Marlene Dietrich in *The Blue Angel*.

He began to type.

The phone on his desk rang, adding its voice to the other phones shrilling on other desks. He picked it up.

The caller was Emmanuel Gold.

Miles shifted the phone from his right to his left side, clamping the receiver between jaw and shoulder. His fingers continued to type.

"Miles, old buddy, I got something here hotter'n hell. But first your guarantee. This is off the record, all right?"

He stopped typing. "Sure, Manny."

He could hear Gold's asthmatic breathing through the line. "Yeah, Manny. You got my word. Off the record."

"Okay. I got a call this A.M., come down to the police medical department at Three-forty-six Broadway, see the dentist."

"You got a cavity?"

"Cram it. Now listen. The dentist wants me to go over all the records they got on cop teeth. Why? To see if I can draw a match with, un-huh, *the Baskin bite mark*."

Miles felt his heart contract. Every corpuscle in his body screamed for the story. "Jesus, Manny. Just Jesus."

"Jehovah. Now, here's the free Cracker Jack giveaway. You listening? You can print the cops're looking for a cop. But no mention of dentists, teeth, bite mark. Agreed?"

"You want me to kiss your ass, I'll do it. Yeah, *agreed*. You go for Coors, don't you?"

"Yeh."

"Expect a case over this afternoon."

"They're back again," Paige MacLeish said.

"What are back, Paige?"

"The damn rape fantasies."

"Tell me about them."

Paige stared down at the blue-tiled table. On it were an appointment book, a bound volume entitled *Medical Aspects of Human Sexuality*, a china dish filled with foil-wrapped Hershey's kisses, and an economy-size box of Kleenex.

There was no ashtray. Someone had told her shrinks forbade ashtrays because smoking lessened your tension.

"Do you want to tell me about them, Paige?"

She looked up. Aurelia was sitting, legs crossed, in the other upholstered chair, a bulky woman nearing fifty. She was wearing an oatmeal linen suit with Ultrasuede patches on the jacket elbows—Ralph Lauren, Paige guessed, and on *my* money. She ran a hand through her cloud of thick, wavy brown hair streaked with gray, her face battered with the effort, Paige thought, of looking infinitely accepting.

"I haven't had them, the fantasies," Paige said, "since Christmas last year. And then that thing happening with Alex. And now they're back."

"What are they about, Paige?"

"It's just that—I'm just so *ashamed*."

"Why?"

"You know."

"I don't know until you tell me."

"Because . . . *I get off on them*. Have an orgasm. I use them for that. And they're disgusting. Degrading and humiliating."

"Why don't you describe one for me."

Paige looked across to the tall windows, which were green

and gold with the sun through hanging plants. There was nothing wrong with Aurelia's philodendrons. It had to be a good sign.

"This is one. I even know where I got it—that damn book *Hell's Angels*. I'm on my back on a green pool table with my Hell's Angel boyfriend. He pulls up my dress and does it. Incidentally, I'm very thin in this fantasy. I like the feeling, but just as I'm really getting excited, he comes. Then he looks up over my shoulder. I look back and see this huge, greasy, potbellied guy swaggering through the door. 'Take your time,' he says. 'I'll wait my turn.' Three other guys crowd in behind him. Then potbelly's on me and I'm screaming, struggling, hollering to my boyfriend, but he just slaps my face. I feel potbelly go in and I get this rush. I wrap my legs up around his back. I hear the men all jeering at me because it's *not rape*, I *like it*. Then I come."

There was a silence. In the other chair, Aurelia was looking out the window.

"I mean," Paige said, "isn't that the pits? A feminist with rape fantasies?"

"Paige, we've discussed this. Many women, probably most, have similar—"

"And then the other, it's from *Pelham One Two Three*. I can't even originate my own rape fantasies. I'm down in the subway and there's a catastrophe, a wreck of some sort. People are running for the exits, screaming, shouting. A black man claps a hand over my mouth and drags me into a filthy men's restroom. Two men see him do this. I'm on the cold, stinking floor and the black man is raping me. I see the two men come through the door. To save me! I scream to them but they just grin and shut the door. One opens his fly and starts masturbating. Then the black man gets off and the masturbator gets on. And then I come."

Paige reached for a Kleenex.

"When do you find yourself having these fantasies?"

"When I masturbate. I get to a certain point, and then I don't want to think about them but I know they'll make me come. But how can I *hate* myself like that—that it's exciting to be degraded and used. *Why?*"

"Paige, remember last fall we discussed your fears about self-assertion? A rape fantasy is a self-assertion fear. Women are brought up to be passive, to feel they'll be punished if they strive for what they want—in sex, work, and in their relationships. By getting yourself gang-raped you get to be passive and feminine, so you don't have to feel any guilt. And yet you still get all the sex you really want. You're perfectly normal and healthy. You have a normal healthy interest in having sex."

Paige wadded the Kleenex in her hand, then opened it, watching the tissue fluff out like cotton.

"But how do you know I don't have rape fantasies because every book and movie shows you rape? You're thirteen, fourteen, the first time you see sex in a movie it's rape. So you think: sex equals rape. The thing is, it's so goddamn unfair! Men don't have to grow up like women do—seeing torture, rape, and death done to them by the opposite sex. Women don't go around raping and killing random men. How am I supposed to love a man, have sex with a man now, after seeing what a man did to Alex?"

The psychiatrist watched the wavering band of sunlight through the panes of glass. "It isn't really all so unequal, Paige. Men are terrified by women, too. That's why they do what you've just said."

Her patient made a derisive noise.

The psychiatrist crossed to a bookcase, withdrew a volume and began leafing through. "Here. This is by Karen Horney. You said she made a lot of sense to you."

Paige blew her nose into the Kleenex.

236

"Quote. 'Is it not really remarkable (we ask ourselves in amazement), when one considers the overwhelming mass of this transparent material, that so little recognition and attention are paid to the fact of men's secret dread of women?' Unquote. Horney says how surprised she was herself to first hear that idea—and from Groddeck, a man, too."

"Surprising? It's just not true. Women are afraid of *men*, not vice versa."

"But, Paige. Every man was once tiny, dominated by an all-powerful, mysterious, and terrifying female—his mother. It's the source of all those menstrual taboos, that the blood can be fatal, crops will wither away, hunters will take nothing. That's fear. Fear of the female genitals. Fear of women."

"But those are primitive societies, Aurelia. Those are uneducated men who don't know physiology."

"No. I'll tell you a little story. About how terrified of women the most sophisticated New York City men can be. And with your understanding of that, maybe you can gain some acceptance of all these unfortunate things."

Paige looked across at her, the anger on her face giving way to curiosity.

"I have a male analysand," the psychiatrist said, "who's high up in publishing. He was telling me about a meeting to consider artwork for the paperback cover of *Jaws*. Various drawings were passed around until they came to one. It showed the skeletal jawbones of a shark, spread wide, teeth all around the edges. Seen through the teeth was a tiny swimmer. Now, these men, Paige, are truly sophisticated. It only took one man to voice the comparison before the others agreed and voted it down."

"What comparison?"

"It looked, he said, like a *'vagina dentata.'* A common but terrifying, often impotence-causing male fantasy. It means a vagina that's armed inside with teeth."

He saw the she come out through the black door with the brass knob, stand a moment under the white-lettered canopy. The she smiled with many bright teeth at the uniformed black doorman, the way she smiled at all men.

All men, Dalroi thought. Except him.

The late-afternoon sun was warm on the red, yellow, and white zinnias planted along the island dividing Park Avenue's four lanes. Paige MacLeish glanced across at the massed ruffled domes of the flowers and then looked north, hesitating as if to make up her mind. She shifted her wicker briefcase from her right hand to her left and walked south toward Seventy-third Street.

Across the island, on the other side of the avenue, Dalroi followed. In the sun the she's legs flashed pale beneath a mid-calf brown dress, hair a brilliant spot of red-gold threading between the passersby, keeping her easily in view.

His heart expanded, pushing the anger through his body. He heard it pounding in his ears.

He was alive, he was safe, he could still feel.

At Sixtieth Street the she turned east toward the homeward-bound crowds thronging Lexington Avenue. Walking quickly, Dalroi crossed Park Avenue and closed the distance between them. The she was directly in front of him. He watched her walk, feet striking heavily in worn stacked heels, bright head bobbing in tandem up and down.

Just as the she reached the corner of Lexington Avenue the flashing "Don't Walk" sign turned a steady red. The she darted across the street with an awkward knee-knocking gait, forcing the first cars through the intersection to brake. There was a cacophony of horns.

Had the she spotted him?

Dalroi stood at the corner, staring across the rush of cars, trucks, and cabs. The she was passing the palsied comic-book hawker and moving toward the revolving glass door of Bloomingdale's, the expensive department store.

There was a cloud of stinking exhaust, the bellows sound of released brakes, and a Lexington Avenue bus erased her image.

When it passed, Dalroi stared at the revolving door, which turned ceaseless as a water wheel, picking up and spewing out a stream of gay men, models, and older women sheltering under designer straw hats. But the she was lost within.

He had time, he thought. Yes. And it would be good.

It would be the way it had been with Alexandra.

8:37 p.m.

Miles walked out of his cramped kitchen with a white towel over one arm, bowed, kissed her hand and began to serve.

"The *plat du jour*," he said, "is sautéed chicken livers with grapes. The selection caressing your eardrums is Telemann: *Musique de table*, Suite Number Two. Appropriate, no?"

Francie laughed. She loved grapes. And if she drank a lot of wine as quickly as possible, she might even get the chicken livers down.

The green candle had guttered beneath the rim of the glass when Miles stood up, clumsily embraced her, and led her into the darkened bedroom.

She lay on her back on the cool striped sheets. On the floor beside the brass bed the heap of fake fur glowed phosphorescent. Like an animal, she thought. After nuclear rain.

Miles was lying between her thighs, darting his tongue in

239

and out, in and out, like the Tom Thumb of penises. She was wondering if she should tell him the clitoris was farther up. But she didn't know how to pronounce the word: was the emphasis on "clit" or on "tor"?

Then she felt the pressure of him between her thighs, the thick hard parting, and tasted herself on his lips.

It was hard to breathe. The desert air rushed from the vent, her chest corrugating over the hot slats as she stared into the bedroom below.

The soles of her father's feet were yellow as egg yolk. There were sounds and her mother's white arched feet fell out to the side, moved back, fell out and moved back like counterweights tied to the sounds.

It was hard to breathe.

They would see her here, wrench her away, smack her, yellow whorls of callus stinging down on her small pink knuckles. She felt them flush angry red.

Bad girl, oh, you naughty hell-bent bad girl, bad girl. You won't learn won't learn won't learn.

She moved her legs beneath Miles, and his thrusts came faster, and then faster.

"Ah," he said in a matter-of-fact tone.

The telephone was ringing.

She felt Miles shrink inside her, first with a jerk, then with a swift, deflating movement. He fell out of her with a belching sound.

"Damn," he said.

She sat up on the bed as he walked toward the living room, back stiff with anger.

"Yeah? Ummm. Yeah. Look, I can't talk right now. Indisposed, you know."

She felt the bumps rise in waves along her naked body, the hairs stirring on each elevation, antennae probing to hear.

"Um. Right. No, really. Can't possibly. I can't, Patty."

Patty? Who was Patty?

The arcing splash of urine sounded from the closed bathroom door. The toilet flushed.

Francie looked up.

Miles stood in the bedroom door, his narrow naked body backlit by fluorescence. She watched his penis quiver beside his thigh, drawing up into the beginning of an erection.

(John 8:44)—Ye are of your father the devil, and the lusts of your father ye will do. He was a murderer from the beginning . . .

She watched his bare toes grip the wood as he crossed toward her. She felt the breath leave her body. She wondered: had she always felt this much desire?

She cried out as he entered her again.

"Good night, chooch," he said at the door to her apartment. He touched his fingers to his lips and then, gently, to her crotch.

She felt a rush of tenderness. "Good night, Miles."

She watched him walk toward the elevator, the backs of his socks still showing. He turned and saluted before stepping in.

She felt very warm, the crotch of her pants sopping. She closed the door and threw the three locks. She felt a sense of elation, independence, freedom. It was like a dull, flickering pain that promised at any moment to flood into the most intense pleasure.

She whirled suddenly, hugging her arms that in Alex's gray crepe-de-chine blouse felt as soft, as silky as the muzzle of a horse groping on your palm for the lump of sugar.

She remembered dressing up in two crinkly white petticoats, one as a skirt, the other veillike around her head, and dancing to *Swan Lake* on the living-room rug. She remembered dancing on the lawn one late evening, the sprinkler

241

hissing, weaving the fireflies into her dance. She had caught one: "Mama, look!" "Let that go now, Francie. That's God's own creature you've got there." It had pulsed in her closed palm, like a candle in a jack-o'-lantern; then her prison fingers had opened, it had crawled to the edge and flown away. She had run after it, flapping her arms.

Then she heard the crying, faint behind the closed bedroom door.

Paige was lying on her side facing the wall, a jumbled heap of brown bedspread.

"Paige, what's the matter? What's wrong?"

The reply was muffled.

They were out of Kleenex. Francie placed a fresh roll of toilet paper beside her fingers. "I've been so selfish, Paige. Is that it? Me going out with Miles, leaving you here?"

Paige unrolled the toilet paper, sat up and blew her nose. "No, Francie. Of course it's not that."

"I understand, really. I'll just stay home. Or we'll go out together from now on, okay?"

"No, really. It's not all that. It's the other stuff. It's just all the other stuff."

"What other stuff?" (*Genesis 3:16*)—*Unto the woman he said, I will greatly multiply thy sorrow and thy conception.*

"To die isn't so bad," Paige said. She scrubbed at her face with the toilet paper. "I mean, we all have to die sometime, right? But it's the *way* Alex died. I just can't accept it. The thought that he could get enjoyment from her suffering, her death. How can I ever accept that? It just seems like the ultimate evil."

Chapter Ten

Tuesday, August 16
8:36 a.m.

John Steinbeck had also started as a lowly police reporter, Miles thought, for the . . . what was it? The old, now-defunct New York *American*. And look the hell how far Steinbeck had gone.

Miles whistled as he walked past the three blue-and-white *Post* delivery trucks backed up to the dock. He waved to the dispatcher with his folded "Metro," the first edition (*his* edition), which had been put to bed at 6:45 A.M. by the lobster shift.

He rounded the Post Mortem Lounge in the southeast corner of the New York Post Building, whose fortresslike concrete was interrupted by windows only above the third floor. Already the air was a saturated sponge. He paused in the shade beneath one of the tall, scaling sycamores, unfolding the paper and glancing again at the front page.

LETTER SAYS
STRANGLER IS COP

by Miles K. Overby III

An anonymous letter addressed to Detective Third Grade Victor Amspoker, of the 4th Zone Homicide Squad, claims that a member of the New York City Police Department is guilty of the strangulation of three young women in the New York area. All were sexually assaulted.

Detective Amspoker, one of the principal investigators in the case, was not available for comment.

A number of policemen or former policemen, possibly as many as nine, it was learned yesterday, are currently under surveillance as possible suspects in the case. . . .

The elevator opened on the fourth-floor hall, whose walls were painted olive green and orange, the ceiling royal blue. Miles followed the hanging blue pipe to the city room, which was a cacophony of telephones and typewriters.

"Hey," Beinsdorf shouted from the copy desk. "Good show, shorty."

"Thanks. *Baldy.*"

"Lowry wants to see you," Kirsten Ray said. "Pronto."

She was leaning against her desk, pelvis tilted in—yes, this time—*his* direction. The twin bones jutted cunningly through the fabric of her skirt.

Well, somebody had said it: success was the greatest aphrodisiac of them all.

"Yeah," Arnold Lowry said as he tapped on the open glass door.

The managing editor's window was green with ferns, beyond which Miles could see a tugboat steaming up the East River. Laminated front pages covered one wall, on another a sign in bold red: THANK GOD FOR THE WASHINGTON POST. On Lowry's cluttered desk sat a silver-and-black plaque presented at a particularly drunken office party following Nixon's resignation. THE OFFAL OFFICE, it read.

"Sit down, sit down," Lowry said, waving at a plastic chair. He continued reading through a stack of papers on his desk.

Miles sat down, crossed his leg at the knee. The muscle in his cheek jumped.

Lowry's gray eyes beneath their jungle of brow darted up at Miles. Suddenly he threw back his head, his narrow chest jerking with laughter. "Hell, Miles. *Hell.* The *Times*, the *News*—we got 'em shitting razor blades over this one."

If only his father could see this, Miles thought, remembering the ass-numbing piano bench, his fingers like wood clunking up and down, the *Times* clipping his father handed him at dinner: "Music has a core of such pure intuition that a child genius can display his powers quite early, not limited by experience, like merely talented children."

Miles attempted a small, hopefully modest smile. "Thank you, sir."

"Now, I know the police shack's a boot camp for you guys. But we may be seeing our way to kicking you upstairs in a bit. If you don't slack off."

Miles constructed the voice on the phone, *basso* with power: "Overby? We sure as hell liked your story over here, Overby. This is Arthur at the *Times*." "*Arthur Gelb?*"

"Now, get the fuck going," Lowry said, "and flesh out this pygmy for the second edition. I want to stick it up the *Times* and break it off."

"My sentiments exactly," Miles said.

9:16 a.m.

"You wanna know what it felt like, *mes amis*, I'll *tell* you what it felt like."

Kandis balanced the pencil on its point, eraser against her palm. Her long fingers flared, like a spider, then closed one by one on the stalk.

"*Betrayal*," she said.

The pencil lead broke with a snap.

Francie Perry looked at her across the bouquet of dried flowers and the copy of the *Post*. There were four of them discussing the headline around Kandis's desk—Ward Yates sitting on the desk across the aisle, drumming his heels against the metal side, Mary Sills and Fred-the-projectionist on borrowed chairs.

Francie's gaze went back to Ward, who was wearing an oxford-blue button-down shirt, unbuttoned on black sprouts that foreshadowed the thicket below. He was giving her the old eyes-from-under-squinting-brows, which were equally black. But then, he seemed always to be squinting, as if peering ahead into what he knew would be a disastrous future.

"I mean," Kandis said, "there he was, our *security* guard, the old douche bag, telling us, 'Oh, girls, my God, *burglary*, oh, my God, dis is terrible, it's dat element, girls, dat ele-

246

ment lives here now.' And all the time *he* was the burglar!"

Francie looked down at the folded *Post* on her desk. *By Miles K. Overby III.* It had jarred her with a thrill, everyone reading the story and talking about it, no one knowing that she was the one Miles K. Overby loved. It was like sitting on the scarred wood benches at the Bitter End, watching the male folksinger in his tight jeans and Frye boots, watching the girlfriend he'd introduced as "my old lady," in the front row, her face up to him trying to reflect some light.

Only now *she* was the girlfriend.

The one all the men wanted.

Francie felt Ward's eyes examining her, down over her thighs, knees, ankles and then slowly back up, suctioning in any detail he might have missed.

"But if you can't trust the cops," Mary was saying, "who can you trust?"

"You just gotta have street smarts about people," Ward said. "But you either got street smarts or you don't. Like sex appeal."

She wondered what his cock looked like.

There was a sudden silence, and Ward eased down to his feet. Walking toward them was Milo Greene, director of creative services. He was frowning down at the circle of lapis lazuli buckled with gold links around his wrist.

After his stiff back passed, the group broke for cover.

Francie turned back to face her desk. There was no letter rolled into the typewriter, no memos scribbled in Nagy's red ink (for immediate action) or blue ink (do by 4 P.M.) stuffed into her In box.

Tibor Nagy, vice-president and group creative director, had not shown up for work since Friday.

His wife had taken ill. A long-term malady, possibly fatal, it was understood.

Of course, there was also the matter of the tardily (perhaps

247

too tardily?) acknowledged affair with his murdered secretary. The calls on New York Telephone records from his Manhattan *pied-à-terre* (as Kandis described it), and from Gurney's Inn in Montauk and from Pensacola, Florida, to their old apartment number. There was also the matter of his mistress, rumors of beatings and rubber garments. His visits four times weekly to a shrink on "Freud Row"—Park Avenue. There was the matter of excessive drinking. His assault on a man in a bar, charges dropped.

The police had interviewed him five times, once invading his broad-windowed office, where it was rumored he had hidden a tape recorder in his calendar pad. They had taken his fingerprints, but word was they did not match the single as-yet-unidentified partial print found in their apartment. *Where* in their apartment? Even Amspoker had refused to tell.

Instead of dying out, with Nagy's exit the stories accelerated, crackling out from Runyan's Onion across town to the tables in the back room of P. J. Clarke's, where (Miles said) Aristotle Onassis used to and Governor Carey still did slum it with reporters, movie stars and other low-lifes, even an occasional ad man who had a certain kind of tale to tell— that success and money and high station bred disaster.

It was called irony, and it went down as sharp and satisfying as the olive in a Tanqueray martini.

In the Monday after-hours halls of Gilbert, Levensky, & Hane, someone said Nagy had been fired, not for the death of his secretary/girlfriend (which made a lot of people nervous), but for the ass of Milo Greene's girlfriend (the new Avon girl, Cari Swenson), which he had grabbed at a soiree in Hampton Bays. Which caused the producer of Cari's last three commercials—a balding man in a tie-dyed leisure suit, gold chains snagging his chest hair—to demand that in the American system of justice, by God, a man was innocent until proven guilty. That Nagy's accusers were a bunch of no-ball friggers, that Nagy had been made the innocent butt of an indiscriminate dirt-eating police investigation.

The producer enjoyed the center of attention for well over ten minutes.

She almost missed them, Francie thought, the monsters of *Nebula* magazine—the she creatures and robotized men. They were innocent by comparison.

A phalanx of late-night television monsters flew, crashed, and slithered through her mind: *Brachyura—Attack of the Crab Monsters; Hirudinea—The Giant Leeches; Mantis Religiosa—The Deadly Mantis.* Even *King Kong, Son of Kong, King Kong Versus Godzilla, King Kong Escapes, Konga,* and now the new, improved, women's-lib remake of *King Kong*—they all had the same thing in common. Girls hanging head down in the monster's paw, feeler, pincers. Girls writhing backward in the torn shreds of a dress away from the reaching paw, feeler, pincers.

But why *that* image?

Why was that the arresting, archetypal image that sold millions of tickets and millions of books? (The nightmares came along for free.)

Why did a screaming woman make you want, no, *demand* to buy?

11:39 a.m.

Paige MacLeish threw the second edition of the *Post* at her wastebasket. It missed, sheets flapping mantalike over the carpet. When it came to rest, the headline stared back up at her: LETTER SAYS STRANGLER IS COP, hateful byline in full view.

Overby was a panderer, a jackal of the worst sort; Francie was making an ass out of herself over him and acting as though Alex had never *been;* she herself was being treated like a secretary by the new prick, Beaham, whose last memo wasn't even *grammatical,* for God's sake.

And now this. A *policeman* killed Alex? Had Alex had a thing for cops (too)? Well, there were Sylvester Stallone groupies and Jimmy Connors groupies and Mick Jagger groupies and Henry Kissinger groupies. As the song went, there was something about a man in uniform. She supposed there must be cop groupies, too.

Outside her office she could hear the staccato hum of the electric typewriters. Her head jumped with the return of each carriage.

She was remembering Monday night, sitting on the subway, the man across from her reading *Newsday,* the headline in the corner that said GIRL ON ERRAND RAPED. Would they say MAN ON ERRAND ROBBED? Of course not. Moral: girls, play it safe. Stay home where you fucking *belong!*

She lit a fresh True, inhaled sharply, reached to put it in the notch of the ashtray and found a cigarette already there.

Do something. When you felt like this, the only way to handle it was to do something. She leaned forward to dial Samuel R. Baskin.

Her hand hesitated above the Touchtone buttons. It was a problem. There wasn't a man on the floor that pushed his own buttons. The secretaries were the watchers at the gate: one dialed another, who flicked the intercom and told her boss that so-and-so (through his secretary) was on the line, then got back and told the calling secretary okay, raise the moat, put *your* boss on the line.

Oh, fuck it all.

She punched the number herself.

"May I speak to Mr. Baskin, please? This is Paige Mac-

Leish. Thanks. Mr. Baskin? This is—"

"Yes, my dear. My secretary told me. How are you feeling today?"

Fucking rotten, thank you, she thought. Throat feels like I've given deep tonsils to a corrugated pipe. And I think I'm being followed (men can't resist me), absurd isn't it, it's why I took karate two years ago in the first place. *Kiai!*

"I'm fine, Mr. Baskin. Much as can be expected. How is Mrs. Baskin?"

"Frankly, I worry about her. I know a call from you or Francie would cheer her up. She's been depressed about the whole thing, understandably, of course. But she just doesn't show signs of picking herself up the way she should."

I know a hunky-dory shrink. A real nice lady who'll convince her that her real problem is she hates her sweet, intelligent, good, liberal, right-thinking parents. Electra complex, deep dark and sexy, don't you know. See, she doesn't hate men. She loves her poppa. And her roommate getting killed has exacerbated her symptoms, you like that word?

"I'm sorry to hear that, Mr. Baskin. I'll give her a call this afternoon."

"You sound a bit upset, Paige. Anything wrong? Anything I can do for you girls?"

"Well, I suppose you read this morning's headlines."

"Yes. Gave me a bit of a turn."

"Well, I just don't see . . . I mean, how can you set cops to investigate cops? If it's one of their own, they'll just draw the wagons around, cover up, who knows what? And you're a man respected in this town, Mr. Baskin. I just wondered if you might . . ."

"Call somebody?"

"Yes. I don't know who—the mayor or someone. Someone outside the police department, who will see this cop is *found*."

"I'm sure the police are doing everything they can to—"

"I want to see him behind bars, Mr. Baskin. In the *chair*. I'd pull the switch myself." Her own voice startled her. The naked lust for revenge, the sound of the lynch mob. And she had laughed, sure of her superiority while reading the leaflet that said "Advanced Methodology in Spiritual and Psychic Growth." The teacher was a man she had once had coffee with, who leaned over his cup to educate her: "Only one thing for it. Bring back public executions for blacks."

"Paige, my dear," Mr. Baskin was saying. "You're giving yourself a lot of worry, but what does it accomplish? Natural, I guess. But the police are the only experts we've got at finding criminals. We have to leave it to the experts, not interfere, and trust that they'll do their best. Now, I know several members of the force—at the top, I might add—and I have been assured, quite firmly assured, that this madman will indeed be caught."

But for whom, Paige thought, did she really want revenge? Was it for Alex? Or herself?

Boys have an external, easily controlled genital they are given permission to touch—when urinating. Girls have only a hole where the baby comes out. A c-r-a-c-k, like in a sidewalk. Menstruation is another example of the lack of control over the vagina (uncontrollable soiling). "You have two ovaries, a uterus, and a vagina, Paige." Yeah, but, Tessa, what about my joy button? "An overcompensation of her intellectual growth has occurred to compensate for the missing penis." Bullshit. But there she was, page 72 of the Sarah Lawrence yearbook, under the caption "Phi Beta Kappa" —hands down in front of her crotch, thumbs hooked, index fingers forming a V. Very interesting, my dear.

"Assurances," she said, "are one thing, Mr. Baskin. But—"

"Even should they find him," he cut in, "it won't bring Alex back, now, will it? None of us will forget Alex, but

252

we must put her behind us, so to speak. Get on with the living, that's my advice."

But how did you put behind you someone who—after she had been told to move out, two women couldn't stand her—sang in the shower the last morning of her life?

"Maybe you're right, Mr. Baskin. Thanks for listening."

"All right. Now, you take care of yourself, Paige."

She replaced the receiver and lit another cigarette. But how did you put behind you *yourself?* That was the big one. She knew if the man were before her now, and she had a gun, she would blast his madness into a pool of blood. How did you put behind you the murderer that was yourself?

She remembered all those debates cross-legged on the dormitory floor—"spreads," they were called, and that's what they did to her thighs: the bowls of buttered popcorn, the chocolate-chip cookies and the paper-cup wine. The mind stirring and coming alive, darting between points and settling back to ponder and reaching, suddenly, the pinnacle of an idea.

It was *right,* she had said, for a criminal to go free because he hadn't received the Miranda warnings: the right to remain silent and so forth. "But what if he *murdered* someone?" Bea had said. "Can that be right, to release a *murderer?*" *Yes,* because it's the principle that matters, she had answered, don't you see, the principle of the thing. One guilty person might go free, okay, yes, but thousands could be saved from police coercion.

Fardface. (It had been her favorite campus epithet— sounding so obscene and yet all innocence: "fard" meant to paint with cosmetics.)

How the others must have laughed at her, back in their rooms.

For how could concern for thousands you had never met

compete with this wild bubbling, this screaming for revenge? She felt scorn for her sweet collegiate liberal concern—as outdated as patchwork, too sweet, too charitable to be true.

Now the principle had died, was buried as Alex.

The only thing alive was the will to revenge.

It was in the Fifth Song of *Astrophel and Stella*, she remembered circling the lines for her thesis with a yellow marking pen:

Revenge, revenge, my muse, defiance's trumpet blow;
Threaten what may be done, yet do more than you threaten.
Ah, my suit granted is, I feel my breast doth swell;
Now child, a lesson new you shall begin to spell;
Sweet babes must babies have, but shrewd girls must be beaten.

Beaten, yeah, she had to admit it.

She stubbed out her cigarette, shook another from the pack.

She had turned out to be—well, almost, she thought—as human as anyone.

12:02 p.m.

It was like watching his youngest, Ninette, stutter on a word: face darkening, eyes glassily outward but focused in where the trouble contorted in a birth spasm. When it arrived, it was exactly what Victor Amspoker had expected.

"Lovely, just fucking lovely!" Chief of Detectives John J. Donoghue said. The front page of the *Post* contracted beneath his huge fingers. "Jimmy, I'm holding your ass, and the ass of all you guys here, responsible. Find the son of a bitch who leaked. I'm going to personally pull his goddamn chain. And flush him."

Lieutenant James C. Reid nodded, his face a set mask. Glances were exchanged around the table. Was it one of *them?*

Deputy Chief Inspector Halle smiled.

Donoghue released the front page, which resembled a starfish. He flattened it and turned it over.

"That second story there, Commissioner Daly is even hotter about that one," Halle said.

BUT WHO WILL WATCH THE COPS?

by Miles K. Overby III

The mental stability of police officers, who are charged with safeguarding our persons, possessions, and homes, was called into question in a new book by a prominent California psychiatrist.

Thirty-five percent of all policemen are "really dangerous," reports Dr. Edward Shev of Sausalito, California, who has screened and counseled 6,700 policemen and applicants in the last 13 years. . . .

Frank Quinn, Sergeant Brune Corolla, and Detective Bill Szkotak sat without speaking, overflowing the narrow green vinyl chairs, faces glum.

They were gathered in the boss's office, Jimmy Reid behind his green metal desk, the gooseneck lamp irradiating the hairs on the backs of his hands, which were clenched.

Amspoker crossed his leg on his knee, the pop of the joint breaking into the silence. The room had always reminded him of the ASPCA, he thought. Clinically modern, green-white-gray cinder-block walls, green linoleum, shuttered white blinds. Still, it was better than the prehistoric rock pile that was the One-Nine—where cuffed trousers went out when the roaches moved in.

"Look," Frank Quinn said, smoothing his mustache between thumb and forefinger. "Only way we turn this around is to get this guy. Old news is dead news. Hell, remember the screams of the press when that fifteen-year-old black kid and then that Kingsborough College student bought theirs at the end of a cop gun? *We* sure as hell remember. But does anybody else?"

"Frank's right," Reid said. "I never thought to hear the end of that seventy-two case—that detective in Robbery. Admitted raping two women on the West Side at gunpoint, three others in Queens. Even my wife was after me about that one. The tactic is, we'll be honest. With thirty thousand cops, no way a few closet nutskies don't slip through, right? But we nail this guy—then the talking stops."

Every face looked up. Standing in the doorway was Dr. Helene Untermeyer, her black-framed glasses dangling from a silver chain against her flat chest. She was holding a manila envelope in her right hand. The hand was trembling.

This is it, Amspoker thought. What they had all been praying for: the fluke, the break, the chance event, the tip-off—without which almost no case, despite the most laborious and exactingly pursued procedures, ever got solved.

"Mrs. Untermeyer?" Brune Corolla said, pulling out a chair.

Jimmy Reid leaned forward. "You got the Cognitor analysis there?"

"Yes, gentlemen. And most interesting it was. Cognitor and Dalroi, you see—they are the same person."

In the silence Amspoker could hear his neck creak. Halle coughed.

"But how can that possibly—?" Chief Donoghue began.

"Permit me to show you, gentlemen," Untermeyer said.

"I have compared the printing, from Dalroi, with the script of Cognitor. To the micromillimeter. But you should know, there are experts who say an absolute match between script and printing cannot be made. I say—*poppycat!* I testified in a forgery trial, successfully, I should say, that a row of numbers the defendant had printed down a page matched his handwriting. Why? The spacings were *exactly* the same.

"Now, with these two samples, I compare the spacings between letters, the length of lines, margins, the space between lines, the quality of the strokes, the slant, many things. I measure the width of each stroke, length of each stroke, whether certain letters lean together in pairs like lovers, or stand apart. Fourteen matches out of twenty indicate you're doing well, very well. Twenty out of twenty, in the legal sense—yes—is absolute. Gentlemen, with Dalroi and Cognitor, the match totals thirty-seven."

"Do you dare . . ." Donoghue said. "I mean to say, we have agreed that the Cognitor letter is from a priest. Do you mean to imply that a *priest* is the killer?"

"The paper and pen used might so indicate," she said. "Rectories are, to my understanding, well-equipped with supplies for the priest residents. Expensive bond papers. Elaborate desk sets of pens. Traditional *fountain* pens, I might add, which Cognitor although not Dalroi has used. But perhaps Cognitor only wishes us to think he is a priest. For some purpose of his own."

"A priest killer," Brune Corolla said. "Think of it—a *priest* killer."

"Maybe you should show us just how you came to such a . . . conclusion," Donoghue said, voice aggrieved.

"Certainly." Dr. Untermeyer drew out two Xerox copies of the letters. "Here. The capital D in Dalroi's signature is the same as the capital D in Cognitor's 'Dalroi.'" She circled each with a sharp red pencil.

There was an intake of breath.

"Not only do they *look* identical, gentlemen. I have measured each portion of both. Now, then, the capital M in Dalroi's 'Dear Mr. Quinn' is the same as that in Cognitor's 'Mr. St. Gryphon.' The t-bar crossing in Dalroi's 'St. Gryphon' is at the same angle, is the same length, width, and height up the letter as in Cognitor's 'St. Gryphon.' Now regard. In both letters, the commas occur at precisely the same distances from the preceding and succeeding words. In Dalroi's 'till I return,' the 'ill' is separated from the 't:' In Cognitor's 'kill an innocent young woman,' the same spacing between 'ill' and 'k.' "

Again she circled each as she spoke.

"Dalroi pauses here, his pen forming a blot after each 'e,' 'a' or 'c.' You see, Cognitor makes the same blots after those letters, the same pauses with the pen, which are generally thought to have a sexual origin."

"Stop. Enough already," Lieutenant Reid said. "You're the expert. But there must be a chance this is just coincidence. Two people writing alike. I mean, would this hold up in court?"

"Handwriting, gentlemen, is considered at least as individual, exclusionary, as fingerprints. Handwriting is really a brain print transferred to paper. Now, what are the chances of finding two persons with identical fingerprints?"

"Someone figured it out once," Quinn said, "on a long lunch hour. A statistician. He used sixteen ridge characteristics in one fingerprint for his base, compared that to the present world population, came up with a probability of" —Quinn took a breath—"four billion, two hundred ninety-four million, nine hundred sixty-seven thousand, two hundred ninety-six. To one."

"And that," Helene Untermeyer said, "is the probability of duplication here."

Chief Donoghue frowned. "Incredible."

"Gentlemen, let me show you one more thing. It is . . . a matter of symmetry. Almost beautiful." She bent over the two sheets on the lieutenant's desk, her freckled hand moving the red pencil.

Her audience pressed closer.

Amspoker was staring down at the symbol Dalroi St. Gryphon had drawn—the x'd circle in the square, the circle with an eye staring from its center. Even with the Xeroxed distance from the original, image drying and spinning into a bin, he felt the same stomach-dropping faintness. The revulsion came again. And then the fear.

But was he using all this as just a scapegoat? Trying to pin some ultimate evil onto one loony psycho killer, like a too-big tail on the donkey? Was he determined to see everyone that had gone wrong and sick and sad in the world staring back at him from a crude scribbled eye?

Dr. Helene Untermeyer sat back in her chair, chest lifting in asthmatic breaths.

"God *damn*," the lieutenant said. "Excuse, Mrs. Untermeyer. But you got something here."

On each letter her pencil had followed the gaps between words, winding down through successive lines.

"The pattern of these spacings, gentlemen—absolutely unique for each individual. They are called rivers. Poetic, is it not?"

No one answered. They were staring at the twin maps, each bisected by a river flowing south, curving out and down toward the west, eddying sharply east and then west once more, emptying red into the white margin.

"What I am wondering," Dr. Untermeyer said, "is if you should now look for a man with a large nose. The one you seek has given us his physiognomy to admire."

Detective Szkotak was staring blankly at her.

"He has drawn his own profile," Helene Untermeyer said.

11:48 p.m.

His fingers turned the dial.

Like surf, the sound of the air-conditioner four stories above and three buildings away rushed through his earphones.

Dalroi laughed.

Child's play, really. A simple wiring change had turned the telephone receiver in the girls' apartment into a live mike. Even when it was hung up, on the hook, to all appearances dead.

It was sitting now in their living room on a pasteboard table—alive as a third roommate. It could hear a whisper within thirty-five feet, send it over telephone wires down here to his listening post—an unsteady wooden crate in the hot basement of a neighboring building.

Of course there were other eavesdrop gizmos he had heard about: space-agers like sonic, subsonic, cesium, and infrared. Even a laser that could be beamed through a closed window to suck out the sound in a room.

But he liked doing things the simple way—relying on his own two quick, muscular hands.

The air-conditioner flowed into his ears, tightening the heat around him. A drop of sweat jetted down his spine. Restless, he spun the dial, turning up the sound.

The air-conditioner crashed through his mind.

It had been cool that night a year ago on the Long Island beach. He had scrubbed his toes through the rough cool sand, watched them disappear in the circular cream of a wave. Ahead, the beach-view hotels and weathered frame houses of Montauk peered out over the Atlantic. Early evening it had been, blue and cool and the air wet with the promise of night.

The she had been sitting on the sand, arms locked around her knees, looking out to sea. The she was alone.

Then they were together, driving, and he was hot again, sweat like thorns in the crosshatchings from the seat. The stoplight red, the she stirring beside him, the gun nudging beneath her breast. The she quiet, while the old man and the couple with the dog crossed in front. Then his foot on the pedal, buildings rushing past, her sneakers flattening the rubber cubes of the floor mat. Trees moving past, faster and faster, a wash of silver green in the headlights, then a blur. . . .

The sound of metal exploded in Dalroi's head.

In the basement he straightened on his crate, fingers yanking the dial.

Soft now through the earphones he heard the apartment door close, then metal again as the locks were thrown.

Two pairs of feet crossed the floor, one tread heavier than the other. They had come, then, the ones he had been waiting for: Paige and Francie.

A voice spoke, and he tensed. It was a man.

He listened to the pair of voices—the female and the male—both a little high, frothing easily into laughter, both giddy at the prospect of anticipation and flirtation.

He followed their steps, followed the laughing, tracing their steps the familiar way past the coffee table to the couch.

It was all exactly like a dance. Elaborate, formal—and it wasn't until now, when he was not a participant, that he could see it as such. That is, it would have been a dance except for the ugly hurt. He concentrated upon the formal outlines and tried to ignore the content and personal meaning which every sound carried.

He wouldn't even have known at all except that he knew what to listen for. He had been there the day before —he knew the graphic layout of the apartment, where the couch was, what particular noises it made as it was sat upon. He knew so well what the precursor was, the follow-up, and the finish.

Anger rose.

Dalroi spun the dials with both hands.

Through the noise of the air-conditioner he could hear the rising and falling of their voices—the magical emotional cadence that told him what was happening—but he could not make out the words.

The voices kept on and on, still light, still laughing, but with a new undercurrent, an intensity spelling out what each was expecting, was waiting for.

It was as if, he thought, they both spoke in a vaguely abstracted way, knowing that this conversation was but a social convention, a marking of time.

He sat on the crate below them, almost lulled by the rising and falling of their voices—the male petulance, the female staccato.

There was a sudden silence.

The preamble was over. The conversation, Dalroi knew, would not be resumed.

He heard the squealing sound of wood on wood as the Danish-sofa legs gave beneath their weight. Now they were both silent, then music, the radio was turned on.

He had always wondered why people turned the radio on—to drown out any possible incriminating noises, to add a certain substance of romance to a situation noticeably devoid of romance?

Again there was silence, beneath the music. Then the

squealing sound of wood on wood, squealing that continued as the sofa legs inched across the floor.

The squealings rocked into a rhythm now, faster and faster. Then they went on and on.

Above the air-conditioner the female voice shrieked into hearing: "Oh. Ohohohoh. Oh, Ward."

It had to be, he thought, the one called Paige.

The she would not escape him again.

From four floors above there came an absolute silence.

After a time his head nodded, jerked awake, then began again its descent toward his chest.

He dozed.

When he awoke, sharp over the rush of the air conditioner he could hear retching sounds.

Chapter Eleven

Wednesday, August 17
4:29 p.m.

She was waiting for Ward Yates to walk by her desk, dial her extension, place his imprimatur upon their evening together by asking her out again.

It was not, Francie Perry thought, a pleasant wait.

She had gone to the restroom six times to put on fresh lipstick and perfume. She had bought a pink rosebud at noon to put in the stitched lapel opening on Alex's beige linen suit, which had a pink heart-shaped linen camisole above which her breasts showed. But he had yet to catch a glimpse.

Of course, his office was all the way down the hall and around the corner past the employees' lounge. On the other hand, maybe he was avoiding her; alcohol closes the eyes and opens the zipper, she was just a good lay.

Or she *wasn't* a good lay. She had maybe nicked his skin as she had struggled to keep her lips sucked down over her teeth while restraining her gag reflex as he pumped on and on into her mouth, his hands on each side, guiding her head.

She had hated that.

"*Oh babe, now you got it, yeah, like that, oh, yeah.*"

But she had known it was a matter of time: if she waited she would care about someone—Miles or Ward or someone —and not be able to make love without caring.

"*Move down to me, babe. Move down, move down.*"

Like a gynecologist.

"*Oh, you feel so good.*"

Was this what it was about—anesthesia?

He had moved her legs—bent them and wrapped them around him—as if she were a flexibly jointed doll deep in ether.

"*What I lack in size I make up in technique.*"

The truth was she hated him.

But she had wanted to *know*, the way she had wanted to know in college when Mary Ellen had come back from her date without underpants. She wanted to know, the way she had wanted to sit on the second floor of Baird Library in the lap of the modern "tulip" chair, legs tucked under her on the soft orange upholstery, letting the other students cross and flow around her, thinking "I've done it I've done it I have finally done it."

265

By the time she had, they had torn the library down.

She had wanted to know. But was the knowing that it could sometimes be nothing?

Under the desk she crossed her legs, squeezing her thighs together. She could feel the ghost phallus. She thought of the sperm still breast-stroking through her.

They had put their clothes on again, were walking toward her apartment door when he had bent her over the back of the couch. She had felt her dress slide above her waist, his hand rounding her naked buttocks in the cool air. She had felt like a wounded marsh, wet trails leading down toward her knees. He had entered her without preliminary from the rear. It had gone on and on, so long she was afraid Paige would walk in, and had faked it.

And then the nausea from the two bottles of wine. Or was it the pebbled balls, the come in her hair?

She was still awake when Paige had come in, irritable after the duty visit with Mrs. Baskin in Manhasset.

They had lain in the two beds, talking into the dark. And then the slow, ragged sound of Paige's breathing, and her own—fast and harsh.

Sleeping was like breathing. It was natural, it worked so easily until you suddenly wondered how it worked at all.

She had stared up at the ceiling, remembering her father's hands behind her on the new red two-wheeler, spinning out from his hands onto the dirt road, the evening air a sudden wet rush in which she knew just what to do. "Don't fall!" her father had yelled.

She had looked down at hands and handlebars, feet and pedals, legs and spokes and wheels. And then the road reaching up.

But sleep—she had always been a natural at sleep. It came in its rhythm like the crickets. Sleep followed day like fullness after hunger, like soybeans after a season of fallow. She remembered the yellow record turning under the lamp: "Good night, toys, sleepy time is here. . . . Good night, Mother and Father, dear." Her face buried in the dry, powdery limestone smell of Kitty-Boy's fur, asleep before the record finished.

Her phone was ringing.

She snatched it up. It would be sly and teasing, mocking and suggestive—Ward's deep nasal voice.

"Francie," Paige said. "I just got a weird phone call. Here, at my desk. I tried to pass it off, but—"

"Obscene, you mean?"

"No. Some man. Sort of prim-sounding. He said something about how he had done everything he could. It was not his fault."

"*What* was not his fault?"

"I would have to watch out for myself, he said. Then he hung up. I don't know what to make of it. Scary, huh? What do you think?"

"Call Detective Quinn. Call Amspoker. This minute."

"Maybe you're right, Francie. No need to take chances. Let them worry about it. But I'm sure it was just some nut who—"

"Just call them, okay?"

"Okay."

"And, Paige. Call me back after. Okay?"

Ridiculous, Francie thought, putting down the receiver. Some nut. Some obscene caller. Some stroke out of the blue, random number, roll of the dice having nothing whatever to do with everything that had gone before.

She felt something thicken in her chest. She waited for Paige to call back.

It was nearing five when Francie dialed the Hornblower, Weeks number.

"Sorry," the research-group secretary said, voice impatient in Francie's ears. "Miss MacLeish has left for the day."

"*Left?*"

"Yes. Left."

"This is her roommate, Francine. Would you put me through to her boss? Mr. Dornbush?"

"I'm sorry, he's in a confer—"

"*This is an emergency.* Put me through!"

"Francine?" the male voice said.

She felt her tension slip a notch.

"This is Mr. Dornbush. Is there some problem?"

"I'm really sorry to bother you. But something . . . well, odd has happened."

"Odd?"

"Paige got a strange call. Told me about it, was supposed to call back, and now she's gone!"

"Well, let me see here. It's five now. She usually leaves at five."

"Francie!" It was Kandis's voice from behind her. "Got a call for you on my line."

Francie mouthed "Hold it" to Kandis.

"Mr. Dornbush? False alarm, I guess. Paige is on the other line now. I'm really sorry—"

"You all right?"

"Yes. Perfectly. Really, it just gave me a scare."

The casters scraped across the transparent plastic mat as she pushed the chair away and ran toward Kandis's desk. She punched the lighted cube. "Paige?"

"Detective Amspoker here. Miss Perry, something strange just happened. Someone called Miss MacLeish, she was upset, called me—"

"I know. I told her to call you."

"I suggested she meet me in front of her building, we'd check it out. But I'm here now and she's not around. Her secretary said she left."

Down the aisle, Francie could see Ward Yates walking in her direction. But one thought had wedged into her mind, which had gone numb, as cold and frictionless as a glacier.

Paige was gone.

8:04 p.m.

Why was it that failure made you feel so old? Made the veins surface beneath your eyes, pulsing blue as old ladies' hair, you could hear the bunged-up rhythm.

In the Homicide Squad coffee room were Frank Quinn, Lieutenant Reid, Sergeant Corolla and five others. Someone slung a sack of bologna and cheese sandwiches on the table. The bread was dry. Someone wanted to know why can't we ever get roast beef, at least pastrami once in a while for fuckin' cryin' out loud?

Victor Amspoker sat slumped over his coffee, feeling the depression seal him in.

They had failed. *He* had failed.

They had taken statements from Francine Perry and every Hornblower, Weeks, Noyes & Trask employee they could find, talked to the newsstand operator in the lobby, the wino sitting hunched on the bench on the tiny concrete island, the subway-token-booth clerks, the transit police, the bus drivers, cabbies, the panhandling student playing his fiddle over on Broad Street, with exactly the same result.

Nothing.

They had looked for anyone trying to conceal his concern: someone whose body faced the street but with head averted, someone whose body was turned away but with head toward them, anyone on the corners examining his nails or staring overhead.

And nothing.

By seven the financial district was deserted, the only signpost of life the cabs and limousines pulled up in front of Harry's, the after-work bar in the old brownstone on Hanover Square. They had questioned the crowd of men within.

And still nothing.

Paige MacLeish had vanished.

Lieutenant Jimmy Reid was sitting, body bent, shoulders hunched, like a man sandbagged in the gut. He looked around the table. "Hell. Maybe we're running off half-cocked here. So this girl got a nut call, hasn't got home from work yet. Maybe she remembered a date with some dude she's after, went tearing off after him. She gets reamed good, she'll be home later tonight."

"No way," Amspoker said.

"Could have been some nut reads the paper about her roommate," Bill Szkotak said. "Traces her, calls to give her a scare. The call could have nothing to do with her being out somewhere tonight."

"Cut the shit." Amspoker rubbed the creases in his forehead. "Why say that when we all know why we just went over Wall Street with a fine tooth."

"Even if this caller is the same guy we're looking for," Frank Quinn said, "what we've got to know—and fast—is why he's after MacLeish too. Something he dropped, left behind? Maybe something she knows that would give him away? Something she's not even aware of, forgotten?"

"Yeah," Jimmy Reid said, "but what the fuck is it?"

Silence.

He would not be home again tonight, Victor Amspoker

thought, drinking his coffee. Next thing he knew, the kids would be calling him Uncle Daddy.

8:22 p.m.

"Braden here?"

"Dean Braden, sir? The university chaplain?"

"Yes. I ride that hobbyhorse, among others."

"Sir, this is Miles Overby of the New York *Post*. There's an emergency. I wondered if you'd be kind enough to notify Willis MacLeish. I understand he's still in his office."

"Emergency? What on earth are you talking about?"

"His daughter, Paige. She's missing. Her roommate was killed ten days ago. The police think there may be some connection."

"Good Lord."

"Precisely. Would you hold, please?"

"Sergeant?" Miles said into the other phone. "Would you say there *was* a connection with the Baskin homicide? Uh-huh. Any ideas where she might have gone, then? Uh-huh. What are you going to do, wait till the body shows up? Same to you, Sergeant.

"Dean Braden? Sorry to keep you waiting. Paige Mac-Leish got a threatening phone call at work this afternoon, then disappeared. Her roommate doesn't know where she is. The police are looking for Paige now. Would you inform Mr. MacLeish, before he hears it on the news?"

"Why, uh, yes. Of course. I'll call Will right now."

"That's very kind of you, Dean."

Miles replaced the receiver and stared along the double row of gray metal desks. The dayside staff had gone, filled ashtrays like calling cards on every surface.

He would give the chaplain exactly three minutes, Miles thought, then dial Willis MacLeish for a quote. He already, of course, had a good opening line from the roommate.

One of the two telephones on his desk was ringing. He glanced at his watch and picked it up.

"Miles? Francie. Can't you get out of there yet? I feel awful. Like I'm just sitting around up here waiting for something to happen."

"Was her car in the garage?" Miles said.

"Yes. Right where she left it last night, the attendant said. Miles, she didn't just go somewhere, to a movie. The police are sort of trying to say she did. I know something's happened. And nobody's *doing* anything about it."

But what, he thought, was there to do?

2:42 a.m.

It was the nape of her neck that remained.

Paige's nape as she had seen it just this morning, bent as Paige started down the steep subway stairs toward the tunnel of the IRT express, dark and full of noise below.

Her hairline was an inverted U, the reddish hairs damp in the heat, crinkled tighter against the white skin that was so different from the burned red carapace of Harold Perry's neck.

She had looked back from the stairs as Francie headed toward the BMT sign. Her eyes were blue, shell-blue as a redstart egg, down-slanting, that made her look sad even when she smiled.

When she laughed, her face always screwed up as if she were crying.

As if she knew it would come to this.

"Bu-bye," Paige had said.

But it was the bent nape, white as winter, that remained.

It remained like the sunlight on the glossy tan hair of Hula, Beverly's dachshund, when the poison bunched his muscles into fists.

It remained and it would always remain.

The light in the bathroom seeped beneath the door—a white bar bending over the furniture. Francie had asked Miles to leave it on.

He was asleep beside her in the twin bed, his breathing slow and deep—his limp arm flung across her abdomen. She could see the sparse reddish-brown hairs that lifted, glinting off his arm. She stirred under the weight.

She looked up at the white ceiling of her bedroom, the bumpy ridge of the many-times-plastered crack. It was the first time they had been together that Miles had not made love to her. He was being considerate, she thought, not wanting to press himself on her at such a time. She would have said no if he had tried.

Still, she felt hurt, abandoned. There was something unfeeling about his ability to sleep while she could not.

She stared at the ceiling until her eyes felt dry.

Fear of sleep—Sir James Frazer had written about it in *The Golden Bough*. Something about the ancient belief that during sleep your soul temporarily abandoned you—out to lunch. Death of course was the soul gone permanently out to lunch.

Gone as Paige.

There were three little roommates who lived in a shoe. First there were three. Then there were two. Then there were . . .

She would have to leave the city, of course. But go where? Do what? With whom? Be alone in some other city?

Walk down some other city's streets, all the men standing on the corners in combative pose: legs forked, hands in pockets, chin under, eyes staring. All the men leaning on "Pizza—50¢ a Slice" windows, leering down from the cabs of trucks—eyes traveling ankles thighs crotch waist breasts face and then back down, face breasts waist crotch thighs ankles.

"Like ta hump ya, doll."

"Suck it, foxy."

"Fuck you, you was *ma-ade* for love."

"Don't say hi, huh? Stuck-up *bitch*."

Incomprehensible slobbering noises falling behind her as she walked—hanging juicy as a wet dream on the air.

"Lorraine!" the old ragged charcoal-dirt-blackened man called to her from the curb. He followed her up Second Avenue, calling in his wounded treble: "Lorraine! I'll break all your fuckin' fingers, Lorraine!"

"Okay, now what would you say a man stops his car, asks you to get in?" Thelma Perry had asked, brushing the pigtail crinkles out of Francie's hair. "No, thank you." The fear biting. But fear of what? Her mother had smiled, brushing harder until the electricity crackled, lifting up the hair on her nape.

She edged Miles's hand off her stomach.

His hand moved back, groping now for her breast.

His hand held and then squeezed her breast. She could feel the heat of the four fingers, and his thumb pressed against her breastbone. His thumb moved up, flicking back and forth across her nipple. Then his knee dented down in the sheet, and he was on top of her, his breath already coming fast against her throat. She felt the hard smooth round knob between her thighs.

She was completely dry.

He released her breast, brought his fingers up to his

mouth, then wiped the head of his penis.

The knob was back but this time it forced her apart. He thrust again, deeper. And then deeper, harder and faster.

She opened her eyes.

Above her his face hung like a mask. His gray eyes stared down into hers, fixed and expressionless, shiny as glass.

She stared back.

His eyes shifted toward the wall. He glared at the wall as his hips bucked, shuddered against her and he came.

The bathroom was cool afterward, white and pristine. Francie sat on the toilet, thighs spread, watching the milky fluid drip in slow drops, clouding the water.

Always before, the sight had been interesting, even precious—a knitting of a man to herself. She should have felt happy. After that first time, Miles had not been impotent.

But she felt nothing but revulsion.

It was just a loss of mood—what appeared exciting a few minutes before could turn ugly. It had once been devastating, that shift of mood, but now she accepted it as just a part of life. She tried to accept it.

Miles was sitting up when she came out of the bathroom, the wrinkled sheet around his waist, a lighted cigarette between his fingers.

She remembered the three ripples of belly when Ward had leaned over, the shiver of his breasts, which were larger than any man's she had seen.

"Get you anything, chooch?" Miles said. He watched the movement of her breasts as she walked toward the bed.

She shook her head. She crossed to the bureau, and from the bottom drawer took a clean white pillowcase.

"Can I have the pillow?"

He looked up at her, pulled it from beneath his back.

She stripped off the case, threw it on the floor and put on the fresh one.

"Whatcha doing, chooch?"

"It helps me get to sleep. A clean pillowcase. I don't know why. I've been putting one on every night now."

She climbed onto the narrow bed, and he held her in silence for a time, one hand about her shoulders, his cigarette a dancing arc of light.

"Presleep ritualist, that's what you are," Miles said. "You and old Charlie Dickens. He would get out his pocket compass, move whatever bed he was in to face north. Some theory about magnetic currents flowing north to south, and they'd pass right through you, cure whatever ailed you."

"The storms at home," she said, "always went from west to east. The sky would get yellow, then gray, and hailstones big as eggs."

Finally she heard him tamp the butt down in the ashtray.

"Maybe you should go back tonight," she said. "Kind of crowded in this bed."

"I could sleep over there." His eyes moved toward the second bed, covered with the matching brown corduroy spread.

"*No!*"

"You mean you want to be alone?"

She wanted to ask: What was it you were depressed about? She was remembering certain words, expressions on his face, fleeting angers and images. *Holes in the walls.* But everyone had them, didn't they—cracks, canyons, wells that made you sick and dizzy peering down?

"You mean you want to be alone?" Miles said again.

"Well, maybe."

"Why can't you just say it, then? Why make me guess?"

She turned on her side, away from him, face buried in the detergent-smelling pillowcase.

"Just let me stay a while longer, then," Miles said.

His arm pulled her back against him.

After a while she heard his deep, even breathing that snagged every so often into a snore.

His arm fell once more across her stomach.

3:20 a.m.

His fingers turned the dial.

But they were quiet up above, the only sound in his earphones the churning churning churning of the air-conditioner. He imagined it smashed, clubbed apart into bleeding wires and fractured metal.

This was how they honored the other she's death. They went to her room. They fucked like rabbits.

Dalroi shifted on the uneven crate. The gluey air stuck to his face, filled his nostrils. Beads of sweat covered his upper lip, which glistened under the bare hanging bulb. The basement walls were caked with dirt, its ceiling a maze of asbestos-covered steam pipes, bare dripping pipes, and the sound, always the sound running tap tap tap like tiny claws in the corners and over his head.

Did someone die? Oh, right. No one cared.

No one had cared in high school. It was Homecoming, there was coffee and a coffee hour, doughnuts and decorations, chicken wire stuffed with tissue, cheerleaders and a football game. And there was one who fitted himself in between crepe-paper shakers and kilted laps, who sat with beaked nose and white-latticed scalp. The call for a doctor went out over the helmeted and ringleted heads, over trophies and cheering and the queen and her court up on the plywood platform. The bleachered ranks parted reluctantly, the dead man was carried away on a stretcher, and the crowd sealed itself up again, tight and hoarse. And kept on cheering and kept on perspiring and kept on watching the game.

And that night *The Lavender Hill Mob* was shown in the school auditorium, followed by an informal dance in the gym.

They went to her room. They fucked like rabbits.

It was starting to unravel. What was starting to unravel? He didn't know.

(*The voice that spoke was very thin and high. It was a young boy's voice. The young boy looked down. He could see the heavy white folds of the choir robe, the ivory-colored crisscrossed threads where a rip had been darned.*)

Dalroi stood up, wiping his sweaty palms down his trousers. It was a matter of time. He knew they would find the she, as they had the other.

But no. Maybe the current had found her already, a tug pushing and pulling, guiding her gently into the channel, then past the twin square-topped towers of the World Trade Center, past Battery Park, the Statue of Liberty, faster now through the Upper Bay and then the Narrows, under the Verrazano Bridge and through the Lower Bay, around the boardwalk of Coney Island and out, the water dense and buoyant now with salt, washing clean and white, and, bleached like the once-red shell of a horseshoe crab, she would pour out into the Atlantic.

But he hadn't wanted to. It was starting to unravel. He hadn't wanted to. Her red hair was so bright against the dark water. The daisies dropped pale one by one against her hair.

Chapter Twelve

The voice through the receiver was a hoarse, high-pitched rattle. Victor Amspoker felt his spine straighten against the desk chair.

"You told me I hear somethin' give you a call."

"Benny?" Amspoker said.

"Yeah, lover."

"What you got, Benny?"

"What *you* got?"

"The usual. Fifty."

The rattle accelerated into a barking laugh. "Uh-uh, baby. This here's not no usual. This here's a spill-the-beans. About that rich cunt you boys're creamin' for."

"Alexandra Baskin?"

"You know, you smartening up."

"Where are you, Benny?"

Benny Gaddis, heroin addict, was slouched in the back booth of the coffee shop at Seventy-third and Broadway. He looked up as Amspoker slid into the seat across from him.

Benny's face had always bothered him. The delicate features had a perspiring translucence that reminded him, Amspoker thought, of the crucifix nailed above his mother's bed. There was a switch that you pressed, and a six-watt bulb that lit up the wax Christ's face.

But Benny was useful, out on the streets all night, a pipeline straight to the gutter. Like the other addicts and whores, he always knew who had a new leather coat, who had forty bucks for the numbers instead of the usual four.

Of course, dealing with the Bennys had been easier once. For years Amspoker had kept decks of heroin, pocketed during a collar that would not be affected by it, in the bottom of his locker. If a pusher had fifty-three bags on him—a misdemeanor—he could add two of his own, making fifty-five, a felony. And the decks were currency to keep Benny and the other informants greased and running.

Today that was corruption.

Today there were forms and hassles and never enough money.

Benny was drinking a bottle of Orange Crush. He smiled over the glass rim, thin colorless lips flattening back from his teeth, eyes studying the detective.

"You lookin' bad, lover. Case got you chasing your ass, gettin' nowhere, am I right?"

"You got the real stuff, Benny?"

"I ever fuck with you, man?"

Benny's black, pupilless eyes widened as Amspoker laid an envelope on the Formica. Benny pulled the envelope to his chest and counted the contents. Then, with a look of disdain, he folded the envelope into the front pocket of his shirt.

"I got the stuff," Benny said. "Junkie name of Carlos Neal. Wanted to know could they trace come from a stiff. I says, why? He says he humped this cunt on Sixty-third Street. And get this: *after* he iced her."

Three faces stared up from Victor Amspoker's desktop—the first a faded Polaroid print of Carlos Dean Neal, age thirteen years, looking like any other scared-as-hell half-Cuban kid. Then the two NYC police mug shots, ages sixteen and seventeen, profile and front, with the metal plate resting on his right collarbone, the chain slung around his neck, weighted end dangling on his left.

The face was disturbing, Amspoker thought, exactly in proportion to its "niceness." Neal looked like the kind of young man you might approve for your daughter's first dance: thick, wavy black hair trimmed short around the ears, clean-shaven unremarkable features, large brown eyes that searched the camera with a gentle confusion.

It was the face that lent credence to the whole thing. It was a face you could imagine Alexandra Baskin opening her door to.

The family bio only added to the portrait. The father had deserted when Neal was two. The boy was devoted to his Cuban mother, with whom official records had him still living. He was known to walk her home from the subway each workday—to protect her from muggers. He was also devoted to animals, having owned two dogs, six cats, birds, turtles, and a collection of Japanese beetles.

"Makes you wanta weep, right?" Jerry Mollegen said. "Now, here comes the rough stuff." The detective from the Two-Three (the precinct encompassing the north side of Eighty-sixth Street up to One Hundred Tenth Street, from Fifth Avenue east to the river) searched through the thick folder. Sex trouble in the Two-Three, he had told them, meant you automatically called on Neal.

"Nineteen-seventy to nineteen-seventy-two," Mollegen was reading. "Neal then aged eleven and twelve. Twenty-eight juvenile-delinquency petitions for purse-snatching, shoplifting, and throwing stones at cars from the FDR overpass. Plus arson, three jostlings, chronic truancy and two possessions of a flamethrower. And, baby, that fucker shot a six-foot blast."

"So?" Frank Quinn said. "I was looking at some city figures yesterday. Twenty-five hundred of these little monsters been grabbed for murder, manslaughter, rape, assault, robbery, burglary, grand larceny. And that's just the *ten-and-under* set."

"Wait a minute," Lieutenant Reid said. "A ten-year-old rape-o? How the hell can a ten-year-old get it up?"

"Eats paint chips," Mollegen said. "Lead'll do it every time. Anyway, now we got Neal, age thirteen. And he's starting off, you should pardon the expression, with a bang."

Mollegen picked up one of his own typewritten notes. "December twelve, nineteen-seventy-two. Marlee Gotschalk, age fifteen, accosted in a hallway outside her apartment at Two-thirty-one East Ninety-eighth Street at one A.M. After forcing her to the roof and raping her, the assailant fled down the stairs with her purse. She was able to describe him. Two days later Detective Jerald A. Mollegen arrested

282

Carlos Dean Neal, thirteen years old. (Remarks: Uncorroborated testimony of prosecutrix. Case adjusted at family-court intake area by probation officer R. L. Zipkin. Neal released in the custody of his mother, with whom he lives at Four-oh-eight East One Hundredth Street.)

"Now we got Neal from seventy-three to seventy-five. Thirteen to fifteen years of age. Charged with nine rapes, seventeen burglaries, twelve robberies, a grand larceny, one riot. Spent two months in the Spofford juvenile facility. Picked up on a Hundred Fifteenth on a burglary charge with the Spofford keys still in his pocket. Transferred for six months to Warwick. Neal turns over a new leaf, makes lamps out of scrap lumber, obeys the rules. He's given weekend passes home.

"November ten, nineteen-seventy-five: Now sixteen, Neal is indicted for the rape and assault of an eighteen-year-old girl in her apartment on East Ninety-first Street. She says he threatened to kill her. The computer comes up with a zero on Neal: he's an adult first-offender. Neal is permitted to plead guilty to a charge of second-degree assault and is paroled in the custody of his mother."

The mother, Amspoker was remembering. *Short and eyes like obsidian in the doorway.* Her son's name, of course, had popped from the state crime computer in Albany when they punched in the query. But most of Neal's offenses were as a juvenile and thus sealed. Worse, Neal had been one of hundreds of names, and no longer resided, when they called on his mother, at the given address. And no, she didn't know where he'd gone, but Chalo was a good boy, a real good boy, why? he hurt some girl?

Lieutenant Reid brought his hand down on the table. "That's enough for me. Out on the streets and let's find this SOB."

Victor Amspoker walked into the adjoining dormitory and picked up his sport jacket from one of the narrow, sheet-covered bunks. He put the jacket on and sat down on the edge of a lower bunk, the springs firing noisily.

Fear burned like salt on the back of his tongue.

Had they blown it?

Had they spent so much time mowing down the weeds of an address book, struggling to strike a path, that they overlooked a highway? Was it the stock answer after all, dull as dishwater, common as dirt: *previous offender, similar modus operandi*?

If so, who was to blame?

First Sally Teising, then Alexandra Baskin. Rita Viseltear. And now Paige MacLeish—who would be to blame when they found her body too?

There is marked cyanosis of the nail beds of the fingers.

Did you blame the psychiatrists, a bunch of roses, the smell of success that sent them up to the fortieth floor?

The mucosa of the upper trachea is covered by a thin, slightly hemorrhagic film.

Did you blame Dalroi, some off-the-wall boyfriend who got his rocks off sending nut notes to the cops?

The left ovary on section discloses a well-formed large corpus luteum cyst with a thick yellow border.

Did you blame a priest who'd heard one too many through the grille and finally flipped? Or his parishioner who thought it was macho to "confess"?

Heart: Not unusual. Autolytic changes, minimal. Brain: Not unusual.

Did you blame yourself?

He picked up the phone, hesitated a moment, and then dialed.

"Yes?" Thin and high again.

"Maddie, just have a minute. Wanted to see how you're doing."

284

Pause. "That's nice. I'm fine, really."

How are *you*, he imagined her saying. But she didn't.

"I just wanted to tell you, I'll be home tonight, okay? I don't care what's going on down here. Plenty of other guys in the department, right? I'll try to make it for dinner."

"I've got some veal chops." Her voice had softened into a lower register. He felt hope flare. "Or ham. Would you rather have ham?"

"Don't go to any trouble, hey? Just want to see you and the girls."

"Ham'll dry out if you're late."

"Veal chops, then. Maddie."

Say it.

But he couldn't say it. She had always said it first.

"Yes?" Thin and high again.

"See you tonight, then, say hello to the girls."

He couldn't say that he loved her. But maybe tonight he would.

When he walked out to his desk, Quinn was leaning over it, talking into the telephone.

"No, no, we'll find her all right, don't you worry. We've got everyone in Missing Persons on it. The Catskills? No objection. Thanks for letting us know. We'll be in touch."

Amspoker looked across at Quinn.

"Perry wants to get out of the city today, not that I blame her. Camping with that reporter, what's-his-face."

"Overby?" Amspoker said. "The one from the *Post* that's taking her for a ride?"

"Yeah, that's the one."

"*Camping?*" Amspoker said. "Frank, you think that's safe?"

It was the knife that bothered her, Francie thought.

It hung from Miles's belt in front of her, moving at eye level back and forth with his thigh. The soft dark brown cowhide sheath was "wet-formed," he had told her, so that it clung to the contours—"not like a common sheath with a snap."

The blade was outlined beneath the thin covering like the bones of a newborn calf.

It was the need for a knife that bothered her.

When they had driven up the road from West Shokan, she had leaned out into the breeze. She had watched the clear brown waters of Malthy Hollow Brook unroll beside them, and the fear had seemed left behind.

Then Miles had pulled the car onto the road's shoulder. Ahead a sign pointed the way north to the Moonhaw Gun Club. She had stepped out and looked up. To the west a creek descended from the ridge high above, which loomed like a wall, dark with trees.

"We follow the creek," Miles had said, pointing upward. "And wait till you get an eyeful of the view from up there, chooch. Like sitting on a goddamn eagle's nest."

"Looks pretty good from down here too, you know. And anyway, no trail?"

"Trails we want to avoid," Miles said. "Nothing but kiddie scout troops all the hell over the place. You ever spend a night listening to twenty cub scouts play Lemme Sticks?"

Even with the three pairs of pebbly wool socks, her toes slid forward in the boots, which were a well-worn one and a half sizes too large. Which caused her to wonder again just who had well-worn them. And why her boots remained in the back of Miles's closet.

He had also unearthed two zip-together royal-blue sleeping bags, a wear-dappled orange backpack on a metal frame, which he was now wearing, and a green canvas satchel with arm straps. Following his example, she walked with thumbs hooked under the satchel's straps, easing the strain forward from her shoulders.

The air was hot and transparent, loud with bees. She could feel the twin springs pumping up beneath her arms. *Slog slog slog*—blank the mind. You couldn't sweat and worry at the same time.

"No trail anywhere *near* this mountain," Miles said over his shoulder. "Called Balsam Cap, by the way. We'll be nice and alone.".

The shallow stream they were following flowed around lichen-covered boulders. Their lug-soled boots cut prints in the soft earth of the bank. They climbed higher, leaving the hot field, ragged with the green stalks and white clusters of Queen Anne's lace, behind them. Francie paused to look back, the sun glinting through spider webs hooked to the tall stems, insect columns bellying above.

The stream arched higher, tumbling now in near-vertical sheets of spray. The weight on her back tugged fiercely, threatening to overbalance her backward, sawing between her shoulder blades. She could hear the panting of her breath, feel the blood flaring up the sides of her thighs. But she welcomed it, the hard physical newness that she had almost forgotten.

Moving relentlessly upward with no pause for breath were the frayed legs of Miles's tan corduroy pants, worn to cream in the seat.

"Hey up there," she said.

"Yeah?"

"Never again will I order a gimlet straight up."

She paused, the blood jerking up now along her cheeks

to her temples. She looked out at the green valley below, tiny houses scattered like Monopoly pieces. She was surprised that they looked so far away.

"You were right, Miles. It's good up here. I'm glad we came."

"Old farmhand like you, I knew you'd go for it."

The blotched blue-gray trunks of the beeches, the white, peeling curls of birch were giving way to evergreens: hemlocks with soft lacy needles, stands of northern spruce, the dense spirelike crowns of balsam firs.

Her face was flushed red when they finally crested the ridge and he led the way out from the cover of the trees. There was a wide ledge overlooking the valley, covered several feet deep with a humus of fir and spruce needles. She sank to her knees, the needles giving spongily beneath her, and eased out of her pack. She stared down at the blue distant glitter of Ashokan Reservoir.

"Three thousand six hundred and twenty-three feet," Miles said.

"Oh, thanks, I needed that."

He sat down beside her, locking his hands around his knees. "I got something I want to share with you, chooch. Only time I've been up here before I was by my lonesome. Let's find a flat spot, pitch the tent, and then I'll show you."

It was hidden between two folds of the ridge, a horizontal lip of pool into which fell a thirty-foot spume, so thin it was as much mist as water. The sound was no louder than a sprinkle of rain.

"Feather Falls," Miles said. "Just a name I decided to give it. To the finder go the spoils."

The bank was thick with overhanging ferns. She stepped down into them. On the stump of a rotted log the fluted edges of a fungus formed a cup, rainwater silver-gray within. A red-spotted salamander flicked beneath, trembling the water.

"Last one in is a fucking ∴.." His words were lost as he yanked his shirt over his head.

Skinny-dipping. Well, she never had. Hardly anyplace to dip in Iowa, although she had once run through the back cornfield with no clothes, the stalks dark, the tassels light with the sun high above. When she had run back, the grasshoppers had claimed the pile of her clothes.

She sat down and unlaced her shoes, pulling off the pairs of socks. Her feet emerged like swollen lumps of dough. She looked up to see the pale circles of Miles's small buttocks lower into the water.

"Ye gods! My privates!"

"Not cold, is it?" She was struggling to get her clothes off before he would turn in the pool, watch her walk—short and shorn—to the bank. He would see that the muscles in her calves stood out like hard round balls.

He turned, and all that was visible was his nose and the upper part of his face. He bubbled into the water, which spun out toward her in rings. Then his head sank beneath the surface, which was dark in the shadow of the overhanging ridge.

Hurriedly she entered the pool. It was chill against her heated body, yet with a depth of softness, like snow. She kicked out toward where his head had disappeared, the furry knots of roots swirling around her ankles. Water striders forked away from her fingers.

Her toes arched down for the bottom but felt nothing. She trod water, turning to look behind her, but the surface was glassy, undisturbed.

"Miles?"

She could feel a colder current move around her legs. She trod faster, staring ahead at the dark green ring of trees. A wave of goose bumps surfaced up her body. She felt suddenly as if she were being watched.

"*Miles?* Come on, now."

She started, her mouth gulping water. Fingers were sliding up the outsides of her thighs. She wanted to laugh with relief. Miles was just teasing her, fooling around. She looked down, saw the mud smoke up with Miles's kick, and then his hands were moving higher between her thighs, one finger probing for the entrance. She felt her open vulnerability, dangling in the thick cold water. His finger pushed deeper. The excitement was like a blow.

She gasped for air as his head broke water and he pulled her against him. She felt the slick cold slide of his body, his legs moving, his erection hard between their bellies. He pulled her harder against him and she tasted the bitter leaf mold on his lips.

Beyond the pool they found a near-level spot beneath fir trees. The needles were dry, crisp and yet spongy beneath her back. The scent was sharp and rising around her, as if she lay in a cedar chest. She felt the chill drops of water slide to the edge of her thighs, then dart downward as he pulled her legs apart.

Then his penis was searching awkwardly, and she arched against him, felt the heat of her lips part around, drawing him in. He supported his weight on his palms, his body slapping faster and faster, deeper, until she could feel the cool pendulous slap of his scrotum. She felt the tremendous urgency rise in her, and her legs broke around him, crushing him in, her nails scratching, but already she could feel the spasms of his coming.

He fell forward across her, his body cold along its edges in the twilight, the sun gone beyond the ridge.

"Hey," he said, raising his head, looking down at her. "Hey. So how do you like summer camp?"

"I like it fine."

He smiled. He thrust his softening penis deeper inside her.

The wind had strengthened, rustling the needled branches above her head. Then there was another sound—short and sharp and finished. A squeal of distress, as from a wounded small animal or bird.

She started up, her weight on her bent elbows, lifting his heaviness off her chest. She stared back into the wall of green, brown with needles beneath.

"What was *that?*"

"I don't know. And frankly, chooch, right now I don't exactly care."

"No, really."

He squatted on the needles, listening. The night air skated across her bare skin.

He shrugged, rubbing his hands up and down his arms.

"Really, Miles. What do you think it was?"

"Coot probably. Mud hen, some people call them. And a.k.a. Blue Peter, which is what I'm going to get we don't hightail it back to some dry clothes."

"What's a coot?"

"Ugly little birds with chunky gray bodies, black heads. You've seen them, all the hell over North America, wherever there's fresh water. They make so many different grunts and cackles and squawks, soundtracks of 'em are dubbed into jungle films. Hey, don't look so worried. Little wildlife is good for the soul. Come on, I'll get us a fire going, we'll dry off, how about that?"

The orange glow, she thought, seemed to draw the woods closer around them, the resin blisters pale ovals against the dark trunks. Her eyes were drawn to the ring of trees, the blackness beyond the firelit circle.

"We are having," Miles said, voice buoyant, as if to lift

her mood, "le beef Stroganoff, le corn, et les green beans avec mushrooms in wine sauce. And wine to sauce us up, of course. In fact, let's get the hell started on the wine. You want to do the honors?"

She pierced the cork with the sharp point, began rotating the screw downward. The label between her knees read "Bodegas Bilbainas Gran Reserva 1955."

Miles was ripping open an assortment of foil envelopes and rattling cardboard packages. A yellow disk, traced with what looked like hoofprints, struck the rim of the saucepan, bounced and rolled across the floor of needles.

"Add water and bingo," Miles said, retrieving the disk. "Freeze-dried corn. In fact, freeze-dried—"

"*Every*thing?"

"Hell, some guys trim the margins off their maps just to save weight. We'll just douse it—and us—in wine."

She was biting into a pink granular chunk of "strawberry ice cream" when she felt the chill, the stiff unwieldiness of her fingers. She got up and rummaged through her satchel, put on the blue sweater over her red cotton shirt. She sat down again on a flat stone, arms encircling her knees, staring at the orange flames, the glowing coals. She thought about a hot shower, how the thunderous roar of water felt beating on her back, dissolving the kinks in her spine. She moved her legs nearer the fire, thrusting her fingers deep into her jeans pockets.

It was better to be here. Better to be here than there, where Paige had disappeared.

"I don't suppose," she said, "there are any bears around here."

"Bears? Oh, shit, no."

"That sign out on the road. Moonhaw Gun Club. I mean, what do they hunt?"

"Deer mostly. Few ducks. Maybe even a coot or two."

"But no bears?"

"They're all farther north, up in the Adirondacks. Hamilton County is supposed to be the bear capital of New York, and that's way the hell up there."

"But none down here?"

"Well, there was no hunting season allowed on bears in the Catskills last year. So that means the population must be pretty low."

"You mean there *are* bears?"

"Why don't you open that second bottle of wine?"

She drew her fingers out into the damp cold air. The bottle of red wine felt refrigerated beneath her grip.

"Something about the way bears move," she said. "The way their head sways back and forth, back and forth. Like a snake. I don't know, I just hate that."

"And where did you see bears on a frozen waffle like Iowa?"

"I worked two summers in Yellowstone Park during college. Old Faithful Lodge, as a waitress. We used to drive out at night, a whole pile of kids in a car, to this little town of West Yellowstone, to the dump. We'd take these washed-out plastic Clorox jugs filled with Purple Passion . . ."

Miles was turning a softening piece of cheese on a twig over the coals. He looked up at her, his face comically quizzical just as the cheese slid hissing into the fire.

He laughed, and she felt a quick answering happiness. She could make contact with others, she could do it without fear and know that they liked her. Miles liked her.

"You know, Purple *Passion*," she said. "Little grape juice, lemon, lot of vodka. Anyway, there were these smoking hills of garbage out at the dump, and we'd wait, lights off, until suddenly this huge bulking shape on top of the hill. Then we'd quick switch on the lights, and the grizzly would rear up. I saw one I know was ten feet tall. Everybody would scream at the driver and we'd go tearing back out of there."

"Didn't want to inspect the inside of a live bearskin?" Miles said.

"You know what was worse?" She took a deep swig from the wine bottle. "I drove out there by myself one day. I walked up on the garbage piles. I don't know why, I wanted to *see*. Beyond was a cleared slope that led down to the circle of trees. And there were these trails coming up out of the trees, deep ruts really, rayed up where the bears walked toward the garbage."

"Bears don't hassle you if you don't hassle them."

"No. That's just it. Campers were always getting mauled, bitten up by bears in the park, but the news never got out. Bad P.R. or something. Bears don't eat people, either, that's what they used to say. But on the same night in Glacier Park two girls were killed by two different grizzlies. They shot one and found human remains in the stomach."

"Dammit all to hell. Chooch, will you knock it off?"

She looked across at his face. His eyes were invisible behind the glasses and the reflected flames. She realized suddenly what she had wanted to ask him all along. What she had been waiting for, hoping he would volunteer.

"Would you tell me something, Miles? Why did you get so depressed? I mean, that you had to take pills for it?"

"You mean, am I crazy? Or *was* I crazy? Am I still?"

"No. I didn't mean—"

"*Christ.* Okay, yeah, I had a nervous breakdown, I was at C. F. Menninger Memorial Hospital, but now I'm making it okay, okay?"

She felt frightened at his tone. "Miles, really, I—"

"Let's forget about it. Sometime I'll tell you. Not now."

Committed. Not the same, had nothing whatever to do

with committing a crime. It wasn't a crime. He might have committed himself. It was absurd, a medieval fear, prejudice against mental disorder, as if anyone were mentally *ordered*. But a nervous breakdown—didn't that really mean what-did-they-call-it—a psychotic episode?

She wished suddenly and entirely that she were back in her apartment.

"It's not as though you're a perfect model of mental health either, you know," he said, poking at the coals with a stick. "No one is."

"What do you mean—I'm not either?"

"Don't you think it's a little odd, you applying for Alex's job?"

"Why? I hated my old job."

"Bullcrap." He stared across at her. "It was definitely unhealthy. Almost as if you identified with her for some reason."

"That's a *lie*."

"Is it?"

No, it was the truth.

She felt the tears start down her face and stood up.

"Oh, Christ, look, I'm sorry." He stood up and pulled her against him. "Let's forget about all this, okay?"

The wetness soaked against the lapel of his chamois-cloth shirt.

"Let's turn in, we're both tired," he said. "Give me a back rub when I'm lying down, would you?"

She wanted to be taken care of, she thought. But it seemed men wanted you to take care of *them*.

"Dammit all to hell, chooch. I love you."

"I love you too."

"Now let's go to hell to bed."

The canvas walls of the tent sagged close to her face, the smell harsh, tickling her nose. The woods air was increasingly damp, heavy with small, indistinct, repetitive sounds. Through the triangle of mosquito netting the coals had died to a dusty gray, only slightly lighter than the surrounding darkness.

She thought: Nyctophobia. From the Greek *nyktos,* meaning "night." Fear of darkness or night. Night, third definition: any period or condition of darkness or gloom. Specifically, (a) a period of intellectual or moral degeneration, (b) a time of grief, (c) death.

Her heart thudded unevenly in her chest. She felt her lungs stop, breathless. She sat up, eyes searching blindly through the silvery netting.

Nyctalopia: night blindness.

Paige was gone. She felt the vacuum quite suddenly, as absolute as she had felt it there in the hall of the Council Bluffs hospital. Her father was gone, her mother had said. On some floor in some room on some bed her father had left before she got there. And she had never told him how much she loved him. Hating him in some illogical, isolated, burnt-out, cauterized but still living nerve end because he had never told her how much he loved her, either.

And now Paige was gone. A woman friend that you couldn't say such things to anyway, even when you had the chance. And now it was altogether too late. And how did you square that with yourself?

She looked down at Miles, his hair pale and damp in strands across the curve of the air pillow. His face was peaceful, mouth slack, closed eyes blots of darkness. She could see the edge of the cowhide sheath beneath the pillow.

The ease with which he slept, oblivious to her, made her feel lonely. She nudged his shoulder.

His fingers twitched on the blue rip-stop nylon sleeping bag. She stared at the brown moles on his arm. She nudged harder.

He turned over on his back. His jaw dropped open like a door on an oven, a snore tearing from within.

She lay again on her back, eyes staring up at the dipping shadowed roof of the tent. She remembered wrapping four fingers in her sheet, wetting it with her mouth, and rubbing the damp mitt across her nose as she sucked her thumb. She had often fallen asleep like that, watching Beverly in the other bed.

The private bedroom was an invention of the fifteenth century. Like love? No, romantic love was invented by the troubadours in the south of France in the ... tenth? No, eleventh century.

And how could she have forgotten the sleeping pill?

She remembered the sound of her mother's voice, reading from the illustrated pages of *Tommy Thumb's Pretty Song Book*:

> Here comes a candle to light you to bed,
> Here comes a chopper to chop off your head ...

2:29 a.m.

They were startling spears of paleness in the mist—a growth of springy dead-white crinkle-capped mushrooms. He stopped in their midst and squatted, heels crushing the round caps and the lace-soft ferns. Pungent green smells rose into his nostrils. On the hill below him, through the balsam firs, he could see the orange rectangle of the tent, phosphorescent with dew.

There was no sound from within, but he knew the she was there.

His ankles ached. He shifted forward onto his knees, the damp coolness soaking up beneath the dry crisp needles. . . .

The magic box—where you were washed free of sin in the blood of the lamb, horrible and yet wonderful—he had knelt so in the blackness of the wooden box, his heart loud, the heavy maroon velvet curtain breathing dust near his face. He could see nothing. He waited, panic thick in his chest. He would scream. Yes, he would scream. Then the partition sliding back, the chinks faint as a night light between the wooden crosspieces. The sagging outline was Father McTeer's face, chin on palm.

His heart louder now, stunning like a drum. "Bless me, father, for I have sinned. This is my first confession."

"Eh? Speak up, boy."

But listening beyond the curtain in the pews was his entire first-grade class, and the she with the man's name, Sister Anthony, named for the first of the desert saints, the tortured flagellant, lewd visions floating in the painted clouds above his face.

"Bless me father for I have sinned this is my first confession."

"And what have you to tell me, my boy?"

"I lied, father."

"Well, how many times?"

"Three times, father."

"Eh? Speak up. *How* many times?"

"I lied three times."

"What else?"

(No. He could never say it. But he must say it, must be washed clean of the dirtiness. In his bath it had bobbed and he had reached for, had touched himself. The she who was his mother had yanked his arm away, his shoulder exploding into pain. *"No. No. That's dirty. Nasty. That is a sin!"* So that was where the dirt was. The filthy slimy dirty dirt. Dirty was the opposite of pure. Sister Anthony had said sins against purity were always mortal. But was this over the line? Was this a venial or a mortal? Was doing the nasty thing big enough to be mortal?)

"I did the nasty thing, father."

"Yes, child."

"Father ..."

"Yes?"

"Father ... I touched. Myself."

"Eh? *What say?*"

(But father would forgive. Jesus would forgive. He was gentle and forgiving: "I am the Good Shepherd. I know my sheep and my sheep know me." The boy tried to imagine himself as a lost sheep, small hooves trotting cold in the mud, looking, looking. But what if the Shepherd *did not recognize him?*)

"I lied one more time I didn't say before. I lied *four* times, father."

When he began reciting the act of contrition, tears rose with the blood to his face. "O my God, I am heartily sorry for having offended Thee, and I detest all my sins ..."

(*But Sister Anthony said if you deliberately and knowingly concealed a mortal sin, you made a Bad Confession. And that meant God did not forgive you and on top of that you had committed a new mortal sin.*)

"... and I detest all my sins because I dread the loss of heaven and the pains of hell, but most of all because they offend *Thee,* my God, Who art all good and deserving of all my—"

At the sound Dalroi looked up. The sliding panel was already closed. He was in darkness.

She must have slept, Francie thought.

For she was suddenly awake with the overwhelming need to urinate. But that meant outside. In the woods, in the dark.

She willed herself to lie back. She looked up at the sagging roof, moisture clinging in globes against the orange canvas.

Gradually the need grew, became a burning sensation that filled her abdomen. She fought against it, muscles clamping against the pain.

It retreated, prickles of sensitivity crossing in its wake.

She would not go out, she thought, no matter what—until dawn. Until the light, the warm early sun, when she would be able to see and it was safe. She tried to relax, but her chest felt heavy, weighed down.

Nightmare: from the Middle English nihtmare. Niht meant night, okay. But mare, now. Mare was a demon, an incubus, thought in medieval times to lie on the chest of sleeping persons, especially on women, for the purpose of sexual intercourse.

Alex had been wrong. Sex could not be tamed, gentled, known. There was a lawlessness about it. The entrance of a man into your body could never be a simple thing. She remembered the mirror that had fallen, the sharp edge striking the top of her wrist. She had stared down into the flared cut edges before the blood welled—a tiny cut, really —but she had felt faint, sucked down, dizzy like peering into a chasm with water swirling beneath.

She saw the feet, Alex's arched, girlish feet, lying spread on the ugly brown bedroom rug.

Why had it happened? When Alex might have hurried with her shower, dressed and gone out the door with them and been on time for work and not been in the apartment at all to cross lines, intersect with the one who had gone there to kill.

What was the explanation?

The explanation was that there was no explanation. Not for Alex, not for Paige. The thought stared at her like a black hole in space.

Abruptly she sat up, jolting the condensation into rivulets across her hair. The need to urinate resurged, like a hot wave up her body. She felt the warmth flush through her toes and her ears, then burn up along the fronts of her ankles and into her fingertips. It pulsated into a steady pain.

Through the silver crosshatchings of the mosquito netting she could see nothing.

She would not go out.

She felt the pain fill her.

She remembered her father and his finger, caught and spinning into the gears, flesh became metal, and he had borne the pain.

She lay on her back, abdomen hard, while the minutes passed.

Gradually the triangle of the netting grew less black, then gray, then light gray. She waited still longer. When the triangle was a dim white she sat up and peered out. The blackness had fragmented into the still-shadowed shapes of trees and rocks, the green of grass. Above the tent, out of sight, she could hear a bird. She pulled her jeans, which felt cool and soggy, over her legs, and felt for the crumpled softness of her flannel shirt, buttoning it across her chest.

Miles was lying on his side, eyes closed. Saliva had dried in thin white flecks at the side of his mouth. His face was soft with sleep. She eased the knife from beneath his air pillow.

She knelt by the netting, unzipped it and went through.

His body was stiff, angry with the long wait bent-kneed in the blackness. He stood up, careless in his tallness. Beside the violets his footprint lay like a vast depression, filling with dark seepage from the forest floor.

He wasn't a knight, Dalroi thought, he was only the squire. But still he wanted to win the joust for Our Lady.

He would eat of the flesh, drink of the blood, Blessed Virgin.

Thighs, white and soft, spreading. The moist soft hot inward pressing. To there. Yes, he would go there.

Happiness, sorrow, pain, breath, ecstasy.

He felt the guilt take him, the blood-hot angry guilt that he had to find a reason for.

He moved toward the reason when it emerged from the tent.

When she had refastened her jeans, the tensions of the night seemed gone. The trees were still in shadow, but the breeze that stroked through her hair was faintly warm against her ears. The air was clear, full of the resinous balsam smell.

She started down the slope toward the ledge Miles had shown her the afternoon before.

The thick cushion of needles crackled beneath her boots' as she stepped out onto the slab of rock. Strands of mist lay over the valley below, floating its features like islands in a sea. She stared down beyond the dropoff, toward the people who slept hidden below. She lifted the tangle of hair off her neck, twisting it, letting the breeze move across her skin.

That crazy tree house—just a platform really—she and Beverly had nailed in the sycamore, remember that? Orange-juice cans for walkie-talkies, herself reading books on the boards swaying with the slim branches in the wind.

Climbing up higher to the thinner branches, the feel of toes cool on peeled bark. And higher to the branches that dipped with her weight when she leaned her head back to let the sunshine, warm blue Iowa sunshine, touch her face. The tree had swung, the skies reeled, and she had thought: Heaven is like this.

Francie stared down at the toes of her boots, scuffed brown against the paler brown of the needles. She drew in a deep breath.

When she exhaled, she heard the sudden snap behind her. She turned, looking up the slope between the dark columns of trees. But she could see no one.

"Miles?"

He remained still, the branch of spruce needles trembling its moisture against his sleeve.

The bar of the she's flesh. Mold the she into a small ball he could get close to, surround.

A voice spoke into the center of his mind: Dalroi. Do you hear me? I order you to stop this. Now.

Blackness loomed at the edge of his thoughts. It spilled, blotting across his mind.

Shut in once more, deep in blackness.

There was panic.

He was wet. His heart filled his body. There was no room. The blackness was full with his body heat. He could not draw breath. His lungs labored, clung together. The air was thin and then thinner, sucked out and gone.

Deer, she thought. Miles had said deer, there had to be deer around here, lots of deer, because the Moonhaw Gun Club hunted them. What she had heard was a deer— pronged hoof pressing the twig, then weight forward, snapping it in two.

"Miles?"

The air was quiet.

The tent was hidden on the slope above her, directly through the thick stand of spruce. She plunged into the drooping, still-dew-wet interlocking skirts of the trees.

The snake in the soybean row rearing suddenly, speckled brown against the dark green. But Ralph had been with her then, she had to be calm, find the calm in the center for him. *Don't run, Ralphie. Just walk. Walk away slowly. See how I'm walking?* Run and it would strike. Run and the poison would pump faster, around your body, coiled like a snake, circle back and into your heart.

She heard the sound behind her, the sound of something large pressing through the trees.

He was going to kill her. They were alone, there was no one to help, he would kill her, and Miles asleep up in the tent.

Unless it was Miles.

The thought cut through her mind cold as a knife. Anger exploded. She felt a wild recklessness, freed by rage. Her fingers pulled at the knife, yanked it from the calfskin pouch, tightening around the handle. She darted sideways behind a tree. And then without thought another tree and another, out toward the perimeter of the stand. She held the knife tightly up against her chest, the blade jerking as she tried to breathe. She bent over, and with her other hand pulled at the lacings of her boots. The needles pricked through her socks, tiny knives against the skin. Her mouth fell open, and she gasped for breath.

The sound came again, the compression of needles, once, twice, again.

Circle back, circle, that was it, dig toes in stand on toes don't crackle dig down among the needles not on them. Where oh God God where was he? She held her breath.

There was nothing, had she passed him? Had to get behind him, go on. Get behind him—and the blue sky of the dropoff hung suddenly in front of her. She was back at the beginning of the trees.

She turned, pressing through the needled branches, flattening herself up against the sticky resin-streaked trunk.

She tried to breathe with no sound, heard the creaks, the gasps, the pulse of her body. Her lungs heaved. He would hear her. He could hear her.

She pushed herself forward along the rough trunk, peering around. Through the intersecting green was a square of black. Straining out farther, she could see the back of a jacket, tight across the shoulders of a tall, heavyset man. He stood in an attitude of listening, head to one side.

The sound of her breathing filled the silence.

She felt violence gather in her, the pressure to scream. She wanted to run, she imagined the release of running, the pulse through her legs. But she stood rooted, as if all her life, all its emotions had been arrows directing her here.

He started, one shoulder went up, hunching, his face twisting around into view. Wedge-shaped nose, meeting black brows, beaked upper lip like a tricornered hat, the familiar face hung like a mask through the branches.

Confusion, relief fought inside her. She stepped out from the trees. "*Mr. Amspoker*. It's . . ."

Why was his face so odd? Her breath stopped.

Why did he stare?

Daddy don't hit me I could kill you for that you little savage Daddy don't.

The heat and closure of hands around her throat was sudden as a door, slamming into darkness. The needled floor fell away, heat seared through to her chest, his breath came raw gasping down into her face.

In the small dark space she struggled but the walls

305

pressed steadily in, tighter, hotter, drier, there was no more space left to breathe. *Please.* Tighter, hotter, drier, pain, panic. The dark exploded into stars.

In her fingers the handle vibrated like a live thing, the blade shivering off something hard. In reflex she pulled back, then drove it in again, then again and again until the hands went up and out, fingers spread, releasing and widening with his scream. She was falling backward, blood was falling, on the woody overlapped scales of the cone beside her face she saw the bright red splash of someone's blood.

And then there was a large darkness, closing its immensity seamless as water over her head.

Someone was bending over her.

"Hey, you're okay, wait a minute, wait a minute now. This is Frank Quinn here."

Her eyes opened fully.

"You're safe now, Miss Perry. Blacked out, but we got him. He can't hurt you now. But you sure tore him up a good turn. Here, feel like sitting up a bit?"

"Miles," she said.

A ring of faces was staring down at her. The air crackled with staccato bursts from police radios.

"I'm here. Right here." Miles was shirtless, wearing his worn corduroys from yesterday that seemed years before. She felt his bare arm slip up under her back, lift her to lean against him. Her throat felt bruised and torn. She tried to swallow. She touched her fingers against her throat, feeling for wetness. She looked at her fingers, but there was no blood.

"Just take it easy now, chooch. We'll be out of here in no time. They're packing some stretchers up. You'll ride down in style, how about that."

It was then that she saw the long heavy body across the

306

grass. It lay doubled up with its back to her, knees bent forward out of sight up to the chest.

A dark circle spread over the back of the trousers.

"So would you mind finishing telling me how in hell you got onto him?" Miles handed Quinn a cigarette, struck a match, leaning forward to light it.

Quinn inhaled, then blew the smoke up toward the cloudless sky. His brow wrinkled. "Through some departmental records. Can't tell you more than that right now." He picked tobacco off his lip. "We put a little beeper gizmo in the sole of his shoe. And bang. He led us right here.

"Goddamn shame, you ask me. How do these things happen? This is not for print, hey? But Vic Amspoker was a damn good cop."

Epilogue

What had that ignominious boy done *now?*

With effort Cognitor raised his head from the thin pillow. His arms were crossed over his chest, his fists lumped like white breasts beneath the canvas.

He let his head fall back. Was he to be spared nothing? Must they humiliate him beyond human reason? Truss him and tie him into a straitjacket, as if he were a wild beast?

Must he suffer until the Day of Judgment for the sins of Dalroi?

His eyes traveled across the bumpy blue-painted wall to the man-high window, whose light was striped with bars.

It was of some solace. Dalroi had not managed to escape.

Cognitor was lying on the gray blanket on the narrow mattress, which was sealed in brown vinyl. To prevent, he thought, the stowing of armament, such as might be made were the supports not welded to the frame. Nor did the beds roll, for a human cannon to launch at an unsuspecting guard.

Careful they were, but careless with one's dignity, which here was all a man had left.

Beneath the straitjacket he lay in a blue-and-white-striped robe, BELLEVUE stamped across the back, blue pajama bottoms (they were not inmates, oh, no, they were *patients*), and one paper slipper dangling from the big toe of his right foot. Backless the slipper was, of course, so that one went shuffle shuffle shuffle to keep it on. Could a man retain his dignity while the sound of his own shuffling filled his ears?

Their only concession had been to leave on his hand the broad gold band. Such farce, why hadn't they asked him? They might just as well have thrown it in the cardboard box with the other personal effects, to be withheld for the thirty days of psychiatric examination. It wasn't *his* ring, he cared not a fig! It had been Victor's wedding, let him take the responsibility for that tragedy, and so of course it was Victor's ring.

Exhausted, he thought. He was exhausted, spent from the constant battle with the others for control over the body. He was nearing seventy, after all, the sap had frozen in his joints when winter came to his hair. But did they respect the wisdom of age here on the notorious "O2" side of the prison floor, this ghetto for murderers, robbers, rapists, sodomists?

The itch began on his ankle, a flick of sensitivity that burrowed in, snapping like mites. His body struggled forward beneath the stiff canvas casing until his bare ankles hung off the foot of his bed, away from contact with the wool.

When *he* wore the body, Cognitor thought, he made sure to remove the blanket and neatly fold it beside the bed before lying down, because he was allergic to wool.

But Dalroi wasn't. And what did Dalroi care now that he had left the body, left Cognitor to suffer? What did Dalroi care for anything besides the constant exercise of his irascible and concupiscible nature, the sins against purity?

He struggled to remember what it was Dalroi had done to deserve this latest chastisement. It was disconcerting. Always before he had known what Victor and Dalroi had been up to. It was his responsibility: he was the Knower, remembering for all three of them, trying to shield the body from harm.

He felt afraid. Had this something to do with Victor's morning sessions with the psychiatrist?

He had waked. Yes, definitely, it had been he, Cognitor, who had been in possession of the body. He was sure of that. Breakfast at 7:30 in the day room with the twenty-four other men, the doctor's rounds at eight A.M., the Thorazine mixed in the orange juice in the white Dixie cup printed with the two blue caducei—the physician's symbol of wings and snakes entwined on a staff. His soul trembling as his tongue reached to receive what he longed for, what should have been. *Corpus Domini nostri* . . . The Host approaching, the wine on his tongue . . . *In vitam eternam. Amen.*

Couldn't the doctor *see*, rectify this grievous mistake? He did not belong on a psychiatric prison ward. Before God, he was entirely innocent.

"On the gate!" the doctor had called. And the officer unlocked the barred metal door and the doctor walked through to the second set of bars—nesting one within another like china Easter eggs. Through those bars he had gone, and out to freedom.

Then lunch, yes, he was sure of it, he had worn the body at lunch.

The men had filed in, guts slack as their eyes, a population of pajamas lining up at the rolling cart with the metal serving pans. On the heavy-gauge aluminum tray he remembered the veal, mashed potatoes, pond of gravy, peas, white bread, mixed fruit, the officer pouring coffee from the metal pitcher into his Styrofoam cup. The fork and spoon distributed one by one (to be recounted later). And it was he, Cognitor, who had sawed, crushed the veal into bite-size pieces with his fork, scraped the triangular partition, picked up the last green pea with his fingers. The food was good—the population went up, the little patient named Henry had told him, on Thanksgiving and especially Christmas, when there was a party.

Out on Rikers Island, Henry had said, they were called Swallowers. Men who would cram down anything not bolted down just to get here to Bellevue. Somebody had eaten a light bulb, somebody had dismantled and swallowed both faucets on his detention-cell basin, just to get to Bellevue and doctors, a recreational aide, an art therapist, two drama therapists, and second helpings.

Cognitor remembered the garbage, hit from the lunch tray against the inside of the tall gray rubber wastebasket, falling and sliding down onto other men's garbage. And then the man who had been sitting on the opposite wood bench at the table, watching him with fingers curled like worms around his chin, had come up behind him, come up too close, breath fogging old evils into his face. "Ay," he had said. "Ay, you, I'm speakin' you. You the rape-o?"

Cognitor felt again the sickening depression, the sudden dizzy downward whirl, sight dimming.

Lying on the bed on the hairshirt of wool, he fought the weakness of his flesh, the attempt by one of the others again to take control.

When he lay spent, still in charge, he felt a deep aged coldness. He felt the coldness stir with the breath from the beating floor fan. Now he remembered. Dalroi's anger erupting, the other patient red-faced, exultant: "*Rape-o! Rape-o!*" His own shrinking weakness as Dalroi wrested control, striking with the tray. The hard sound of metal against skull.

And thus the straitjacket.

But what if the doctor could really cure them, the way he had told Victor? Which one of them was the real personality? Which one of them—Dalroi, Victor, most deservedly he, Cognitor—which would survive?

He did not want to die.

And now there was a fourth, a new baby that smelled still of milk, emergent, with no name. It was so odd, so unexpected, so terrifying—he thought it was a girl. But who would be left to look after the baby?

Cognitor stared up at the ceiling.

He did not want to die. He had never had the opportunity to follow his own life, the studies in book-lined rooms, the warmth from the grate, the deep soft incense and the flickering of the sanctuary light—white candle in the red glass cylinder, purity in flesh.

No, he had always to worry about the others, keep Victor from working the body until it dropped, turn Dalroi from as much violence as he could. There had been no scrap left for himself—a life unlived, and now he was old.

"Amspoker. You feeling any better?"

Cognitor turned his face toward the voice. The man wore a blue shirt, navy pants, a silver badge, and a large clanking ring of keys hanging off his belt. He had no gun.

"Yes, officer. Much better now. Could you possibly release me from these bonds?"

"You gave Johnson a pretty good clip with that tray. You feeling any friendlier now?"

"Yes, officer."

Cognitor struggled up into a sitting position, a placating look on his face. The backs of his calves shrank from the hard texture of the wool.

He felt the sudden give of the fastenings behind his back, and then the joints of his shoulders rolled achingly free.

Cognitor stood up, flexing his knees, rubbing his nails down over the itching calves. He scratched until the blood came.

His right hand pulsed with pain. He raised it nearsightedly closer, beneath the fluorescent ceiling light. Teeth marks—pockets of purple—ringed the reddened skin. *Mother of Mercy.* That animal Johnson had *bitten* Dalroi.

He felt the others pressing behind his eyes, struggling through him to see the bite. He could hear their gibberish through his brain.

Enough.

They had owned, used, dominated—they had brought destruction on the body—for too long.

Now it was his turn. Was it too much to ask that he should have his turn, to make of the body what he might?

"I am like a pelican of the wilderness," the psalm went. Was it the 102nd? "I am like an owl of the desert. I watch, and am as a sparrow alone upon the house top."

Yes, he too would be alone.

Manresa, the peaceful Jesuit retreat house on Staten Island, came into his mind.

Yes, Cognitor thought, that was it. He would take the body, restore the body and the spirit at Manresa.

When he had given the doctors their thirty days of prying into Victor, when they would see that Victor knew nothing of the other selves and that he, Cognitor, knew but was innocent, perhaps he could persuade them to give *him* thirty days, too. A month's retreat at Manresa, to make the spiritual exercises of St. Ignatius.

Yes, he would use the afternoon's free telephone call—at the small Formica table with the officer sitting beside on the blue chair—to call Manresa and ask if there would be room.

The first week would be devoted to penitence. How gladly he would make the examen. Then the hard work of the second week, the probing of motivation. The sadness of the third week—meditation on the Passion of Christ.

Tears crowded his eyes as he thought of the happiness of the fourth week, the meditation on the Resurrection and Redemption.

It was true, there was hope still.

The voice spoke into the center of his brain, shattering the image of Manresa like a stone into a pond.

"You think you'll walk right out of this loony bin, you phony motherfucker bastard?" Dalroi said. *"We're in this together, you know."*